To Robert Taylor
my Smiling Preacher
and
Excellent Teacher
Enjoy

[illegible]
2-3-18

My America is Back

Thoughts from a Patriot

BJ Melton

BookVenture Publishing LLC
1000 Country Lane Ste 300
Ishpeming MI 49849
www.bookventure.com
Hotline: 1(877) 276-9751
Fax: 1(877) 864-1686

Ordering Information:
Quantity sales. Special discounts are available on quantity purchases by corporations, associations, and others. For details, contact the publisher at the address above.

Printed in the United States of America.

Library of Congress Control Number		2017963693
ISBN-13:	Softcover	978-1-64166-363-2
	Pdf	978-1-64166-364-9
	ePub	978-1-64166-365-6
	Kindle	78-1-64166-366-3

Rev. date: 01/10/2018

Preface

My name is Buster Jack Melton, but, for good reason, I like to go by B.J. When I was born I had two older brothers, one was 10 years old and one was 20. My Mother was 40. Raising two boy 10 years apart, take patience, tolerance, discipline, endurance, and correcting a lot of mistakes. AND THEN, I CAME ALONG!

I think, having a child at age 40, was a surprise. When I was 25, my Mother finally admitted I was supposed to be a girl. They were so sure they had no boy names selected. After I had been in this world about 8 days, I still had no official name, but I had acquired two nicknames, so I was hung with Buster Jack. Do not misunderstand, they are good names, but in my mind, they did not fit.

Since I was born in 1925, I become a child of the Great Depression. I remember when I was about 7 years old we had a house, a 50-acre farm, plus a cow, hogs, chickens, an old grey mare for pulling the plow, AND two automobiles.

When I was 8 we were renting part of a house from a widow lady. Papa lost everything and until he died in 1944 we never had another car. Walking is what we did.

We were poor, we had no welfare, but Papa saw to it that we never missed a meal. He worked at whatever to make money, and I inherited his work ethic. At age 12, I got a job sweeping out the local dry goods store at 6 AM. Took an hour. Paid me $3.00 for 6 days, plus I got 10% off of clothes I bought.

In 1942, at age 16, I graduated from Merkel High School and started to Texas Tech University. I turned 18 in October of 1943 and joined the navy. Most of my friends in high school and in college, were older and already in service. Sadly, some never came back home. I was honorably discharged in February 1946 with no claim to fame, no heroics, and I returned to Texas Tech to get my degree. I graduated from 1947 with a degree in Electrical Engineering. With the help of a football scholarship, the GI bill and odds jobs, I had no debt. But World War II etched something in my soul that remains to this day- PATRIOTISM AND LOVE OF MY COUNTRY.

Our generation was a proud generation. When the call for service came, we voluntarily volunteered, never looking back. We said the pledge, we saluted the flag, we were proud of America and what we stood for. As for me, and those of my generation remaining, we are still proud.

However, in the 1960's my country began to change, and not for the better. With the Vietnam war. Patriotism and love of Our Country began to wane. A new generation of young people began to immerge with different values and formed a different appreciation of the country they inherited, much different than the one I hold to this day.

Finally, Barack Obama came along appearing a promise to Paradise. He was elected President and his promised "Paradise" turned into lies, and the deterioration of America began to accelerate.

It seemed we had no way to turn the tide. In the 8 years of his presidency, more and more of my values were stomped on. America was turning into an insignificant part of a world in chaos. To make matters worse a person like mind to Obama, Hillary Clinton, was guaranteed to succeed him and finish the destruction.

But the best laid plans of mice and men often go astray.

Along come a man preaching what I preach and what I believe, and promising to MAKE AMERICA GREAT AGAIN!

It was my thought that we could not, as a country, stand another 4 or 8 years like Obama. So immediately after Donald Trump announced his candidacy in 2015 for President, I began publishing, on e-mail and Facebook, a "Thought for the day", promoting Donald for President.

This book chronicles my thoughts from the beginning. It covers the campaign and the first 6 months of his presidency. The theme, of course, is about electing Trump President, but sprinkled among the Thoughts, is a little humour, a joke or two, or three, and some "imagining". Enjoy!

Foreword

We all have thought and opinions.

In this book,

My America is back, thoughts from a Patriot,

I am exposing for all to read,

my thoughts and opinions from

June 16, 2015 to July 2017

about the process of electing our

President.

You will see my obvious bias in favour of

Donald Trump.

And, hopefully,

you will understand the reasons for my bias.

If you agree with me,

I will take it as a compliment.

If you disagree with me,

Que sera, sera.

Mixed in with the political stuff

is a little humour and some of my personal life,
of which I am both proud and thankful.

The Lord has blessed me beyond measure.

Enjoy

Contents

Chapter I

The Beginning

JUNE 16, 2015 TO DECEMBER 31, 2015

June 16, 2015

Donald Trump Announces

2016 Presidential Campaign:

'We Are Going to Make our Country

Great Again'

Sic 'em Donald!

Tuesday, June 22, 2015

The government and the loons tell you,
there is no wrong or right.
If it feels right, It's right for you.
You don't need to sacrifice at all... ever!
If you have all the equipment of a male
but feel like a female, that doesn't matter.
You can change it! If you feel like a female
and you want to be male then change it!
If you are born to a white family and
you want to identified as black, no problem!
Lie on your applications and writings and change it,
Truth is debatable. Absolute truth is a fantasy.
Whatever!

Tuesday, June 23, 2015

AMERICA'S #1 MUSLIM

IF THERE WAS EVER ANY DOUBT.........

An Iftar Dinner to Celebrate Ramadan:
President Barack Obama hosts an Iftar dinner
celebrating Ramadan in the East Room
of the White House, June 22, 2015.
AND YOU PAID FOR IT!

Thursday, June 24, 2015

Trial day for our Supreme Court.

On the morning of that day,
the lawyers and spectators enter a large courtroom.
When an officer of the Court bangs his gavel,
the people in the courtroom stand.
The nine justices walk through a red curtain
and stand beside nine tall, black-leather chairs.
The Chief Justices take the middle and tallest chair.
"Oyez! Oyez! Oyez! Shouts the marshal of the Court.
(It's an old Court expression meaning hear ye.)
"God save the United States and this Honourable Court."

I find it interesting that the court begins by asking a blessing of GOD

when many of their "deeply deliberated" decisions

treat GOD as a non-entity.

Thursday, June 25, 2015

IT IS NO LONGR OBAMACARE,
OR AFORDABLECARE,
IT IS NOW SCOTUSCARE,
AS REWRITEN BY
THE SUPREME COURT OF THE UNITED STATES.

Friday, June 25, 2015

Let the lions in ……………..

AND NERO FIDDLED………
AND OUR SUPREME COURT PUT ANOTHER NAIL IN THE COFFIN.

Sad day.

Friday, June 26, 2015

As with Obamacare,
the court is engaging in what I propose we call
'outcome-based adjudication.'
The majority decides what policy it likes,
and then rationalizes it, however clumsily."
Shame!

Saturday, June 27, 2015

The Supreme Court is comprised of 9 unelected judges,
all lawyers, with lifetime appointments,
and cannot be fired for any reason,
no matter how incompetent.
Theoretically, they swear under oath to judge,
solely by the law of the land, the Constitutionality
of laws passed by Congress, and do so impartially.
So much for theory.
These 9 judges,
wearing their black robes signifying wisdom,
sitting in their high back chairs,
looking down on the people begging for justice,
supposedly dispense JUSTICE.
But they do so,
NOT according to the Constitution,
but what is called 'outcome-based adjudication'.
The majority decides what they want the answer to be,
then rationalizes it,
NO MATTER HOW CLUMSILY,
the Constitution be damned!
Words change their meaning,
imagine intent replaces reality,
personal biases replace reason.
These 'Judges' took an oath.
Violating that oath is betrayal of trust,
a breach of faith, and seemingly,
an act of treachery.
Result? Rome is burning!

The OATH

"I,__________________, do solemnly swear or affirm that I will administer justice without respect to persons and do equal right to the poor and the rich, and that I will faithfully and impartially discharge and perform all the duties incumbent upon me as________________, According to the best of my abilities and understanding, agreeably to the constitution and laws of the United States. So help me God."

Tuesday, June 30, 2015

Fake news

The world is full of FAKES

Monday, July 13, 2015

Keep an eye on this 'woman'. She sure has an eye on you!

Sic 'em Donald!

Tuesday, July 21, 2015

There's now no doubt about it. The establishment cronies at the RNC are trying to rig the Republican primaries to nominate a "moderate."

Just the other day, RNC Chairman Reince Preibus, the man who supposed to be natural in this entire nomination process, called Donald Trump to berate him and demand that he "tone down" his rhetoric.

It's not the place of the Republican National Committee to censor what a candidate says or believes. That's true no matter whether the candidates is Ted Cruz, Carly Fiona, Donald Trump or anyone else.

But you can be sure that Reince Preibus would NEVER presume to tell Jeb Bush or Lindsay Graham to change their rhetoric or ideals

No way

Sic 'em Donald!

Thursday, July 30, 2015

The onslaught to discredit Trump
is picking up steam.
They are merciless
when their money
and power is threatened.

Sic ’em Donald!

Saturday, August 8, 2015

Killing Jews was legal in Nazi Germany.
It would have been insane not to use their skin for lamps.
Killing babies is legal in the United States.
It would be insane not to sell their body parts.
HAVE WE REACHED THE BOTTOM?

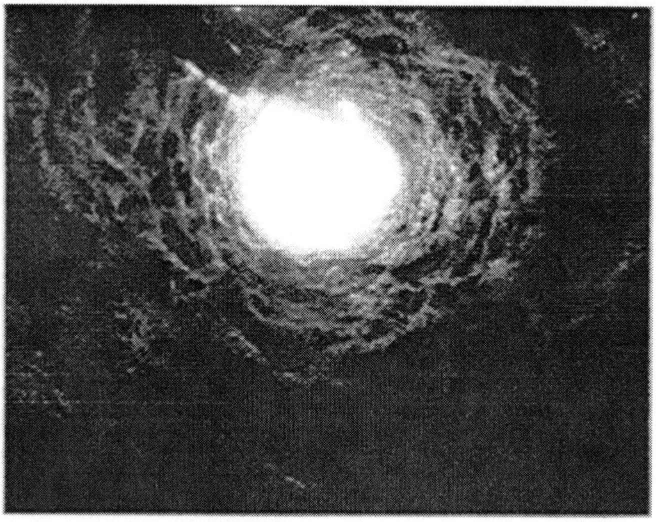

Sic 'em Donald!

Monday, August 10, 2015

A 'TRUE STORY" ABOUT
'GENERAL McChrystal's resignation in Obama's office
from General McChrystal's book!
NEVER STAND IN LINE AGAIN
Some men carry and handle their diplomacy better than others.
When former U.S Military commander in Afghanistan,
General McChrystal,
was called into the Oval office by Barack Obama,
he knew things weren't going to go well
when the President accused you as a politician, Mr. President,
it's my job to support you as a Commander-in-Chief," McChrystal replied,
and he handed Obama his resignation.
Not satisfied with accepting McChrystal's resignation,
the President made a cheap parting shot:
"I bet when I die you'll be happy to piss on my grave."
The General saluted and said,
"Mr. President, I always told myself
after leaving Army
I'd never stand in line again."

Sic 'em Donald!

Wednesday, August 12, 2015

This is just for laughs.
Have one!

HA HA

Monday, August 17, 2015

Who is Donald Trump?

Donald Trump is a bodacious
quick thinking talking machine.
And he is also all of these:
Compassionate, uncompassionate,
(Rosie O' Donald), lucky, (billionaire), smart,
unfortunate, rich (most of the time),
a diehard capitalist, a blue American,
and he thinks and talks like I do,
(but faster), so you can take it to the bank—I like him.

Sic 'em Donald!

20 Aug, 2015

Got this through the mail.
Ingenuity at work!

Took down our rebel flag and peeled the
NRA sticker off the front door.

We've discounted our home alarm system
and quit our Neighbourhood Watch.

Bought two Pakistani flags on eBay
and raised them in the front yard,
one at each corner,
plus a black flag of ISIS in the center.

Now the local police, sheriff, FBI, CIA, NSA,
Homeland Security, Secret Service
and other agencies are all watching the house 24/7.

I've never felt safer and we're saving $49.95 a month.

Friday, August 21, 2015

I just heard that Hillary's e-mail server
was located out west
some place in the closet of a bathroom.
Sure made it convenient to wipe it clean.
I guess you could call that Planning ahead.

Sic 'em Donald!

August 22, 2015

Another Muslim on Obama's payroll
How many does this make?

Fatima Noor

President Obama appointed Fatima Noor as the head of

U.S. Citizenship and immigration Services

in the Department of Homeland Security.

HARD TO BELIEVE, BUT TRUE.

Tuesday, August 25, 2015

I hate to admit it but this may have some merit.

Thursday, August 27, 2015

Liberals have you pegged. See where you fall
in the pecking order!

So PROUD! Makes you want to wave the  doesn't it?
Right now, in America, patriots are terrorists,
Christians are the bigots and all white people are racist.
Veterans are a threat to national security,
radical Muslims are first class citizens,
as are militant homosexuals, LGBT's and illegal immigration felons!

Sic 'em Donald!

September 1, 2015

Trump is in danger of attack from his own party?
Trouble is brewing.

"It's no secret the Republican establishment is unnerved by Donald Trump and his lead in national and key state polls," reported CNN.

Party elites had hoped that Trump's support would have fizzled out by now.

Instead, he's the clear leader of GOP candidates with nearly a quarter of the vote.

But who will sponsor the attack against Trump:
Super PACs, rival candidates, or some other group?

There are rumours of anti-Trump television ads in the works.
"There are a lot of donors out there who see it as much too dangerous, obviously, for the candidates, or their allied super PACs, to go after Trump,"

"So, they're looking to more establishment PACs to potentially take him down in post-Labor Day adds."

According to Fox News' Charlie Gasparino, the other Republican candidates think Donald Trump has gotten away with too much and are planning to bring him down.

Gasparino reported that GOP donors, especially those associated with Marco Rubio and Scott Walker, are planning "attack ads" in an effort to "reset the primary."

THEY ARE AFTER YOU, DONALD!

Sic 'em Donald!

Sep 2, 2015

Hill in her best southern accent…
"I don't feel no ways tried, I come too far from where I started from, nobody told me that the road would be easy"
….I am give slap out.

Sic 'em Donald!

September 7, 2015

How did it happen?
Humans began slaughtering babies in the womb or
immediately after birth by the millions.
Men married men and women married women
and they had no regenerative ability.
The negative birth rate continued
until mankind went the way of the dinosaurs.
And the year of THE LAST MAN STANDING WAS____________?

Think About it!

Saturday, September 12, 2015

Texas has 4 seasons
To my friend in Boston:

Haven't you heard? It is no longer Global Warming, which is false. It is now climate change, which is true. Happens every day. Been happening for eons.
Sure was true about your Northeast this year. Record cold and record snow, followed right on schedule by melting snow and warmer temps.
So...... how can anyone dispute "climate change"?
Words are tricky.
For example: "BJ told Bob he had a problem." Who had a problem?

Sic 'em Donald!

Saturday, September 19, 2015

Sorry, Beck has lost it!
Glenn Beck Accuses Trump Supporters of Racism

Conservative talk show host Glenn Beck has had it up to here with Donald Trump, even going as far as to accuse his supporters of talent racism.

Beck, who hasn't been shy in his opposition to the Republican frontrunner, said Tuesday that any Tea partiers who jumped on the Trump bandwagon were probably not genuine in their beliefs.

"The media's making this look like Tea Party people."

Beck said nothing the press coverage of Trump's enormous rally in Dallas.

"I don't think these are Tea Party people who are following him.

Some of them may be, but if you were a Tea Party person, then you were lying. You were lying.

It was about Barack Obama being black.

Beck said he didn't understand what his friends Sean Hannity and Sarah Palin were thinking when they defended Trump.

Thought his remarks on the integrity of Tea Partiers who support Trump are offensive and ignorant.

It might be a stretch to say that Republicans will take "anyone,"

But it's definitely true that the Tea Party is ready for a win.

A movement built out of outrage against the establishment must either grow or die. At some point, it gets tiresome to simply point out the same old things year after year.

Ho hum, another Republican Congress fails to stand up to the Obama agenda.

Ho hum, another boring establishment candidate loses to a failing president.

No one is fooled by Donald Trump. This guy's on television around the clock, and you can't watch ten minutes of punditry without being reminded of his liberal positions through the years. Voters aren't blind.

They see what the deal is. But what are the alternatives?

Jeb friggin' bush? The guy who sounds just like Obama on a number of important issues facing the country? Rubio, his padawan?

Chris Christie? Come on.

Beck endorses Ben Carson for the conservative voter looking for an outsider, and that's all well and good.

It's not hard to imagine Carson- who in his delivery is the anti-Trump-siphoning votes from the brash frontrunner.

Of course, that would be very difficult to imagine if Trump's voter base really was made up of racists who opposed Obama because he was black.

In veering down this strange path, Beck sounds more like a liberal than ever.

That's their job, pretending like every Tea Partier is a closet racist.

He should be ashamed of himself for playing that game, even if he doesn't care to get on board the Trump Express.

Sic 'em Donald!

Tuesday, September 22, 2015

Selling baby parts
Obama wants to put the man who made the videos
exposing planned parenthood's baby organs selling in prison
THE OBAMA ADMINISTRATION AND OTHER POWERFUL PEOPLE
WITHIN THE GOVERNMENT WANT THE MAN
WHO MADE THE VIDEOS EXPOSING
PLANNED PARENTHOOD'S BABY ORGAN SELLING
IN PRISON.

PLANNED PARENTHOOD SUPPORTERS
IN POSITIONS OF GOVERNMENT POWER ARE LOOKING
TO JAIL AND FINANCIALLY DESTROY
THE PRODUCER OF THE UNDERCOVER STING VIDEOS
THAT HAVE BROUGHT ATTENTION TO
THE ABORTION GIANT'S ILLEGAL PRACTICES,
A PRO-LIFE LAWYER CLAIMS

Monday, September 28, 2015

JUST ONE MORE DAY
as a boy 6 years old, I remember getting up at 6AM
and walking with my Papa to his cafe in town.
He fed me breakfast and I went to school.
One morning everything was covered with ice.
As we walked Papa held my hand
because I was slipping and sliding,
but he walked steady without falling.
I remember, too, how unafraid and proud I was
that this big strong man was my Papa.
As I grew older that feeling never left me,
but sadly, the need for him to hold my hand
became less important.
I graduated from high school when I was sixteen
and left home for college.
In November of 1944 Papa had a stroke.
It partially paralysed his right side
and he could hardly say a word,
so his working days were over.
I don't know what I was thinking.
Papa had always been there for me
and I suppose in my teenage mind
I thought he would recover and be like always.
When I turned 18 I joined the navy.
After discharge I went directly back to college.
Papa told me many times his desire was for me
to graduate from college and, In my mind,
getting back in school was most important
so I did not even go see Mama and Papa.
Why am I saying all this?
Because my brother that Papawas dying
and asking for me.
I got on a bus and got home about 1 AM on June 2nd.

Papa died about 30 minutes before I got home.
I am 89 now and for 69 years I have regretted
not having JUST ONE MORE DAY with my Papa.
As you read this you can probably recall
one more similar events in your life,
and wish you had JUST ONE MORE DAY
or maybe just an hour.
As for me I hereby resolve to do my best
to have no more regrets because
I did not have JUST ONE MORE DAY.

Friday, October 2, 2015

No comment necessary!

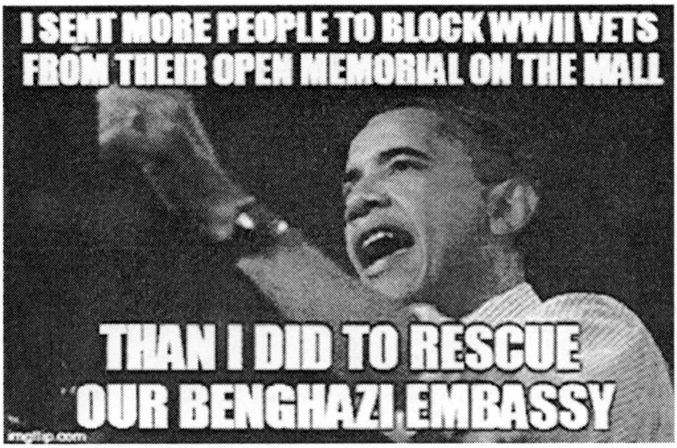

Sic ’em Donald!

Thursday, Dec. 17, 2015

Today a General................
Tomorrow—an Obama ex-General?
Listen up.
General Robert Abrama is the man who decided today
to charge Bowe Bergdahl with desertion.
He did this knowing his career will probably be over
because of his decision.
I imagine that Obama is tonight plotting to ruin his reputation
for upsetting his attempt to whitewash what Bergdahl did
so he had an excuse to free the 5 prisoners from Gitmo.
Please share this with all the Patriots you know.
Show the General Abrams how much you support his courage.
He is the son of General Creighton Abrams,
namesake of the M-1A Abrams tank,
former Army Chief of staff
and another American Hero.....

Sic 'em Donald!

Friday, 18 Dec 2015

You can depend on me. I tell it like it is. I am a dyed in the wool, conservative, red bloodied old time religious, flag waving, American.
I have answers for questions nobody has asked yet.
Rinos are politicians with their hand in the cookie jar.
Fortunately, there aren't many of them.
Unfortunately, they in the wrong places.
Gotta lump them and the socialists.

Sic 'em Donald!

Thursday, 24 Dec 2015

Paul Ryan.........
You are so brazen. After you have betrayed your oath of office and sold us down the drain, you have the nerve to wish us Merry Christmas.
Disgusting!!!

Sic 'em Donald!

Sunday, December 27 2015

Another RINO out of the closet!!

Rep. Trey Gowdy (R-S.C.) is expected to endorse
Sen. Marco Rubio (R-Fla.) for president
when he campaigns with him in Iowa next week,
Townhall.com reported Saturday.

Sic 'em Donald!

Monday, December 28, 2015

Obama's slogan "Hope and Change"
Reached its climaxed this year, 2015,
when A MAN WAS ELECTED WOMAN OF THE YEAR.!

Sic 'em Donald!

Tuesday, December 29, 2015

Glenn Beck is not a favourite of mine, except
when he say something I agree with.
This is one of those times.
Glenn Beck said:
Lamenting the president's recent focus on climate change
at the COP21 summit in Paris, Glenn Beck addressed Obama
on his radio program in the wake of
Wednesday deadly massacre in San Bernardino, CA.
Beck might be a smidgen too far to the right, but.......
"Mr. President, I say this with as much respect as you deserve,"
Beck began. "Screw global warming."
"What the hell is wrong with you?" he asked.
"If you actually believe that global warming is the biggest problem
we face,
with terror all over the world,
and 18 trillion dollar debt-nine of which is yours—
no real allies left that trust us, riots in our streets,
riots in our university campuses,
race relations worse than I've seen since the 1960's,
and a distrust of our fellow Americans
unlike anything I've ever seen,
you, sir, are either delusional or
you're the dumbest SOB on the planet."

Sic 'em Donald!

December 30, 2015

The best philosophy:
Believe nothing you read in the paper,
or hear on radio and TV, and
only half of what you see,
and test that 50% carefully.
Exception: believe 100%
of what I put on internet and Facebook.

Sic ’em Donald!

December 31, 2015

Think about this.
There has been a giant New Year's Eve celebration
in Time Square since 1904.
This will be the 111th anniversary.
In the past it was a moment to celebrate for all America.
In short it was one big party.
Tonight, there will be 1,000,000 or so souls
gathered around Time Square waiting for the ball to fall.
But, It will not be the same as in years past.
Everyone their neighbour,
hoping not to see a terrorist
with intent to kill as many Americans as possible.
There will be an additional 5000 policemen
scattered among the crowd doing the same thing.
There will be many snipers on roof tops doing the same thing,
And helicopters flying above doing the same thing.
All this costing several million dollars.
Why? Because we are afraid. Muslims terrorists are winning.
Why are they winning?
Because our "leader" in the White House doesn't give a hoot!
He is spending millions of our taxpayer dollars
on another vacation in beautiful Hawaii playing golf.
Muslims are his friends. Like he said "I am one of them".
Better believe it.

Sic 'em Donald!

Chapter II

The Campaign

JANUARY 1, 2016 TO NOVEMBER 8, 2016

Friday, January 1, 2016

Elect Donald Trump!
And have a
HAPPY NEW YEAR!!!

Sic 'em Donald!

January 1, 2016

Looks like New York City escaped any major problem, but Rochester, NY is another story fortunately, the FBI arrested the Muslim terrorist before he could carry out his plan. He had purchased a machete and planned to enter a nightclub full of revelers with the machete swinging, decapitating as many as he could.

No harm done, thankfully, but the expensive fireworks show was cancelled, for fear there might be others.

And our "leader" in Hawaii couldn't care a rats putty tail.

Sic 'em Donald!

Jan. 1, 2016

Tonight, I watched a news program on TV which showed
a number of homeless people living under an overpass
in tents and makeshift box huts,
with no water or electricity, or heat.
It really tugged at my heartstrings and I wondered WHY?
How did they come to this?
Well, I don't know. But you know "out of sight, out of mind"
so I just went back to football.
Later I went about my routine of getting ready for bed.
You know-washing hands and face,
brushing teeth, taking my pills,
putting on warm sleepers to get in my warm bed.
The last step was taking my water jug to the frig
for ice from my automatic ice maker,
and filling it with filtered water.
Suddenly the homeless that I saw earlier
flashed through my mind and I thought-
HERE I AM IN A WARM HOUSE WITH ALL THESE LUXURIES
THAT I JUST TAKE FOR GRANTED,
AND THEY HAVE PRACTICALLY NOTHING.
IT MADE ME REALIZE HOW EXTREMELY BLESSED I AM,
AND I STOPPED RIGHT THERE AND GAVE THANKS
TO THE LORD FOR ALL MY BOUNTY.
THEN IT OCCURED TO ME—
SOMETIME IN MY EARLIER LIFE WHEN I CAME TO A FORK IN THE ROAD, IF I HAD TAKEN THE OTHER FORK,
ONE OF THOSE HOMELESS FOLKS MIGHT BE ME.
I be grateful

On Jan 4, 2016

Me and Jordan Spieth plan to play golf Friday,
me at Canyon Creek,
Jordan in Hawaii.
Would you like to play? We only have 3.

Tuesday, January 5, 2016

When you come to a fork in the road, take it!
Life is not so simple as fork in the road may imply.
As for myself I can recall 8 distinct forks in the road where I had to take one.
Each time I thought I took the right one, but each time it was a step backwards.
But I did learn from my mistakes. I learned about attitude, morals, honesty, sincerity, and most of all I learned a lot about people. I learned respect for people.
Everyone has their own can of worms and I certainly had mine. Respect and be respected.
Maybe love is a better word. Why we shy away from LOVE I don't know.
I digress. My 8th fork in the road I took, turned out to be the road I was looking for.
It brought happiness, contentment and peace of mind, but without the love, help, and encouragement of others,
I NEVER WOULD HAVE FOUND THAT ROAD BY MYSELF.
OTHERS were many people, among which were
Tom Blakey, Leon Loveless, Mark Gordon, and Mike Spence,
people who helped many others along the way.
And last, but really first, The LORD has made life's journey with me, walking beside me in good times and bad.

Sic 'em Donald!

Wednesday, January 6, 2016

Very Interesting.
Clinton Mercilessly Grilled on MSNBC:
'What's the Difference Between a Democrat and a Socialist?'

Democratic frontrunner Hillary Clinton was mercilessly grilled Tuesday evening by an MSNBC host over the difference between the ideology of a Democrat and socialist.
"I want to try to help you tonight... locate yourself politically," Chris Matthews, host of "Hardball," told Clinton before noting that her chief 2016 rival Bernie Sanders identifies as a socialist.
Matthews then asked,
"What's the difference between a socialist and a Democrat? Is that a question you want to answer, or would you rather not?" See, I'm asking you! You're a Democrat. He's a socialist. Do you like someone calling you a socialist?"
"Well, you see, I'm not one," Clinton replied.
Matthews still wasn't pleased with the answer.
"Well, I can tell you what I am," Clinton said. "I am a progressive Democrat."
"How's that different than a socialist?" Matthews fired back.
Clinton didn't answer, but only said, she's a Democrat who "likes to get things done."
SO HILLARY, IS THERE A DIFFERENCE?

Sic 'em Donald!

Saturday, January 9, 2016

Terrorist knocking at the door, Obama?
"Hey, don't knock. Just come on in."
In America today, patriots are terrorists,
Christians are the bigots, white people are racist,
Veterans are a threat to national security,
and radical Muslims are peace loving
first class citizens.
And ISIS is just junior varsity?
Remember Paris and San Bernardino?
Did the slaughter really happen?
In the world of Make Believe, Chicken Little said
""The sky is falling"!
AND SHE WAS RIGHT!

Sic 'em Donald!

Monday, January 10, 2016

Unless Hillary gets put in jail, which she might, Sanders won't be on the ticket.
Who is next in line?
Everyone needs to study the philosophy of Socialism and communism, they are about the same.
We have got a lot of socialism now, the welfare programs being classic examples.
We have almost 20 trillion dollars in debt now and growing because we (Gov) spend money we ain't got and have borrow from some country, such as China.
The interest we have to pay on this debt will eventually equal, then exceed revenue from all sources
UNLESS OUR GOVERNMENT SPENDING IS BROUGHT UNDER CONTROL.
Otherwise, the source of borrowing will dry up and somewhere down the road it will be bankruptcy and a dollar won't be worth 2 cents.
Sanders is a professed Socialist. He touts free health care and free college education which sounds wonderful, until you realize there AINT NO FREE LUNCH.
So, who does pay for your "free" health care? Not me.
It is a sucker game designed to appeal to the naive and uninformed.
Finally, one last comment.
Debate can be a useful tool to resolve disagreements.
However, being disagreeable for the sake of being disagreeable is foolish and unproductive.
Facts, not opinions. should resolve disagreements.

Sic 'em Donald!

Mon, Jan 11, 2016

YOU WILL HAVE FUN WITH THIS!!!
Just something I received. Not an endorsement of any candidate...

The PERFECT DAY - .January 20, 2017

1. President Donald Trump and Vice President Ted Cruz are sworn into office.
2. In a rare event on inauguration day, Congress convenes for an emergency meeting to repeal Socialist healthcare farce known as Obamacare. The new Director of Health and Social Services Dr. Ben Carson announces that an independent group of healthcare management professionals is hired to handle health care services for poor and low income people. The move saves billions of taxpayer paid dollars. Healthcare service in the U.S improves 100%.
3. Trump announces the immediate deployment of Troops to the U.S. Mexico border to control illegal immigration and the immediate deportation of illegals with criminal records or links to terrorist groups. Birthright citizenship is abolished. All immigration from countries that represent a threat to the safety of American citizens is terminated indefinitely. Several prisons are closed.
4. Newly appointed Secretary of Business and Economic Development Carly Fiorina eliminates more than half of the Government agencies operating under the Obama administration saving taxpayers billions of dollars.
5. Newly appointed Director of Government Finance Rand Paul announces the abolition of the IRS and displays a copy of the new Federal Tax Return form. It consists of one page.
6. Hillary Clinton is in jail. Her cell is directly across from. Jesse Jackson and Al Sharpton who are serving time for "Hate Crimes". She bitches at them constantly from behind the bars of her cell in what some might call cruel and unusual

punishment. Bill interrupts his philandering once every 6 months to visits Hillary

7. Bernie Sanders is in the nuthouse, where he belongs. His room is directly across from Nancy Pelosi, Debbie Wasserman Schultz, Chris Matthews and Al Franken. They meet for tea every day at ten and discuss the success and benefits of Communism and Socialism throughout the world.
8. Windows 12 is released.
9. Barack Obama flees the United States under cover of darkness and returns to his homeland of Kenya before his trial for treason begins.
10. Oscar Meyer announces the introduction of a new cholesterol and fat free pepperoni that tastes just like regular pepperoni.
11. A committee is not established to determine what is causing global cooling. Billions of taxpayer dollars are saved.
12. Dead people no longer vote in Chicago, a huge blow for the Democrat Party in the State of Illinois.

And this my friends constitutes THE PERFECT DAY

Sic 'em Donald!

Monday, January 12, 2016

"Navy looks to remove 'man' from all job titles"
If you Call a skunk a kitty, it is still a skunk.
In our new armed services ''gender'' disappears.
The services now become sexless.
How sad.
The word seaman has been with us for thousands of years.
Now by the idiotic, senseless, stupid whim of an Obama appointed nut, we will no longer have "semen".
Can you believe this *IMPORTANT Obama THING* has come to this, but does nothing about ISIS, immigration, unemployment, or terrorists?

Being a man, and I still call myself a man, I think women are wonderful, marvelous, forever to be treasured, and loved.
I pray women will be women forever!!

Sic 'em Donald!

Saturday, January 23, 2016

Genius

The USA paid Iran $150 billion to sign a bogus “”please don’t build a nuclear bomb” treaty.

Genius

The USA gave Iran an additional $1.7 billion for release of illegally held American hostages, who should have been included in the bogus nuclear bomb treaty.

Genius

Jan. 21, 2016, John Kerry admitted some of the $150 billion would go support terrorist organization dedicated to KILLING AMERICANS.

Genius.

WASHINGTON -In a series of secret night time flights in the last two months, the Obama administration made more progress toward the president’s goal of emptying the military prison at Guantanamo Bay, Cuba. In .January alone some 22 terrorists have been released to join ISIS or other terrorists groups, dedicated to killing Americans.

Genius

In the meantime, ...

The Iranians masses are shouting “DEATH TO AMERICANS”.

???Treason: “.................. giving aid and comfort to the enemy.”

Sun, 31 Jan 2016

"THE BATTLING BOYS OF BENGHAZI"

We're the battling boys of Benghazi,

No fame, no glory, no paparazzi.

lust a fiery death in a blazing hell,

Defending our country we loved so well.

It wasn't our job, but we answered the call,

Fought to the Consulate and scaled the wall.

Mail - kcaj85@hotmail.com

We pulled twenty countrymen from the jaws of fate

Led them to safety and stood at the gate

lust the two of us and foes by the score,

But we stood fast to bar the door.

Three calls for reinforcement, but all were denied,

So we fought and we fought and we fought "til we died.

We gave our all for our Uncle Sam,

But Barack and Hillary didn't give a damn.

.lust two dead Seals who carried the load

No thanks to us... AS OBAMA SAID... we were just

"Bumps In The Road"".

And SHE said: "What difference does it make?"

And SHE wants to be the next President! The epitome of GALL

Sic 'em Donald!

Mon, 1 Feb 2016

♫Getting to know him # 1

There's no shortage of people taking cheap shots at The Donald these days.

If history tells us anything, however, it's that if you take it too far, you may be sorry.

In 2013, comedian Bill Maher did just that when he joked that Donald was "the son of a monkey" and offered $5 million

if he could prove that his father was a real human being.

Not only did Trump release his birth certificate, but he also released his lawyers.

The suit was dropped several months later

Sic 'em Donald!

Mon, 1 Feb 2016

♫Getting to know him #2

Published over 50 different books over his lifetime.
Most politicians have written at least one book to give them some credibility,
but Donald Trump is an overachiever in nearly everything he does.
Trump has published over 50 books in the past 25+ years,
and his books have reached #1 Bestselling status.
In fact, his first book, "The Art of the Deal", released in 1987
was a New York Times Bestseller and his book royalties alone
are higher than most American's annual household income.

Sic 'em Donald!

Mon, 1 Feb 2016

♫Getting to know him # 3

Donald Trump doesn't back down to other countries.
Donald Trump owns Turnberry, the famous golf course in Scotland which hosted The Open Championship in 1977, 1986, 1994, and 2009. He has been battling both the Scottish ministries
and the neighboring townspeople for years over environmental issues and particularly as they relate to land rights and energy policy.

Sic 'em Donald!

Mon, 1 Feb 2016

♫Getting to know him# 4

Trump The Teetotaler., Trump may take risks
in business and is known to do well with the ladies,
he doesn't mess around when it comes to what he puts into his body.
A lifetime teetotaler, not only does The Donald not drink,
but he doesn't smoke cigarettes or do drugs. His brother, Fred, was an alcoholic
who ultimately died of his addiction and Trump took his warnings very seriously

Sic 'em Donald!

♫Getting to know him# 5
Presidential Aspirations

Didn't choose to run for president on a whim.
Donald Trump didn't just wake up one day in early 2015
and decide that he might run for President.
In fact, he has considered doing so four other times in the past.
Never one to sit on the sidelines,
Trump has considered the possibility of
pursuing the Presidency in 1988, 2000, 2004, 2012, and now in 2016.
He also contemplated running
for Governor of New York in 2006 and 2014.

Sic 'em Donald!

Mon. Feb 1, 2016

FAIR IS FAIR

Donald Trump was born to a German immigrant named Fred Trump. Fred worked hard, became well to do. He had 5 children. One of them, Fred Trump, Jr. became anti-role model for Donald. Fred, Jr. became an alcoholic, had a miserable life, and died young.

Seeing what alcohol did to his brother, Donald has never drank or been a druggie.

When he became of age he worked for his father, and eventually took over the business.

By applying his talents and hard work, his wealth increased substantially.

Along the way he made some mistakes as everybody does. He learned from his mistakes and became very adroit at managing people and in the art of making money.

His "empire" went international and he obtained very valuable knowledge about tricky financial dealings with foreign entities. (Mexico will pay for the wall).

Apparently, his religious upbringing was minimal and his knowledge of the bible sorely lacking, hence his faux pas about two Corinthians. But he does claim to be Presbyterian. At least Presbyterians believe in Jesus Christ.

Donald married the first time at age 31. The marriage lasted 15 years and they had 3 children.

We know little about the marriage except it seemed to be a congenial separation with equal responsibility for the children who have become very outstanding citizens and love their Father very much.

His second marriage in 1993 lasted 6 years and they had one child.

Again,the separation appeared congenial.

In 2005 he married Melania Knauss and they have one child.

So, Donald has 5 children just like his father. There has been no hint of scandal, and apparently all involved are compatible.

Do 3 marriages disqualify him to be President? No.

Does having five well educated and outstanding children Qualify him to be President? No.

Then what Qualifications, at this point in history, do we need?

1. We need a doer, someone who can get things done.
2. We need someone who understands money... lots of money!
3. We need someone who recognizes the many problems we face and has a plan to solve them.
4. We do NOT need a good ole boy or a Casper Milktoast to just get along.
5. We need someone with GUTS to fight for us, the people, REALLY make America great again.
6. We need someone who is not beholden to any lobbyist or bureaucrats.

Trump qualifies for all of these
He does have an ego, but that is a good thing. He has demonstrated his ability to get things done.
He has good character, and he is not a MANIAC!!

Sic 'em Donald!

Thursday, February 4, 2016

The picture of an old geezer with a super inflated ego,
and a Polly-wants-a-cracker mouth who
screeches like a banshee. He wants
to be your custodian and take care of you
and your $$$ for the next 4 years.
Makes your heart beat fast
And your palms sweat, doesn't it?

Sic 'em Donald!

Feb.6, 2016

SIMPLY AMAZING WHEN YOU THINK ABOUT IT.

Isn't it amazing that, within only one week of Tiger Woods crashing his Escalade, the press found every woman with whom Tiger has had an affair during the last few years?
And, they even uncovered photos, text messages, recorded phone calls, etc.!
Furthermore, they not only know the cause of the family fight, but they even know it was a 9-iron from his golf bag that his wife used to break out the windows in the Escalade.
Not only that, they know which wedge!
And, each & every day, they were able to continue to provide America with updates on Tiger's sex rehab stay, his wife's divorce settlement figures,
as well as the dates tournaments in which he was to play.
Now Barack Hussein Obama has been in office for over seven years, yet this very same press:

- Cannot find any of his childhood friends or neighbors;
- Or find any of Obama's high school or college classmates;
- Or locate any of his college papers or grades;
- Or determine how he paid for both a Columbia & a Harvard education;
- Or discover which country issued his visa to travel to Pakistan in the 1980's;
- Or even find Michelle Obama's Princeton thesis on racism.

<<Or find out who were the actual birth parents of his two daughters.>>

They just can't seem to uncover any of this.
Yet, the public still trusts that same press to give them the whole truth!
Don't you find that totally amazing?

NOW TELL
ME THERE IS NO CORRUPTION IN THE AMERICAN PRESS.
Remember, you cannot get the water to clear up until
you get the pigs out of the creek.

Sic 'em Donald!

Friday, February 19, 2016

In the MEDIA's nonstop effort to find new ways to tell us
that Donald Trump is not a "true conservative,"
they seem to have forgotten that we're not electing a replacement for Rush Limbaugh.
We're electing a replacement for Barack Obama. The worst President in our history.
He has made Jimmy Carter look like an Einstein!
We're looking for someone—anyone!—
who can turn back this evil administration's nausea-inducing lurch to the left.
And we're going to mess that up because Trump invited the Clintons to his wedding?
Come on.
Bunch of dirt baqs!!

Sic 'em Donald!

Fri. 19 Feb 2016

The Vatican Wall
The Pope is against the Trump Wall.
Hypocrite?
Pretty formidable wall. Who's he figuring on keeping out the Mongol hordes???
Has Swiss Guards. Does not trust Italians!
IN THE WORDS OF RONALD REAGAN "POPE FRANCIS, TEAR DOWN THAT WALL."

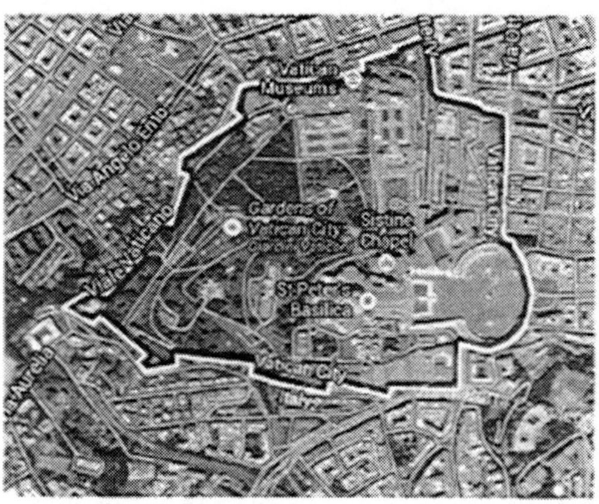

Sic 'em Donald!

Feb.23, 2016

My secretary the last years I worked was a black lady.
Since I retired she comes to my house and we go have lunch about twice a year. I have several black friends from work and at church.
One who is still working at TXU had a birthday
on Nov. 21, same as .Jan's, and we took him and his wife to dinner.
Color is not important to me, it what's inside that counts.
This you must know.
Republicans fought the civil war to free the slaves owned by Democrats.
But the Democrats to this day have never
recognized blacks as free and equal people.
They passed laws forbidding blacks to use white rest room,
or drink from a white only water fountain,
and made them ride at the back of the bus.
They had white only schools and black only schools.
The democrats fought integration of schools to the death,
but Republicans finally prevailed LEGALLY, but democrats to this day have not accepted it.
Don't let the bleeding heart socialist liberals make you believe otherwise.
It is just smoke and mirrors.
THEN THERE WAS THE LB.J 'war on poverty' which was just the democrats
method of permanently re-enslaving black people.
There was welfare for just about everything-having babies out of wedlock was a boon to increasing the fatherless black babies.
Today the % is over 70. Welfare pays for each one.
Need a raise in your welfare check? HAVE ANOTHER BABY.
THEN THERE IS UNEMPLOYMENT COMPENSATION,
AID TO DEPENDENT CHILDREN, FOOD STAMPS, AND THE LIST GOES ON AND ON.
The result? Today the poverty rate is higher than is was in 1965 when they passed the" "War on Poverty... Welfare payments are a pidley amount but they have gotten by" on it so long, and have not been

motivated to better themselves, so they get scared when the democrats say "you better vote for me so I can keep those checks coming. Those Republicans want to take them away." It is a lie but like their masters say

VOTE FOR ME. So the slaves on welfare have become a guaranteed voting block for democrats. When the percent of slaves goes over 50% you can kiss the America you know goodbye. And you won•t like it. Where does all this money for welfare come from? Take a guess. Some of it comes from taxes, my taxes, your taxes, a lot of people pay taxes.

But the sad part is about 51% of the people are paying

their taxes to support the 47-49% on welfare. When that is not enough, the Government just prints

more money, which just reduces the value of a dollar.

Sic 'em Donald!

Thursday, February 25, 2016

$$

There are thousands of insiders making billions on the status quo.
If Trump wins, that will all disappear, and they are getting desperate.
It is bad because desperate people will do anything for money,
and Donald's life right now is not safe.
If Rubio or Hillary win, nothing changes.
Scalia's death was a staged "natural"" event.
These people are merciless. Just look at the Clintons and Obama's graveyard

February 25, 2016

I see where Romney, the ultimate loser, has come out of the closet to bash Donald Trump.
Of all the "Establishment•• tricks so far, this has to be the biggest joke.
No-guts Romney had the 2012 election won (he thought), so he stayed smug and refused
to challenge Obama EVEN on his weakest points. He could have buried Obama, WHO was so inept in his first term.
Instead, the Romney campaign spent most of the fall from Labor Day to November
firmly convinced that they were comfortably on their way to victory.
No matter that most national polls showed nothing of the sort,
or that state polls showed, if anything, an even tougher road to an Electoral College majority.
The Romney campaign just coasted through the fall campaign with a smug. unshakable feeling of confidence.
Consequently, NO-GUTS Romney was directly responsible for 4 more years of Obama's socialism.
And he has the gall to bash Trump.
He is my #1 ENIGMA!!!

Sic 'em Donald!

2.26.2016

I do not believe Trump views himself as a conservative, nor do I think that is the end of the world!
In my opinion that Trump is a pragmatist. He sees a problem and understands it must be fixed.
He doesn't see a problem as liberal or conservative, he sees it only as a problem.
That is a quality that should be admired and applauded, and is one America desperately needs at this point in time.
And we have Problems.
EXAMPLE: Immigration isn't a Republican problem - it isn't a liberal problem—
it is a problem that threatens the very fabric and infrastructure of America.
It demands a pragmatic approach,
not an approach that is intended to appease one group or another.

So, it is my opinion that what America needs right now is a pragmatist, not a liberal or conservative, just pragmatist!
To repeat myself a pragmatist sees a problem and understands that it must be fixed, not patched,
and has a willingness and boldness to get it done.

You think Trump is arrogant?
Sometimes people are too quick to mistake confidence as arrogance,
Arrogance is common among those who have never accomplished anything
in their lives and who have always played it safe, not willing to risk failure.
Trump has confidence. Been there, done much.

Sic 'em Donald!

Saturday, February 27, 2016

Kerry the wimp.
When confronted with the fact that a terrorist released
from our detention center at Guantanamo Bay
returned to fight for Al Qaeda,
Secretary of State John Kerry responded,
"He's not supposed to be doing *that:*•
You cannot make this stuff up.
What a wimp! Stupid, too!

Sic 'em Donald!

2.27.2016

Trump is a pragmatist. He sees a problem and he dedicates himself to solve it.
He doesn't understand "Kick it down the road">
YES, Trump speaks like a bull wandering through a china shop, but he is telling it like it is and the truth is that the borders do need to be sealed;
we cannot afford to feed, house,
and clothe, 200.000 Syrian immigrants for decades
(even if we get inordinately lucky and none of them are ISIS infiltrators or Syed Farook wannabes); the world is at war with radical Islamists; *all the world's glaciers are not melting; and Rosie O'Donnell is a fat pig.*
Is Trump the perfect candidate? Of course not. Neither was Ronald Reagan.
But unless we close our borders and restrict immigration,
all the other issues are irrelevant.
One terrorist blowing up a bridge or a tunnel could kill thousands.
One jihadist poisoning a city's water supply could kill tens of thousands.
One electromagnetic pulse attack from a single Iranian nuclear device could kill tens of millions.
Faced with those possibilities, most Americans probably don't care that Trump relied on eminent domain to grab up a
final quarter acre of property for a hotel,
or that he boils the blood of the Muslim Brotherhood thugs running the Council on American-Islamic Relations.
While Attorney General Loretta Lynch's greatest fear is
someone giving a Muslim a dirty look,
most Americans are more worried about being gunned down
at a shopping mall by a crazed Islamic lunatic
who treats his prayer mat better than his three wives and
who thinks 72 virgins are waiting for him in paradise.
The establishment is frightened to death that Trump will win,
but not because they believe he will harm the nation. *They are afraid he will upset their taxpayer-subsidized apple carts.*

$$$Billions of your tax dollars are at stake and the Establishment will pull out every stake and
tell any lie to prevent their losing their stranglehold on all this money. Desperate people will do desperate things.
Scalia was a thorn in Obama's side. Scalia is not with us anymore. How convenient for Obama to have a SOTUS vacancy in last year of his term.

Sic 'em Donald!

Wed, 2 Mar 2016

As the Primaries and debates began to take their toll on Republican candidates,
we have seen many drop out of the race.
In each instance, the media latched on to the candidate
they wanted the public to vote for,
not the most publicly popular one.
For instance, when it became apparent to anyone
with an IQ above moron that contrary to the media's fixed polls,
..Jeb Bush was not wanted by the public,
they latched on to the next candidate
they thought they could manipulate us into supporting,
this being Ted Cruz and Marco Rubio.
With the prospects of a Rubio win becoming an impossibility,
Ted Cruz will garner the media support.
When it becomes apparent Cruz is going nowhere f ast,
the media will begin to slightly support Donald Trump
while wildly praising the Democrat candidate
whether it be Clinton or Sanders.

The bottom line is

the media will support the candidate
who represents the current socialist establishment.

Sic 'em Donald!

March 3. 2016

Romney the Loser's speech is over and his two-faced lies will live in infamy.
The prophet Romney the Loser descended into the abyss, selling his soul
to add money to his rich inheritance.
Shame. It was pitiful and even sickening to watch and listen to him espouse the words, written
by someone else, as though they were his words.
Sounded like the same words Cruz and Rubio have been aping.
What we have to understand is The Establishment will do
anything, and I mean anything, (Scalia), to maintain the status quo.
They are determined that the next president be a socialist subject to their
beck & call. It matters not whether it is an in-name only democrat or republican as long as the president thinks socialism.
§o book this. It was the great divide speech~
designed to split the remnants of the Republican party asunder,
Thus guaranteeing a Socialist president.
Our only hope you gotta believe!

Sic 'em Donald!

Saturday, March 5, 2016

I find it strange.................

1. In 2008 The Washington Establishment ran McCain against Obama.

   Other than surviving as a POW, McCain had accomplished nothing.

   Other than being a rabble rousing Community Organizer, Obama had accomplished nothing.

MCCAIN LOST.

2. In 2012 The Washington Establishment ran Romney against Obama.

   Romney used his inherited fortune to buy the govern-ship of Massachusetts where he was successful in installing socialized medicine. His only other accomplishment was having a 4 car garage, with elevator, installed in his multi-million dollar house.

   Obama proved to be a woefully inadequate President and was gasping for breathe.

   He was a sitting duck to be easily defeated.

ROMNEY LOST.

3. It is now 2016. What will The Washington Establishment do?

   The Democrats will either run a dyed-the-wool Socialist giving away fried chicken, or a dyed-the-wool Socialist with tons of baggage.

   To run against a Socialist The Washington Establishment has two remaining possibilities: Cruz and Rubio.

   Rubio has accomplished absolutely NOTHING.

   His main talent is memorizing pleasant, high-sounding phrases and rattle them off at a rocket speed pace. In the pocket of The Washington Establishment and they love him.

   A LOSER.

   Cruz has experience in practicing law and apparently knows the constitution.

   He is a staunch conservative

but lacks the finesse to sell his conservative agenda. _
Questionable but far better than a Socialist.

Not in The Washington Establishment camp is Trump, the outright leader and America's favorite to become the Republican nominee.

Trump is an anathema to the Washington Establishment.

Why? Trump is a doer. He turned a million dollars into billions. He has built things, run a business, hired thousands of people. He gets things done. Trump is a pragmatist, someone who sees a problem and sets about to fix it.

The good-old-boy Washington Establishment Club is a cesspool of crooked politicians and lobbyists filling their pockets with taxpayer money. Trump will destroy their house of cards and they know it.

BILLIONS OF DOLLARS ARE AT STAKE AND SPENDING $25-#50 MILLION TO DESTROY TRUMP IS ~UST CHICKEN FEED.

4. Finally, I said all of this so you can understand why I say: WE CANNOT AFFORD TO LET THE WASHINGTON ESTABLISHMENT PICK THE REPUBLICAN CANDIDATE!

Sic 'em Donald!

Thu, Mar 10, 2016

Billionaires, tech CEOs and top members of the Republican establishment flew to a private island resort off the coast of Georgia this weekend for the American Enterprise Institute's annual World Forum, according to sources familiar with the secretive gathering.

The main topic at the closed-to-the-press confab? How to stop Republican frontrunner Donald Trump.

Apple CEO Tim Cook, Google co-founder Larry Page, Napster creator and Facebook investor Sean Parker, and Tesla Motors and SpaceX honcho Elon Musk all attended. So did Senate Majority Leader Mitch McConnell (R-Ky.), political guru Karl Rove, House Speaker Paul Ryan, GOP Sens. Tom Cotton (Ark.), Cory Gardner (Colo.), Tim Scott (S.C.), Rob Portman (Ohio) and Ben Sasse (Neb.), who recently made news by saying he “”cannot support Donald Trump:’

Sic ’em Donald!

Sun. Mar 13, 2016

Chicago Thugs Shoot and

Kill Black Trump Supporter

Obama I know you will leave no stone untumed

to bring these THUGS to justice!

Mar 18, 2016

Greed is a powerful force. It will tum brother against brother, father against son,
daughter against mother, Christian against Christian, and
POLITICIANS AGAINST POLITICIANS, TURN ENEMIES INTO "FRIENDS",
AND “"FRIENDS"” INTO ENEMIES.
If this election proves nothing else it will prove the old adage
Politics makes strange bedfellows.
A month ago Lindsay Graham held Ted Cruz in such low esteem
he said if Ted Cruz were killed on the Senate floor, no one would notice.
TODAY Lindsay is campaigning and fundraising for Ted Cruz.
The American people are yelling loud and clear “"We want an outsider who will
rout out the corruption that is consuming our government and our country."
“"Trump is our choice. We think he can and will do it".
So why are so many spending millions and millions of dollars in an attempt to thwart
the will of the people?
Greed. Consuming GREED!
Greed is like a snowball.
Once it starts rolling it just gets bigger.

Sic 'em Donald!

March 19, 2016

Crucify Trump!
The problems America faces are huge.
Since they are the direct result of the political elites
it seems obvious that only an outsider can hope to curb the power they have.
Can Trump?
We can't know, but we should recognize that neither Democrats,
nor go-along-to-get-along Republicans,
have done anything to make things better.
At least with Trump there is a chance for change.
If there wasn't, would he be attacked as viciously as he has been?
It seems to me that sometimes you can judge the value of a man
by the enemies he makes.

Beware! There will be Moveon.org protests, and millions spent on advertising.

All for one purpose: to generate negative thoughts in your mind about Donald!

Sic 'em Donald!

Tuesday, March 21, 2016 1:30PM

The snake

Brussels March 21, 2016
The snake was invited into Europe.
The snake is now biting and killing people.
Obama is inviting the snake into America providing it
with food, clothing, a snake pit to live in, and money.
Would you like to guess how this snake will thank America?

Correction. Have you noticed how this snake <u>IS</u> thanking America?

Sic 'em Donald!

Wednesday, March 22, 2016

I, like most people, am neutral with most, and dislike a few,
But I am developing an intense dislike, almost a hatred for Glenn Beck.
He keeps comparing Trump to Hitler and If I were Trump I would sue Beck for every
penny he has or will have in the future.
As far as I am concerned, Beck is a pompous, overweight blowhard who, like Cruz,
will tell a lie when the truth would serve them better..
You really need to remove your blinders.
Beck is not a Christian or a Mormon and I am beginning to think he only pretends
to believe in GOD for mercenary reasons. i.e. $$$$

Sic 'em Donald!

Mar 23, 2016,

If you parrot what others say that doesn't make you smart,
it makes you a parrot.
As the word Christian is used today, Trump is a Christian.
He believes in GOD and Jesus Christ.
Unlike Bernie who professes to be a communist atheist.
QUOTE:
What we choose today will determine who we are tomorrow.

Sic 'em Donald!

March 26, 2016

The snail darter
You won't like this

In the early 70's a small minnow like fish called a snail darter stopped construction of a multimillion dollar hydro electric dam in Tennessee for several years.
Environmentalists discovered it in the river water and declared it an endangered species
and filed suit to prevent its habitat from being destroyed.
After several years it was decided to capture the little creatures and move them to another location. They are doing fine and reproducing like mad.
Since then thousands of creatures and plants
have been added to the ENDANGERED SPECIES list and *must be saved at all cost.*
ALSO, SINCE THEN, ABORTION OF MILLIONS OF HUMAN BABIES,
DESTROYING MILLIONS OF HUMAN BABIES,
CRUSHING THE SKULLS OF MILLIONS OF NEWBORN BABIES,
THROWING MILLIONS OF HUMAN BEINGS IN THE GARBAGE,
HAS BECOME A NON-EVENT!!!!!
So our culture has become 'SAVE THE LITTLE CREATURES. BUT KILL THE BABIES'!
I told you would not like this,
BUT HOW LONG ARE WE GOING TO PLAY THE OSTRICH GAME AND KEEP OUR HEAD IN THE SAND?
Sorry, but somebody had to say it.
And we need to say it and keep saying it over and over.

Sic 'em Donald!

Monday, March 28, 2016

My least favorite ENIGMA
If hard work and success
ARE rewarded with
higher taxes,
more government regulation,
and intrusion ----
and not working
IS rewarded w ith
    Food Stamps,
    WIC checks,
    Medicaid benefits,
    subsidized housing,
    and free cell phones,
—you might I live in a nation
that was founded by geniuses
but is run by idiots.

Sic 'em Donald!

March 29, 2016

When I was working and had employees under me, we had an agreement.

If I disagreed with something an employee said or did, I would say so.
If an employee disagreed with something I said or did, he was to challenge me.
In the end we might do things my way, OR maybe not.
All of us did better and were happy with this understanding.
What I am saying is if you disagree with something I say,
then please say so, and why.
We are a product of our environment and I have had 90 years of it,
So, my brain has been twisted, jolted, reprimanded, cajoled.
"Facts" have been digested, accepted, and rejected.
Knowledge has been stored, sometimes in recall,
sometimes in secret and locked compartments,
never to be seen or heard from again.
So, my friends, the last thing I want is for you to think of me
as a babbling old coot who has passed his prime.
Advice is free, and often it is worth about what it cost.

Sic 'em Donald!

Thursday, March 31, 2016

Tail wagging the dog!
A Bible and Bible verse have been removed from a POW/MIA display inside an Akron, Ohio Veteran's Administration clinic after a complaint from atheist Mikey Weinstein.

For decades, these items have long been a part of a “”Missing Man Table .. commonly displayed at military functions and installations all across the nation.

Weinstein said he intervened at the request of nearly a dozen, mostly Christian, military veterans who said they were offended by the Bible display. As usual, Weinstein failed to provide proof that these people actually exist.

Although clinic administrator Brian Reinhart said no one ever complained to him (other than Weinstein), he violated military protocol and took it upon himself to remove God's Word from the display.

According to OneNewsNow, military and base commanders have been instructed on how to respond when Weinstein comes calling with his anti-Christian demands: “”Tell him “Thank you for the call” and then send it up chain of command so [we] can start making correct decisions early on.””

In caving to Weinstein's hateful demands, Mr. Reinhart has shown a lack of courage, a poor knowledge of the Constitution, contempt for tradition, and a disregard for the families of the MIAs and the POWs themselves.

Sic 'em Donald!

Tuesday, April 5, 2016

Hillary Clinton says It's Okay to Murder Babies because the Preborn have NO Rights

On Sunday's episode of NBC's *Meet the Press* Hillary Clinton once again
articulated what is one of the most extreme positions in the abortion debate.
The Democrat frontrunner for President argued that
women should have the ability to kill their children
right up to the moment of birth and that living human beings
do not have any rights until the moment they escape their mother's womb.
Chuck Todd: *When or if does an unborn child have constitutional rights?*
Hillary Clinton: *Well, under our laws currently, that is not something that exists.*
The unborn person doesn't have constitutional rights.

In other words, the mother's vagina has some magic mojo.
The thing she has been carrying is just a thing,
until it escapes the mother's womb

Sic 'em Donald!

Saturday, April 9, 2016 8:32AM

Roseann '"Rosie'" O'Donnell Is a 52 year old part time "comedian".
In the past she has had choice critical words about George Bush and Donald Trump.
Donald responded, of course, with choice unflattering remarks.
(She once weighed 240 lbs.)
So....... Rosie and Donald do not like each other.
Rosie started it, but Trump now gets blamed falsely for not liking women. But IF you think Rosie, (who is actually the Husband in her lesbian relationship),
her WIFE and 5 adopted children are Typical of American women, the degeneration of America is far deeper than I realized.

Sic 'em Donald!

Sun, 10 Apr 2016

Why is Donald Trump is doing so well on the American political primaries?
He is vulgar, abusive, nasty, rude, boorish, and outrageous.
He is also saying what he thinks and, more important,
teaching Americans how to think for themselves again."

""No one could be a bigger contrast to the spineless
and undeserving Barack Obama,
who has never done a thing for himself and
is entirely the creation of reverse discrimination?
The fact that he was elected President - not once, but twice -
shows how deep - set the rot is and how far along the road to
national impotence the country has traveled."

""Under Obama, the US - by far the richest and most productive nation on earth -
has been outsmarted, outmaneuvered and
made to appear a second - class power by Vladimir Putin's Russia.
America has presented itself as a victim of political and
economic Alzheimer's disease.

Sic 'em Donald!

Monday, April11,2016

Greediness is everywhere.
Greediless* is nowhere.

***new word**

Sic ’em Donald!

Tuesday, April12,2016

Not a Tough Choice: Democrats are Evil
It is amazing to see so many Republicans and Independents stuttering and stamping about, and wringing their hands about the prospect of voting for Donald Trump. It has been unbelievable to see so many Republican women say they would never vote for him. It has been depressing to watch conservative icons draw a line in the sand and insist they will stay home or vote third-party in November if Trump is the nominee. Some have even gone as far to claim they will vote for Hillary Clinton.

I cannot understand what is going through the minds of these people?

If you really look at the two candidates, the choice is self-evident.

Our nation is starving and Hillary Clinton will not feed it.

Let's not forget where the real evil lies.

Sic 'em Donald!

Saturday, April 16, 2016

Just a thought..........
The world order, and the universe is all so incredible,
it blows the feeble human mind. Just the process of "reproduction"
of all living things, is mind boggling.

Disconnected thought..........
Everybody, well maybe not everybody, but a lot of people,
including me, have said
""God helps those who helps themselves.""
Thinking they are quoting scripture when they are not.
What it really says
"'God helps those who help others"
Therefore, encourage one another, build one another up,
do all you can to promote Donald,
just as I am doing.

Sic 'em Donald!

April 16, 2016

Today I realized I am not who I thought I was.
I GOT TO THINKING:
I have no appendix
My tonsils and adenoids are long gone.
My left knee has been replaced with a piece of metal.
My prostate is gone
As well as 6 inches of colon.
A small piece of backbone is missing.
I have cataracts in both eyes
And sound magnifiers in both ears.
Then there are my teeth.
I say my teeth but. all though I have a mouth full.
I know some are not original with me.
The originals are mostly patched
And the others were purchased. at a dear price.
From my dentist.
And. finally but sadly. I have added 20 lbs of latent enemy.
So today I realized
I am just an overweight shell of my former self.
Amen

Mon, 18 Apr 2016

Congress is 545 people
representing US the people.
SUPPOSEDLY!

BUT, NOT REALLY. It is the people in the shadows who pushed their agendas all these many centuries that are not counted because they are hidden. If you look closely, those who have opposed have been eventually pushed out sometimes so quietly you don't even notice they are missing. There are strong powers at work who may never fully be exposed. They are the ones truly running this country. 100 senators,

> 435 congressmen, one1President, and 9 Supreme Court justices
> equates to 545 human beings out of the 320 million
> that are directly, legally, morally, and individually responsible
> for the domestic problems that plague our countrv.
>
> It is inconceivable to me
> that a nation of 320 million
> cannot replace 545 people who stand convicted -
> by present facts -
> of incompetence and irresponsibility ..
> There is not a single domestic problem
> that is not traceable directly
> to these 545 people.
> When you fully grasp the plain truth-
> 545 people ALONE
> exercise the smothering power of the federal government.
> Then it must follow that what exists
> is what they w ant to exist!!!!!
> Are we stupid or what?
>
> **Sic 'em Donald!**

Monday, April 18, 2016

Obama Buddy and benefactor

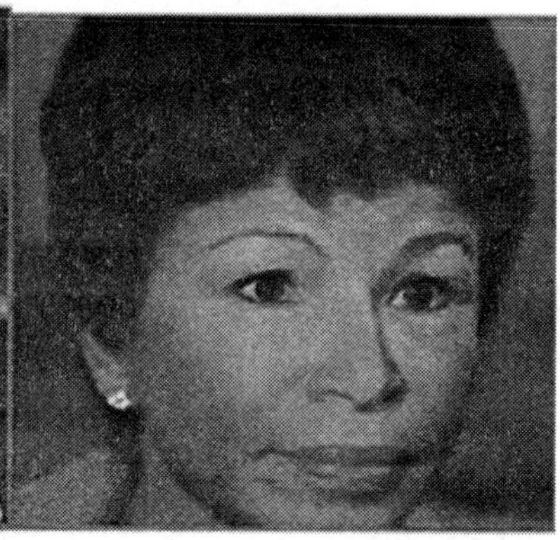

Obama Muslim Advisor

Sic 'em Donald!

4.25.2016

CULLING THE NOMINEES

There are now, just barely, 5 people left in the race for the Presidency.
4 of them have been for years, and still are, on the Government payroll, ie: paid with your tax money.
Are they attacked as the lechers and freeloaders that they are?
No.
Who gets attacked?
Why, a hard-working entrepreneur who pays himself and whose taxes have put bread on the table for the four freeloaders, THAT"S WHO!!

Sic 'em Donald!

Wed, 27 Apr 2016

The First "Earth Day" predictions of the 1970s

Check out these scientific prophecies

"Civilization Will End Within 15 Or 30 Years!
"100-200 Million People Per Year Will Be Starving to Death During The Next Ten Years"
"Population Will Inevitably And Completely Outstrip Whatever Small Increases In Food Supplies We Make!!
"Demographers Agree Almost Unanimously...
Thirty Years from Now, The Entire World... Will Be In Famine"
"In A Decade, Urban Dwellers Will Have To Wear Gas Masks To Survive Air Pollution"
"Childbearing [Will Be] A Punishable Crime Against Society, Unless the Parents Hold a Government License"
By The Year 2000... There Won't Be Any More Crude Oil!"
HOW DID ALL THESE WORK OUT?
Today the crisis is "Climate Change" and melting of Arctic ice!
Don't you realize that with "climate change"·· Florida will be under water by 2020 and students at TEX. A&M
will be able to take a morning dip in the Gulf of Mexico.

IF I BELIEVE THIS STUFF, WHAT KIND OF FOOL AM I?
GOES FOR "FAKE NEWS", TOO!!

Sic 'em Donald!

Tuesday, May 3, 2016 8:43PM

Trump sticker

Today my Trump "Make America Great Again" stickers arrived. My cars wear them with pride!

Sic 'em Donald!

Friday May 6, 2016

Pathetic Paul Ryan

Speaker Ryan says he is not "ready" to support Trump.
What is this RINO thinking?

He obviously wants to make a deal with the Deal Maker.
Thinking he can use his "precious" endorsement as an ace in the hole and tum Donald into a RINO and get him to adopt his agenda.
One other thing. As I have said, he was Romney's VP nominee and they blew it.
He has been counting on a contested and maybe a deadlocked Convention where
he would emerge as the PRESIDENTIAL NOMINEE. Now that has fallen by the wayside
He is crushed. His warped soul is playing hard to get, hoping to salvage something.
RINO Jerk!

Sic 'em Donald!

May 11, 2016

It IS, **when it isn't!**

Let's see...........
Legal is always legal except when it is not legal.
Illegal is always illegal except when it is not illegal.
The constitution is always our law, except when it's not.
The Supreme Court always rules according to the constitution, except when it doesn't.
The President always enforces the laws, except when he doesn't.
Our Congress always represents We the people, except when it doesn't?
I am confused, except when I am confused, which is always.
Think about this:
A truism:
Corruption is only corrupt when it is caught in the act.

Sic 'em Donald!

Thursday, May 12, 2016

Don't Underestimate Trump

From the Elite slander and lies about Trump keep coming.
Words are powerful, especially for the unwashed, which,
unfortunately, represent the majority of Americans.
So, if I were so minded, I could together a set of words
which would destroy someone like a preacher, for instance.
I would not have to lie, just maybe insinuate, or infer,
or maybe just ask a question.
"Did I hear someone say he still beats his wife?"
"Is he a 'closet' drinker?"
All I would have to do is mention this casually
to a few selected members over and over again,
The rumors start and there is no stopping them.
The elders hear them and now there are questions,
then denial, then unbelief, then you have destruction
of a perfectly innocent human being.
WHAT YOU HAVE HERE IS A PERFECT EXAMPLE
OF THE ELITE TRYING TO PLANT SEEDS OF DOUBT
TO BRING ABOUT THE DESTRUCTION OF DONALD TRUMP!
BESIDES YOU,
HOW MANY OTHERS HAVE THEY CAUSED TO
"STEP BACK AND......"?

Sic 'em Donald!

Saturday May 14, 2016

U R What U R

It is all in the mind. If Elizabeth Warren thinks she is an Indian, she is an Indian.
Just like Bruce. He thinks he is a woman, so, he is a woman.
Obama thinks he is a good President, so, oops. didn't work this time.
Elizabeth's Indian name is Liarwatha.

Sic 'em Donald!

May 17, 2016

HILLARY CLINTON-IN THE POCKET OF--

in June 2014, Hillary made a jaunt to sunny San Diego, where she made a speech to the Biotech Industry Organization (or BIO), THE LOBBYIST FOR BIG PHARMA!

Her compensation: $335,000 for one speech.

Talk about conflict of interest. Talk about a scam. And it's just the tip of the iceberg.

On March 13th, 2014, Hillary traveled to Orlando, Florida to make a speech to the Pharmaceutical Care Management Association.

She was paid $225,000...

Also in March 2014, Hillary jetted to Manhattan, where she received $250,000 to talk with Drug Chemical & Associated Technologies.

In October 2014, Hillary collected a quick $265,000 for a speech to the Advanced

Medical Technology Association (or AdvaMed).

In February 2014, Hillary made a speech to Novo Nordisk, the $130 billion Big Pharma mammoth.

It's bad enough that Novo Nordisk sells Victoza, a blockbuster diabetes drug that has been linked to 300 deaths.

But the kicker is, Novo Nordisk paid Hillary $125,000 to make a brief speech via remote satellite.

In other words, she didn't even have to show up! And yet, she collected $125,000 from a drug company that has killed people.

All told, that's $1.2 million from the world's biggest known killers... for a measly 5 hours of "work."

Talk about blood money

Sic 'em Donald!

Wednesday, May 18, 2016

The future of women's toilet.
Can you imagine-after years of practice, men
still walk up to a simple urinal, get all set, then pee on the floor.
I hate that, but if they can't hit a urinal, how much worse
will it be for toilet seats.

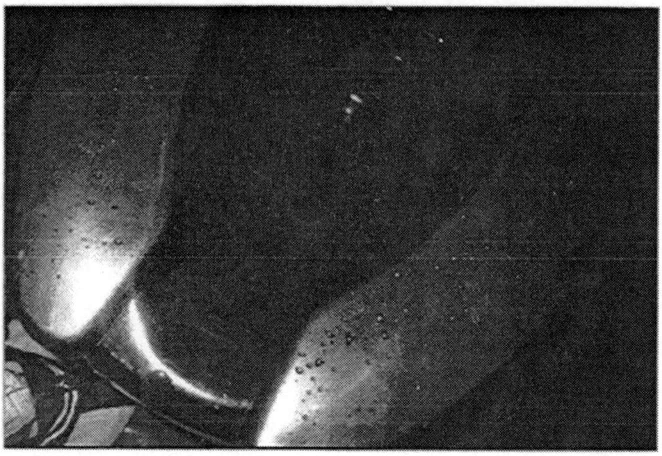

Ladies, you can thank Obama.

Sic 'em Donald!

Wednesday, May 18, 2016

Where no men have been

On May 25, 1961 President Kennedy made a promise to send a man where
no man had been before.
On July 20, 1969 Man landed on the moon, where no man had been before.
On May 13, 2016 President Obama made a promise to send men where no men had been before.

Sic 'em Donald!

Monday, May 23, 2016

It is a fact.
The United States faces a Muslim terror threat
...............because a certain percentage of the Muslim population
...............will kill Americans!
It is their religion. DEATH TO AMERICANS!
It is a fact.
Every increase in the Muslim population
...............also increases the number of potential terrorists.
It is a fact.
Muslim immigration increases the terrorism risk to
...............Americans every single year.
These are undeniable facts.
When you're in a hole, stop digging.
Muslim populations are a hole.
Immigration is the shovel.
Dig deep enough and you're *six feet under.*
IT IS A FACT.
FACTS DON"T LIE!

Tuesday, May 24, 2016 1 0:37 AM

WE ARE SO BLESSED, MY BEST SARCASM!
President Barack Obama, his administration, liberals, progressives, and nuts-whatever,
are basically at war with

1) traditional Americans,
2) the Judea-Christian value system,
3) common sense, and
4) millennia of history.

Progressivism is a worldview, fundamentally based on the philosophy of humanism.
Christianity, Humanism, Buddhism, Islam, Voodoo, and Hinduism can all be true at the same time.
That is completely and obviously illogical,
but you will hear some otherwise really smart people
insisting that all teachings of all faiths can be true.
Well, every faith except Christianity - because Christianity is exclusive,
It must be relegated to the trash heap of contemporary religions.
SO.......... LET THE GOOD TIMES ROLL.

AND..........ROT IN HELL.

Tuesday, May 24, 2016

I have to tell you a story.

God has been watching over me since I was a little boy. At 5 years old I had a ruptured appendix.

The nearest hospital was 30 miles away.

A Dr. Becton (and God) saved my life, which is a story in itself.

Since then there have many "miracles".

The latest happened last Thursday night.

Clarene & I went to Sonic, ate a hamburger in the car while listening to the radio.

You know Sonic is a drive in, park and eat place. Nobody gets out of their car.

When we finished I hit Start and the little solenoids just made a click-click noise. The battery was **DEAD**!.

But at that very instant a man walked in front of my car and heard the click-click.

Recognizing what it was he raised a finger, indicating he could help.

He had not parked at a regular spot, but away from the drive ups.

He moved his car close enough to mine and his jumper cables were long enough

to start my car. We drove home. Saturday, I purchased a new battery.

What a wonderful Samaritan you say. Yes, that's right.

BUT..... HAD I TRIED TO START. JUST 5 SECONDS LATER, HE WOULD NOT HAVE KNOWN WE HAD TROUBLE. TWO "ELDERLY" PEOPLE WOULD HAVE BEEN STRANDED.

Think about the odds.

Wednesday, May 25, 2016

Making millions is easy.

Mom-and-Pop bakery wouldn't bake you cake.?
Sue and be rich.
Small time wedding photographer wouldn't take your picture?
Sue and be rich.
Restaurant sells the fast food you cram down your kids" pieholes?
Sue and be rich.
Chain store won't let grown men use the same bathroom as little girls?
Sue and be rich.
Boss won't pay for your abortion?
Sue and be rich.
Company that made the firearm the nut stole and used in a violent crime?
Sue and be rich.
Small time florist wouldn't do your wedding?
Sue and be rich.
You spilled hot McDonald's coffee in your lap?
Sue and be rich.
You were late for your flight and the plane did not wait?
Sue and be rich.

There are many other possibilities. Stay alert.
Sue and be rich.

May 28,2016

Things I TRUST MORE than Hillary:

Mexican tap water
A rattlesnake with a "pet me"" sign
OJ Simpson showing me his knife collection
A fart when I have diarrhea
An elevator ride with Ray Rice
Taking pills offered by Bill Cosby
Michael Jackson's doctor
An Obama nuclear deal with Iran
A Palestinian on a motorcycle
Gas station Sushi
A Jimmy Carter economic plan
Brian Williams news reports
Loch Ness monster sightings
Prayers for peace from Al Sharpton

Sic 'em Donald!

May 30,2016

Today I can't help but remember My memorial of WWII.
I joined the navy when I was 18.
Since I already had 2 years of college I was considered Officer training material,
The Navy sent me to Officers training school in June 1944.
As fate would have it, Germany surrendered in May, 1945, and Japan,
reluctantly, in August, 1945. At that point the Navy did not need any more officers, or seamen.
So I was hung in limbo and discharged honorably, but without distinction,
in February, 1946. I had no heroics, not even a purple heart
for a pin prick like John Kerry in Vietnam.
If you have read this far, I know you are beginning to wonder
what is the deal about my •memories•.
Well, first of all, I was proud Americans were willing to fight, to the death if necessary,
to destroy two terrible evils that existed. I sang our national anthem, and saluted our flag and gave thanks to God that I was born an American.
THAT I still do. But sadly, I also remember some of my boyhood friends
who paid the ultimate price.
There were two brothers we nicknamed Jackrabbit and Cottontail because they
could run so fast, but in the end, not faster than a bullet.
There was Smitty, our all-star fullback from high school, son of a preacher,
and not afraid of the devil, but the devil got him.
Then there was, a big running back on my college football team.
He went off to Germany and never came back.
Then there was President Lyndon Johnson's Vietnam war that sacrificed thousands of young men. For what?

Nothing really. But my son, Rick, got sucked into the draft and spent over a year
in the jungles of Vietnam. After two Purple Hearts and Silver Star he survived and came
home. He had it bad, very bad, but his parents did also, wondering where he was,
was he all right, and hearing nothing. It was agony. The kind of agony millions of American parents have suffered since America was born. Fortunately, he survived, but the memories.

Today, thankfully, he is happily married and doing fairly well health-wise, but has to visit the VA hospital fairly regularly.

These are all things that make me glad and sad at the same time.

Suddenly, today's current events hit me in the face.

Sorry Obama, who is uncontested for being the sorriest President we have ever had,
is over in Asia apologizing to the Japan for stopping a war they started with
a surprise attack at Pearl Harbor, killing thousands of Americans.

And he went to N. Vietnam, still a rogue nation, and said we are sorry for all these years
you were not allowed to buy guns and ammunition. I, the big 1, am lifting your quarantine, so have at it!

He spends his time apologizing for Terrible America, at our expense.

Sic 'em Donald!

June 1, 2016 12:27 PM

Pig slop is disgusting stuff that people can't eat,
but pigs love it.

Bill Clinton, a disbarred lawyer,
an impeached former President,
who was fined for lying under oath,
asks the American people to believe him
when he says the best thing for the Country is
4 years for Hillary.
Pig slop! Uneatable!

Sic 'em Donald!

Thought for the day June 2, 2016

A strange thing is happening.
Paul Ryan, our illustrious Speaker of the house, a RINO Republican, is lukewarm toward Donald Trump, withholding full endorsement.
Then about 4 weeks ago, out of the blue, I started getting e-mails from him-touting Ryan. Multiple photo ops, and useless information.
Last week I received in the mail this huge survey which, supposedly, would give him information to help him guide the country to bigger and better days--followed of course by Send Money.
Today I received 10 beautiful photo opt pictures of him doing wonderful things.
Curiosity has got me. WHAT IS HIS GAME?

Sic 'em Donald!

Thought for the day June 3, 2016

The game continues. Yesterday Ryan issued an op-ed to his local paper, 806 words, 666 about ME, Ryan. He concluded by saying, with tongue-in-cheek,
he would vote for Trump.
What a ringing endorsement! What an evil web we spin!
Watch your back, Donald!

Sic ’em Donald!

June 6, 2016

UNBELIEVABLE
Sad facts... *THIS IS "0-Day'"*
Every year the French have a 4-day celebration in Normandy complete with American uniforms, tanks, jeeps and guns.
They still honor the Americans who died there....
June 6, 2016, the 72th anniversary of "'D-Day"",
the largest invasion ever attempted, where 200,000 Americans stormed the beaches at Normandy to begin the final push to defeat Nazi Germany in WWII.
D-Day marked the turning point in WWII in Europe.
Today, European heads of state make it a point to recall and honor the sacrifices of those who landed in Normandy,
as do our Presidents--<u>well, most of them ....</u>
In the 72 years since D-Day, there are eight occasions when the President of the United States chose not to visit the D-Day Monument that honors the soldiers killed during the Invasion.
The occasions were:

1. Barack Obama, 2009
2. Barack Obama, 2010
3. Barack Obama, 2011
4. Barack Obama, 2012
5. Barack Obama, 2013
6. Barack Obama, 2014
7. Barack Obama, 2015
8. Barack Obama, 2016

Today's Obama Schedule
Monday, June 6, 201610:00 am, he received the Presidential Daily Briefing.
4:24 pm He Honors the Super Bowl Champion Denver Broncos; Rose Garden
America - Aren't you proud?

Sic 'em Donald!

Thought for the day June 7, 2016

Paul Ryan was quick to chastise Donald Trump for claiming the judge in The Trump University trial is bias against him because his parents are Mexican.
IT WAS A RACIST COMMENT?
Why? What are the factors behind Trump's comment?

But Michelle Obama just gave a commencement speech in which she said she lives in a house BUILT BY SLAVES. RACIST COMMENT? Yes, one of a non-ending stream of racist comments made daily by Obama.
Nothing is said. Why don't you say something Ryan?
What is your game?

Sic 'em Donald!

Thought for the day June 8, 2017

To: THE DALLAS NEWS
I see by your headlines you are still promoting socialism. Is it Hillary or Bernie? No matter. Either one would finish Obama's job of dumping America into the sewer.
I find it difficult to believe how utterly un American you are. Have you checked out Venezuela lately, your favorite socialist country? Good old socialism at its best!

Sic 'em Donald!

Thought for the day June 9, 2014

I know what Hill's game is. It is played with lies, dirty tricks deceit, lies, all out of her Communist mentor's play book. But Ryan has suddenly taken the ball and running for glory, not for the party, for himself.
And I have to ask, What's his game?

Let's face it: people know what Republicans are against. Now we are giving you a plan that shows you what we are for. Our vision for a confident America is a full slate of ideas to tackle some of the biggest challenges of our time:

../ Poverty
../ National Security
../ The Economy
../ Health Care
../ Tax Reform
../ and perhaps most importantly, restoring the Constitution after decades of executive overreach.

America is on the wrong path, but there is a better way.
Lt's time to start a debate and look past this president to what we can achieve in 2017 and beyond.
In the coming days, you can find all these ideas on a new website Better.gop-starting today with a better way to fight poverty.
I hope you"ll check it out.

Thought for the day June 10, 2017

SOMEBODY FINALLY SAID ALL THE THINGS I BELIEVE!!!!!
I am the Democratic, Republican Liberal-Progressive's Worst Nightmare.
I am a White, Conservative, Tax-Paying, American Veteran, Gun Owning Citizen.
That's me!
I worked hard and long hours to earn a living.
I believe in God and the freedom of religion, but I don't push it on others.
I believe GOD made a Man and a Woman, not a Transgender,
I served my country in the US Military,
I believe in American products and buy them whenever I can.
I believe the money I make belongs to me and
not some liberal governmental functionary.
I'm in touch with my feelings and I like it that way!
I think owning a gun doesn't make you a killer;
it makes you a smart American.
I think being a minority does not make you noble or victimized,
and does not entitle you to anything. Get over it!
I believe that if you are selling me a Big Mac or any other item,
you should do it in English.
I believe there should be no other language option.
I believe everyone has a right to pray to his or her God
when and where they want to.
I don't hate the rich. I don't pity the poor.
I know wrestling is fake and I don't waste my time watching or arguing about it.
I've never owned a slave, nor was I a slave.
I haven't burned any witches, shot any Indians,
killed any Mexicans or been persecuted by the Turks, and neither have you!
I believe if you don't like the way things are here,
go back to where you came from and change your own country!

This is AMERICA... We like it the way it is and more so the way it was...
So, stop trying to change it to look like Russia or China,
or some other socialist country!
If you were born here and don't like it,
you are free to move to any Socialist country that will have you.
I believe it is time to really clean house,
starting with the White House, the seat of our biggest problems.

Sic 'em Donald!

Thought for today June 12, 2016

A lot of hogwash is being slopped around about being what you think you are, regardless of what your really are.
You know, like, if you were born a boy but think you are a girl, then miraculously, you are a girl.
I saw Hillary barking like a dog in one of her speeches, so does that make her a dog?
You decide.

Sic 'em Donald!

Thought for the day, June 14, 2016

The Gun
I read a story about this gun.
It was a prize gun, with a high powered telescope,
designed to be shot and could hit a target 1 000 yards away.
The owner was so proud of his gun and they went on many
Hunting trips. The gun performed as it was designed to do.
It obeyed its owner and only fired when the owner
Wanted it to fire. They were the best of friends.
It was very domesticated.
Then the owner heard how guns were going on a rampage
And killing people. He became quite concerned
So,he locked his friend in a gun cabinet.
Then remorse set in.
His friend never hurt anybody and only did what it was told to do.
One day he decided to test his friend.
He took his friend out of the gun cabinet, loaded it,
And left it on the front porch when he went to work.
Being freed from the gun cabinet, it was at liberty
to do whatever it wanted to.
Did it go on a rampage? NO!
When he came home in the evening, there was his friend, right where he left it.
It had not moved or fired a shot.
He concluded-Guns don't kill people. People kill people.
Moral: We have a people problem. not a gun problem.
Think about it.

Sic 'em Donald!

Thought for today 6.15.2016

In his book *The Audacity of Hope,*
Barack Obama stated of Muslim Americans,
"I will stand with them
should the political winds shift in an ugly direction."
The winds have shifted and he is keeping
his promise.
Think about it.

Sic 'em Donald!

Thought for the day June 16, 2016

Christians teach and practice:

You shall not kill

You shall not commit adultery

You shall not steal

Love your neighbor as your self
Do unto others as you would have them do unto you.
God loves the peacemakers.

Islam teaches and practices:
Death to the infdel.
Off with their heads.

Obama, Hillary, and liberals scream:
Christians and Trump are to blame for a crazed maniac muslim, with a head full of 70 virgins crap, killing 49 people.

Go figure.

Sic 'em Donald!

Thought for the day June 16, 2016

Trump was criticized for calling Elizabeth Warren "Pocahontas".
Yesterday he apologized.
He said "I apologize to Pocahontas"

Takes a big man to do that.

Sic 'em Donald!

Thought for the day June 17, 2016

They want to pass a law to prevent a Terrorist from buying a gun.

A terrorist is a terrorist. A terrorist is looking for a time and place to ply his trade, that is-Kill people.

My question:

If we know a terrorist is a terrorist and we just let him walk the street, would a law forbidding him to buy a gun, prevent him from acquiring a gun, or many guns, or hand grenades, or a machette
or dynamite, or maybe just a hammer?
If they pass such a law, will the terrorist think
"If I can't buy a gun, I might as well go back home where people love me...
YEAH! RIGHT!

More political HOGWASH!
Think about it.

Sic 'em Donald!

Thought for the day June 19, 2016

Father's Day, June 19, 2016
My Papa
As a little boy
I remember my Dad
My memories are glad
He was so tall
I was so short
I looked up at him
With a smile he looked down at me
He was so strong
I was so weak
As we walked he held my hand
My Dad was a real man.
He was gentile and kind
I am so glad he was mine.
He was my friend.
On Father's Day, and every day,
I look up and say
"Thank you, Papa,
For making me ME!""

B..J. Melton

Thought for the day June 20, 2016

A True Lie
How can a lie become truth?
Hillary knows. Saul Alinsky, the communist organizer, taught her.
It is so simple.
Tell a lie often enough and it will eventually become truth.
Man is such a Simpleton.
He hears what he wants to hear and disregards the rest.
The fact the media feeds us BS day after day, and we know it,
but cling to every word like gospel, just demonstrates
one real truth: We have become completely desensitized to
what is good and what is evil,
It is like
"I don't care if it is true or not, I just like to hear the words."
Come to think about it, that attitude defines a Socialist Liberal.
i.e Hillary personified.

Sic 'em Donald!

Thought for the day June 21, 2016

If all goes as planned America will have a new President on ..January 20, 2017.

Will the new president make America great again, OR will we continue down the slippery slope to mediocrity? SCARY!

Sic ’em Donald!

Thought for today June 23, 2016

Today is an odd day for me. No earthshaking news to report or tidbits of “wisdom” to express.

This morning I have stopped to count my blessings.

In my 90+ years the Lord has walked beside me, holding my hand, protecting me, providing for my well-being, and giving me hope for tomorrow.

My happiness is boundless. I have a beautiful loving wife, wonderful children

and grandchildren, many cherished memories,

and all the material things I could hope for.

And........... I have been blessed by being born in America.

Sadly, my America is changing, not for the better. I am afraid.

There is a song that apply describes today...

♫The future is not ours to see♫

♫Whatever will be, will be♫

AMEN

Sic ’em Donald!

Thought for today June 24, 2016

Consider the following:

1. EPA agents are armed
2. IRS agents are armed
3. FBI agents are armed
4. Homeland Security agents are armed
5. Bureau of Land Management agents are armed
6. Bodyguards for politicians are armed
7. Border patrol agents are armed
8. Police are armed
9. Secret Agents are armed

So, like Hitler's Germany, we have our own Gestapo, and guns are still killing people.

Question: 1. If the people, you and me, had no guns,
WOULD THE KILLING STOP?
2. If the people, you and me, all carried guns,
WOULD THE KILLING STOP?

Answer: 1 ____________________. 2 ____________________

Sic 'em Donald!

Thought for the day June 25, 2016

Are Americans screwed up or what?
This year abortion will kill, no, not kill, slaughter
over one million-that's MILLION- BABIES.
It is a non-event. Ho Hum.

A gorilla was killed to save a 3-year-old child.
Millions thought the stupid child should have been
sacrificed to save the gorilla.

A gay Muslim terrorist went on a rampage in a
gay nightclub, which had no armed security,
killing 49 and injuring many more.
Liberal democrats yelled "take away
everybody's guns·· (except mine).

A bunch of Democratic monkeys staged a
sit-down on the floor of Congress demanding more gun control
and elimination of our 2nd amendment.
The sit-down reminded me of a 2-year-old spoiled brat
having a temper tantrum!

Not a word about eliminating Muslim terrorists.

But Hillary said "WE need more Muslim immigrants!"
To paraphrase she said "we need more invaders!"

Sic 'em Donald!

Thought for the day June 26, 2016

We have had many Presidential elections, but none like 2016.
On one side we have a woman candidate, who is a professional politician.
We have never had a woman candidate for President.
On the other side we have a successful American business man who is not a professional politician.
We have never had such a candidate before.
In 2008 and 2012 America elected for the first time a man who is half black and half white and the white man's conscience was purged of guilt about slavery and he walked with head held high. See what we did! Hogwash!
How did that work out for us?
So many are in a quandary.
Women, out of loyalty to their sex, may be inclined to vote for the woman. They will have a tendency to sweep under the rug the facts about her character. It is well known that she is a habitual liar, a crook, a total failure as Secretary of State, and responsible for the deaths of many servicemen and our ambassador to Benghazi.
A woman's argument with their conscience might be ""But we have not had a woman president!"

If you have ever been to a rodeo and watched professional cowboys trying to ride a bull, you know the bull usually wins.
Our business man is like that bull. He may be a little unorthodox and shoot from the lip
sometimes, but he plays to win. Lose is not in his vocabulary.
The professional Elite politicians won't ride this bull!!
He plays to win for you and me!
We have never had a president like this before!
So how will you vote?
Make your decision as wisely as possible, but not emotionally.
Then don't look back. You cannot be certain about anything.
The moment of absolute certainty never arrives.

Be as for me and my household we will serve God and vote for Trump!

Sic 'em Donald!

Thought for the day June 27, 2016

Last week I saw a bunch of idiots sitting on the floor of the House of Representatives.
They sat there for 26 hours eating pizza and trying to sell their coolaid about gun control.
And we pay them about $900 a day, plus expenses, to do this!!!???
Today I asked myself "Self, what happens when the people do not have guns?"
I found this soft sell on gun control from none other than Adolf Hitler himself:

Quote:" *This year will go down in history. For the first time a civilized nation has full gun registration.*
Our streets will be safer, our police more efficient, and the world will follow our lead into the future!"
—ADOLF HITLER
So, what happened?

1938: Germany established gun control.
From 1939 to 1945, 13 million. Jews, Catholics and others who were unable to defend themselves were rounded up and exterminated.
There were many other BADDDD examples---
1929: Soviet Union established gun control.
From 1929 to 1953, about 40-60 million citizens, unable to defend themselves, were rounded up and exterminated or starved to death.
1966-1976: China still has gun control. 50-100 million civilians, unable to defend themselves, were killed in Mao Tse Tung's "Cultural Revolution".
In America the last time somebody tried mass gun confiscation was on April 19, 1775, at Lexington and Concord.
How did that work out?

Sic 'em Donald!

An unpleasant thought, June 28, 2016

Monday night I bowl in a league. As I left the alley last night
I felt pretty good after bowling better than normal.
Standing by my car was a lady I have bowled against for years.
She is in her 80's and carries a 140 average.
Her red car was parked next to my red car.
She said "I like your car but I don't like your bumper sticker",
referring to my TRUMP sticker.
"Are you for Hillary?
"Yes I am. She is for women. Trump hates women".
"Are you pro-choice or pro-life?"
"I am pro-choice. A woman has a right to choose."
Sensing an unpleasant confrontation, I contemplated
ending the conversation, BUT did not.
''Can you describe Abortion to me?''
"NO!" (emphatically) "I have studied all about it
and it is not anything like they try to paint it!"
"But aren't you murdering a child?"
Blank End of conversation.
Don't bother me with facts. My mind is made up.
Unpleasant thought. Deflated my ego.
Has America really sunk this low?

Sic 'em Donald!

Thought for today, June 29, 2016

Yesterday Radical Islamic terrorists preached their religion of peace by blowing up the Istanbul airport~ *killing or injuring about 200 people.*
As Obama would say "it was just "workplace violence".
We desperately need an AMERICAN PRESIDENT.
WE ARE JUST STUMBLING ALONG WITHOUT ONE!
Maybe we need to re-think what it means when we sing

♫GOD BLESS AMERICA♫

While the storm clouds gather far across the sea
Let us swear allegiance to a land that's free.
Let us all be grateful for a land so fair
As we raise our voices in a solemn prayer.
God bless America, land that I love
Stand behind her and guide her
Through the night with a light from above
From the mountains, to the prairies
To the oceans white with foam
God bless America My home sweet home!
Amen

Sic 'em Donald!

Thought for the day June 30, 2017

DEAD CROWS

Researchers for the DALLAS NORTH TOLLWAY
found over 200 dead crows recently, and there was concern that they may have died from Avian Flu.

A Bird Pathologist from Texas A&M examined the remains of all the crows, and, to everyone's relief, confirmed the problem was definitely NOT Avian Flu.
The cause of death appeared to be vehicular impacts.
However, during the detailed analysis
it was noted that varying colors of paints appeared on the bird's beaks and claws.
By analyzing these paint residues, it was determined that
98% of the crows had been killed by impact with trucks,
while only 2% were killed by an impact with a car.
DNT then hired an Ornithological Behaviorist from Baylor University to determine if there was a cause for the disproportionate percentages of truck kills versus car kills.
He very quickly concluded the cause:
When crows eat road kill, they always have a look-out crow in a nearby tree
to warn of impending danger.
They discovered that while all the lookout crows could shout "Cah", not a single one could shout ""Truck."

Just for fun.

Thought for today July 1, 2016

Bill Clinton, Loretta Lynch meet on tarmac in Phoenix
Coincidence?
What is a coincidence?

"A remarkable concurrence of events or circumstances without apparent casual connection"

This week we had a Great coincidence!
Bill Clinton flew to Phoenix supposedly to play golf. (But was it REALLY golf?)
Loretta Lynch flew to Phoenix supposedly on "company" business.
By chance their paths crossed on the tarmac and Loretta
Says "Fancy meeting you here, Bill. Would you like a cup of tea?"
"That would be nice" Bill says so she invites Bill into her company plane for a chit-chat and a cup of tea.
For about 30 minutes they bored each other drinking tea and talking about grand kids.
golf. and travel.
No one mentioned the Presidential campaign, or Benghazi, or Hillary's possible indictment.
And there is beach front property for sale in Arizona-CHEAP!
Also I Betcha didn't know there really was a Cinderella, a Rip Van Winkle and
a talking log of wood named Pinocchio whose nose grew every time he lied.
Anything is possible in Fantasyland where we live!

Sic 'em Donald!

Thought for the day July 2, 2016

Wisdom is such a nebulous thing.

As incomprehensible as the **universe** is, there it is, and there you are.
No amount of irrational thinking will make it go away.
Man, with his finite mind, knows it did not just happen.
But then we ask "How did it happen?"
We do not know and cannot know.
Man, since the beginning (whenever that was), has conjured up the idea that a god, a supreme being, created everything.
Once we rationalize there was and still is a Great Creator, a God, everything becomes simple-until.......
You ask "Where did God come from?"
Suddenly we realize-oops-we don't want to go there.
It messes up our comfort zone.
So as for me, I believe in God the creator.
He made the rules that I try to live by. He set the moral and ethical standards I am to go by.
If everyone followed His rules, what a wonderful world it would be, Boring, but wonderful.
However, He created us with a mind and free will. We are free to follow his rules or make our own rules.
But there are consequences if we make our own rules, that I find unpleasant.
Today the thinking is You are what you are, and If it feels good, do it.
In politics today, the rules are out the window.
Our country has gone straight downhill the last ten years.
First, we had a House Speaker with no balls, then one with no guts, followed by a sneaking, backstabbing RHINO.
Greed and power have taken control, so people like me, who fantasize about the way it used to be, are probably spitting in the wind.
BUT I HAVE HOPE, FAINT THOUGH IT MAY BE>>>>>>>

Sic 'em Donald!

Thought for the day July 3, 2016

You know we have a Muslim government, don't you?
The president and all of his major staff are Muslims.
They celebrate all Muslim holy days, such as Ramadan,
which is now. The month of Ramadan ends July 4th or 5th, then
the big feast of EID (no bacon or pork chops) is the next day,
This is a big deal for Obama and his Muslim friends.
But there is no celebration for Christmas.
Obama flies off to Hawaii AND HIDES.
HOW DID THIS HAPPEN?

Sic 'em Donald!

Thought for the day July 4, 2016

Count your blessings.
Name them one by one.
See for you what the Lord has done.
Look up and say '"Thank you".

Sic 'em Donald!

Thought of the day July 6, 2016

Yesterday proved the theory-
Hillary Clinton is above the law.
FBI director James Comey told the American people
to go swallow a nanny goat.
Shudder@#$%&*

Sic ’em Donald!

Thought for today July 7, 2016

The Declaration of Independence... says...

“We hold these truths to be self-evident,
that all men are created equal,
that they are endowed by their Creator
with certain unalienable Rights,
that among these are Life, Liberty and the pursuit of Happiness. That to secure these rights,
Governments are instituted among Men,
deriving their just powers from the consent of the governed, -
That whenever any Form of Government
becomes destructive of these ends,
it is the Right of the People to alter or to abolish it,
and to institute new Government,
laying its foundation on such principles
and organizing its powers in such form,
as to them shall seem most likely
to affect their Safety and Happiness...
I wonder--Are we there yet?

Sic ’em Donald!

Thought for today July 8, 2016

In times past, God has used many people for his purpose.
Some I would not like, or agree with, But God did not consult me.
I'm not sure I would have liked Moses, but he was the right man for the time.
I know I would not have liked Pilate.
He could have saved Christ from the cross,
but it was God's plan that Christ be sacrificed for all of mankind.
So, God provided Pilate.
Winston Churchill was one of our greatest national leaders in the 20th century.
He was a bombastic, cigar smoking, at times crude, even misogynistic leader.
A woman once told him he was disgustingly drunk.
His response was "My dear, you are disgustingly ugly,
but tomorrow I shall be sober and you will still be ugly!"
But he had exactly what was needed to stop Hitler at the Channel,
to rouse a nation to never give up, and to partner with America to find final victory in Europe.
You wouldn't want him as your preacher, maybe not even your father,
but he was the right leader for that moment in England's history.

Do we have a Jesus were running for President?
Of course not, but we do have a devil like person running,
A candidate we know will continue taking America into the abyss.
So, we must consider someone else who is imperfect,
someone who will shape the culture in America for the next 30 years.
So, then, where will Donald Trump take us?
I ask myself will Donald be good for America?
I honestly believe that he has been already.
He has shaken the political system to its greedy roots!
Do his comments offend me? At times.

Do I agree with all he says? Not at all.
Is he being raised up by God to preserve America? Time will tell.

This I know. Donald is the only choice for Americas" survival.
so ..

Sic 'em Donald!

Thought for Today July 9, 2016

Today is Saturday, once known as the Sabbath,
a holy day for the Lord, and one of the 10 commandments.
Which reminds me, what happened to the 10 commandments on which America was founded?
Those of us who cling to our bible and guns and still try to do what is right, are laughed at, and ridiculed.
The 'anything goes' crowd has a new set of commandments:

1. Sex is my god
2. Lying is a cultivated art. (see Hillary)
3. Adultery is the spice of life.
4. Abortion is just population control.
5. Babies don't need no man around.
6. What's mine is mine, what's yours is mine.
7. Life is cheap. Who will miss a few dead cops?
8. If it feels good, do it.
9. You are not what you are, you are what you think you are.
10. Use God's name in your profanity. Adds shock value.
11. LGBT IS NORMAL

FINALLY

12. There is no God.

The sex deviates of Sodom and Gomorrah
would be proud of today's America.

Sic 'em Donald!

Thought for today July 10, 2016

The fools are here, there and everywhere.
And Obama is delighted with his creation.
In his 7 and 1/2 years he has run rampant with his socialist and Muslim ideas,
And nobody raises a finger to stop him.
Why? because he is black.
So, what have we fools got for tolerating him for 71/2 years?
Obama says we are no longer a Christian nation.
And you know what? He's right.
Think about it.
He has taken the bible out of schools. Any mention
of God or Jesus is forbidden.
Prayers are anathema, except to Allah. Muslim
prayer rugs and prayer rooms are everywhere-in airports,
work places, government buildings.
The bible and God have been removed completely from
military bases. Even their mention is forbidden.
The 10 commandments have been given an unceremonious burial.
Immorality has become the norm.
The list of Obama blessings go on and on.
Can you name them
one-by-one?

Sic 'em Donald!

Thought for today July 11, 2016

Writing today is difficult. Normally I am a happy guy
and look for any opportunity to laugh. But the slaughter in Dallas
last Thursday is weighing heavy on me.
Oh, I know I have no kindred involvement
with any who were killed or injured, but I hurt emotionally.
Since I was a boy I have had great respect for those
who choose a dangerous lifeto protect innocent people from the bad guys.
I never liked the word "Cop". For some reason
to me it shows disrespect. So I taught my children
to always say "Policeman·.
This is a sad time for Dallas and America.
Our leaders are quick to blame guns and how easy
is to buy guns, and refuse to acknowledge
the real problem.
We have a sickness in America and it is called racism.
And it is being fed and promoted by Obama and those who literally want to destroy our country.
Off hand, and this is very important, is chaos just around the comer?
If so, will martial law follow?
If Obama declares martial law, will he cancel the elections
and take the roll of Dictator OFFICIALLY?
Don't sluff it off.
Ask yourself "Why is Obama so giddy happy these days?"
THERE IS NOTHING FOR ME TO LAUGH ABOUT.

Sic 'em Donald!

Thought for the day July 13, 2016

Most days we have some kind of encounter with other people.
It may be a stock man or woman at Walmart, a clerk,
a greeter, maybe a waitress, a cashier, someone at church,
or someone you just make eye contact with
that you do not know, and you speak.
Maybe the only encounter you have today
will be with your mate, or perhaps a child.
Will you be loving, kind, thoughtful, polite, or rude and thoughtless?
We need to realize and remember:
PEOPLE MAY NOT REMEMBER EXACTLY
WHAT YOU SAID, OR WHAT YOU DID, BUT
THEY WILL ALWAYS REMEMBER
HOW YOU MADE THEM FEEL

Sic ’em Donald! (This goes for you, too, Donald)

Distressing thought for today July 15, 2016

Today could be a black letter day for America.
I don't mean to be an alarmist, but what I see alarms me.
What I see and what Obama has been doing, and is doing,
to divide the races in America,
pitting black against white, everybody against the police,
tells me his goal is chaos. followed by declaring martial law, followed by
assuming the role of DICTATOR.
To add gasoline to this fire, there is evidence that there will be a PROTEST OF HATE in about 38 American cities
TODAY JULY 15, 2016, many of which could be violent.
IF it happens, batten down your hatches because things are really going to get nasty.
IF it does not happen, I will be glad to be wrong.
Hopefully I am wrong.

Sic 'em Donald!

My thought for the day July 16, 2016

Who am I? Come to think about it, that is an interesting question.
So, really, who am I?
In writing these thoughts for the day, it has caused me to pause and just think. Think about people, family, current events, my life, and this world that GOD made.
Mostly I think about people. People are made by GOD in the image of GOD.
We were given intelligence and dominion over all living things.
We were given emotions...... love, happiness, sadness, hate, jealousy, envy, joy, thankfulness, regret, pride, lust, conceit, and ego.
We were given the ability to think, to reason, to tell the difference between good and evil.
Other living things do not have these things.
We rule the world.
Why then, with all this power and intelligence, do people
KILL OTHER PEOPLE AND SLAUGHTER THEIR BABIES?
WE ARE THE ONLY ANIMAL THAT DOES THIS!!
Why do People go to war with people and kill people by the millions?
Other animals don't do that.
The answer? I don't have one.
So, I come back to the question "Who am I?"
I think I am a people who tries to make a difference,
infinitesimal as it may be.
Final thought: People are really stupid.

Sic 'em Donald!

Thought for the day July 18, 2016

5 policemen killed, 7 wounded in Dallas
3 policemen killed, 3 wounded in Baton Rouge YESTERDAY!
Hatred is running amok.
When did all this start?
When did patriotism, freedom, the “”Grand Old Flag”,
and IN GOD WE TRUST, disappear from our vocabulary?
Madalyn Murray O’Hair, the most atheistic of atheists, was partially responsible
for kicking God, Jesus, Christianity, prayer, and any religion out of schools in 1963.
The onslaught on religion, and our ‘unalienable rights’, (which were endowed by our Creator)
has continued unabated by atheists, ACLU, communists,
liberals, and our own beloved Supreme Court.
Love Thy neighbor, Do unto others…, has been changed to
“Do it to them before they do it to you!””
The divisiveness and hate Obama and party have been fostering the last 7 ½ years
is coming home, not to rest, but to foment more hatred, and violence.
5 policemen killed. 7 wounded in Dallas
3 policemen killed. 3 wounded in Baton Rouge YESTERDAY!
When will it end?
Our police are the only thing between us and anarchy.
Somehow, someway, we must put GOD back in our lives and
restore Law and Order!

Sic ’em Donald!

Thought for today July 19, 2016

There are good people in this world. I know some of them.
There are bad people in this world-lots of them.
I don't personally know any of them, but I could name quite a few
that are bad, really bad, and will be bad until they die.
I hear a lot these days from the "good"" people
about how we should treat the bad people,
the people who want to kill the good people.
We should love them, show compassion, be understanding,
and demonstrate by our actions how nice it is to be good.
When they see how good it is to be good, they will change their ways
and be good! What a wonderful world it would be.
CLAPTRAP!
History tells us there have always been good and bad people,
starting with Cain who killed his brother Able.
There have been thousands of wars-good VS bad.
The bible tells us in Matthew 24:6
"You will hear of wars and rumors of wars, but see to it
that you are not alarmed. Such things must happen.
but the end is still to come ...
Jesus came to earth offering everyone eternal life.
He did wondrous things to show he was the long-awaited Messiah.
Thousands of good people followed him.
He demonstrated unbounded love and compassion.
AND THE BAD PEOPLE KILLED HIM!!!!!!!!!!!!!!!!
So, in the end, our behavior depends on what
the definition of LOVE is!
And common sense tells us when to "tum the other cheek".

Sic 'em Donald!

Thought for the day July 21, 2016

Next month my house will be 49 years old.
It is very good house and has served me well.
But day before yesterday it developed a plumbing problem.
Yesterday the plumber told me how bad it is.
It is a $10,325 problem.
Add to that that House insurance and car insurance is due next month.
What a lick!
Plumbing repairs will start today.
I woke up this morning kinda feeling sorry for myself.
Then I said to Self "Self, you have so much to be
thankful for. Thank God."
So, I took a happy pill and said a prayer to GOD
for the blessings He has showered me with.
I have my health, My sweet wife Clarene, good credit,
and Donald Trump should be our next President.
How can I not be happy?
I will pay the bill, but it will take a while (like a year).

Sic 'em Donald!

Thought for the day July 22, 2016

Strange, strange, strange, really strange.

During the Republican presidential campaign Cruz and company posted on the internet a nude photo of Melania when she modeled professionally for a living.

Trump, in typical Trump mode, fired back something about Cruz's wife.

Cruz was "devastated" and has never forgiven Trump.

Trump was considerate enough to let Cruz have prime time Wednesday night for his speech.

Cruz and 16 others took an oath to support the eventual winner of the Republican Presidential campaign.

To date 4 "honorable" men have reneged on that oath:

Jeb Bush

Lindsey Graham

John Kasich

Ted Cruz

A man's word should be his bond.

Cruz's word is now trash.

Wednesday night he laid an egg

Thought for the day July 23, 2016

Our plumbing problem is fixed.
I never realized before how much it is worth to be
able to flush the pot without worrying.
Well, you can believe me, it is worth

a huge amount!

Sunday is Clarene's birthday and for her present I told her
she could flush the commode as many times as she wants.
She is thrilled, no, not just thrilled,
she is ecstatic beyond words!
She plans to get up early Sunday morning to start flushing!
It is amazing what it takes to make some people happy.

Sic 'em Donald!

Thought for the day July 24, 2016

Well the joy of flushing the commode, fizzled out
pretty quick after about 5 or 6 flushes.
So, I made her Birthday card with a picture of roses on it.

That fell flat also, but the money inside saved my skin.
She likes money.
I am looking forward to a wonderful birthday for
My Pretty Woman!
That's my thought for the day -ALL day!

Thought for the day July 25, 2016

I have heard all my life that difference of opinion
makes the world go around.
Last week during the Republican convention
I listened to millions of words, most of which I agree with.
Today the Socialist convention starts.
There will be millions of words spoken,
most of which I will disagree with.
I predict: There will be enough differences of opinion to
make the world go around and round for many years to come.
PS: Like it or not, politics will be our life
until the election. Hopefully, there will be life after that.

Sic 'em Donald!

Thought for the day July 26, 2016

Last night curiosity got me and I forced myself to listen to Pocahontas.
At last count, if I didn't miss any, she had told 63 lies, half-truths,
and fantasized to poor gullible souls how you can
make a silk purse out of a sow's ear.
Then I listened for a very short time to the Messiah of the millennials
Give me, give me, give me what I cry for.
There were some in the audience who were literally crying
because their hero and savior is being left by the wayside.
It was heartbreaking.
It is a phenomenon of human nature I guess.
The Democrats have been promising Mansions for decades
and delivering outhouses.
With each new generation the cycle repeats.
This new generation has been promised everything
FOR FREE, AND THEY ARE STANDING IN LINE WITH THEIR HAND
OUT SHOUTING “”GIVE ME MORE, GIVE ME MORE!”
“Vote for me
and you will see
how wonderful living on
the Plantation can be.”
A pig is a pig is a pig.

Sic ’em Donald!

Thought for the day July 27, 2016

I listened to Bill Clinton's speech last night. If you did,
you have got to realize he did not get the name Slick Willie
by accident. It was incredible how he took a lie or half truth
and embellished it by 10-fold, converting crooked, lying Hillary
into Mother Teresa. No! that's not right.
Even as slick as Slick Willie is, he couldn't do that.
Maybe Florence Nightingale. And the ignorant souls in the crowd
swallowed it like Blue Bell ice cream.
You know IF Hillary is elected President,
A PERSON WHO HAS ABUSED COUNTLESS WOMEN
WILL BE FIRST LADY.
I hear women say they are for Hillary because she is for women,
and I wonder:
Is she for Bill's women that She ruined for life,
OR for the ones he never got around to?
Neither Hillary or Bill have any shame.
What a mess. Makes me think of Hiroshima.

Sic 'em Donald!

Thought for the day July 28, 2016

They say Trump is running for President to improve his status.

He wants to trade this

For this?

And this

For this

And this $$,$$$,$$$ For this $0/00
Give me a break!

Thought for the day July 30, 2016

I am deeply concerned.
Millions of Americans are preparing their minds to willing
Participate in the biggest scam ever. The magnitude boggles the mind.
On Wednesday night Bill Clinton, a married man.
who has committed adultery with countless women,
wove a romantic story about a marriage of bliss,
a marriage of best friends, a marriage for the ages.
This fairy tale was built on lies, half-truths, and omissions.
Don't question anything, just take your sleeping pill.

On Thursday night Hillary Clinton appeared on Stage in
her white jump suit, so clean, so pure, so elegant, so innocent,
SO POMPOUS, and poured out her soul to millions of panting souls,
who hung on every word about her fairy tale.
Question nothing, just take your sleeping pill. It is all a facade.
It is not about helping the '"little' People, the sick, the poor, the minorities, the unemployed. It is not about Making America better and safer.
The DNC, Hollywood, the Media and Academia have, for years,
been ignoring the scandals, lies, gross mistakes, incompetence,
and human bodies laid by the wayside, while at the same time
drawing pictures of bliss, love, hope and caring for the masses.
"I'M WITH HER" cried the grossly uninformed as she stood on that stage braying like the jackass she is. Yeh man. I believe. Save me from my ignorant self. Sick, sick, sick.
It is not about the people. It has never been about the people.
It is all about Hillary, and power, a gigantic EGO, a glass
ceiling, and money, money, money.
Ask yourself '"How did two people who have been on the public dole become multi-millionaires. almost billionaires?"
The whitewashing is just about complete. The justice department has declared her criminal acts are not of consequence, and, therefore, eligible to run for President. The many past sins have been swept away, and she is pure and clean as the driven snow.

Only if, GOD forbid, she is elected President, will the facade be stripped away and we will finally see Hillary for what she really is. The SCAM will be complete.

HURRY DONALD. RUN FAST.

WAKE AMERICA UP!

Thought for the day July 31, 2016

Bernie Sanders-The sacrificial goat.
As unlikeable as he is, you have to feel a little sorry for Bernie.
From the beginning the system was rigged.
From the beginning Queen Hillary was going to be
the nominee.
From the beginning Bernie was to be the sacrificial goat
on the altar of Her Highness.
Bernie fought a good fight and finished the race.
He added spice to an otherwise boring, boring, Democrat "campaign".
Bernie ran as a democrat, but he has never been a democrat.
He is an Independent Socialist who promised everything free
to everybody. Come to think about it, Hillary and Bernie
really have all things in common.
But I Repeat-from the beginning the system was rigged and
Bernie knew it.
So, he dutifully laid himself on the altar, a perfect sacrifice.
He had his moments of glory. Not bad for an old goat.

Sic 'em Donald!

Thought for the day Aug. 1, 2016

When I woke up this morning, I thanked the Lord for ONE more day. I got up, went through my usual routine, which I suspect is similar to most people on my mailing list. I looked in the mirror. I should not have turned on the light. Wow! How could a bed do that much damage in 8 hours!.

Then I came to my common senses.It is what it is, so make the best of it. Be HAPPY.

I am normally a happy person, but all last week I know I was a down-in-the-mouth scrooge, and a pessimist,thinking my better-than-it-should-be world is coming to an end because of world events.

So today I sat down at this machine and thought to my self
""Self, count your blessings" and I did.

The list is far too long to bore you with, but my attitude
has improved dramatically, and I have resolved that
TODAY IS GOING TO BE A HAPPY DAY.
Hope yours is, also.

Sic 'em Donald!

Thought for the day Aug. 3, 2016

Well, I had one Happy day-Monday.
Obama ruined yesterday and I have carry over today.
Obama had the gall, and audacity, to say Trump
"is not fit to be President...
This from a man who soaked up *REV. Jeremiah* Wright's
hate for America for 20 years A man who sat at the feet of Bill Ayers. who had been a domestic terrorist who planted bombs in public places, including the Pentagon. A man who is a self-confessed Muslim who bowed to the King of Saudi Arabia,
A man who has filled the White House with Muslims and Muslim sympathizers,
A man who has dedicated himself to reducing America to 3rd world status.
A man who is flooding America with muslim immigrants, some of which are terrorists.
Obama was elected, not because he was qualified, but solely because he is half black.
He was not fit to be President when he was elected,
And he has severely deteriorated with ON-THE-.JOB-TRAINING.
So, I repeat:
Obama had the gall. and audacity, to say Trump
"is not fit to be President ...
Lies are a way of life for socialist. communists and Muslims.

Sic 'em Donald!

Thought for the day Aug. 4, 2016

Put your seat belts on. Charges against Donald Trump,
innuendoes, inferences, allegations, accusations, lies, TV ads,
and propaganda you can't imagine at this point,
have now begun to increase in intensity.
Where they will go no one knows,
but the billionaires with their hands in the cookie jar
will not give up easily.
Below is one example of STUFF that showed up Wednesday.

Rep. Karen Bass, an ultra-liberal California Democrat in her 3rd term,
on Wednesday launched a change.org petition
calling for Donald Trump to undergo mental health evaluation,
insinuating he may have NPD, Narcissistic Personality Disorder,
(like Obama has.)
Her qualifications to make this charge: She is a member of the black
caucasian. Congress and she was once a physician's assistant.
PS: She also introduced a bill in Congress to rename a post office.
I don't know if it passed.

Sic 'em Donald!

Thought for the day Aug. 5, 2016

Think about this.

There are 435 Representatives and 100 Senators in Congress.
How many can you name? How many are ever in the news?
I am a newshawk and by trying real hard I can name 17.
The other 500+ are just in the shadows. What do they do?
Good question! Really! What do they do?
If you let a dog represent Congress (not a bad analogy, really)
and the 17 represent the tail,
Does the tail wag the dog, or Does the dog wag the tail?
You know the answer to that.
So what do the 500+ do? Make phone calls to raise money,
and ride the gravy train.
Now you know why Congress never gets anything done
and has a 1 0% approval rating.

Sic ’em Donald!

Thought for the day Aug. &, 2016

The DEAL maker

Obama to the Iranian Ayatollah

Obama: "You are holding one of our soldiers who deserted: "We want him back"

Ayatollah: what's it worth to you?

Obama: "Name your price"

Ayatollah: "You are holding many of our good people in

Guantanamo. Send them all back to us."

Obama: "I can't do that. America would go berserk. How about one for one swap?"

Ayatollah: "You funny man."

Obama: "Ok. How about two? or Three"?

Ayatollah: "I feel generous. Make it five and I name the five."

Obama: "Deal".

Obama to the Iranian Ayatollah

Obama: "You have 4 kidnapped American citizens and I am under a lot of pressure to bring them home. What's your price?"

Ayatollah: I am running low on spending money. Had a lot of expense equipping my terrorist organization. How about 100 million per person?"

Obama: "I hate haggling so it is a deal, But we have to keep it secret. We don't pay ransom money."

Ayatollah: "Fine with me. Convert it to Swiss francs and let me know when you ready."

Sic 'em Donald!

Thought for the day Aug. 7, 201&

After Obama got caught (again) with his hand in the cookie jar, he smiles, flashes his teeth, and denies that ransom is ransom. In politically correct terms, it was just a coincidence, and not ransom.
"We don't pay ransom."
Liar liar Pants on fire!

Sic 'em Donald!

Thought for the day Aug. 8, 2016

I have never been a fanatic about gardens or raising flowers,
so my flower beds do not get the attention they should get.
But I am a proud person and I like pretty things.
My beds got so bad, shame finally motivated me to do something.
So... Yesterday I worked my flower beds, removing weeds and trimming the few flowers I have. For a 90 year old it was work.
Today I got up thinking about those weeds, and I wonder:
Why is it that weeds will grow anywhere with no attention at all.
You don't have to water or fertilize. They seem to be happiest if you do nothing. And if you do nothing, they will take over and choke out any good flowers you have.
On the other hand, the flowers we love require tender loving care.
Water, fertilize, and weed out the bad stuff, and talk kindly to them.
Suddenly I realized, AMERICA is like a beautiful flower, the envy of the world.
GOD has blessed us with freedom and prosperity. For over 200 years we guarded with jealousy what we inherited and fought wars to preserve our inheritance.
But now, deliberately it seems we are planting weeds in our garden.
Immigrants by the thousands are being brought to our America.
Immigrants who not love America, immigrants who have vowed to kill the flower that is America.
These are the weeds that. left unabated will destroy America.
"Thanks Obama"," Thanks Hillary

Sic 'em Donald!

Thought for the day Aug. 9, 2016

Simple Definition of *coincidence*

- :a situation in which events happen at the same time
- in a way that is not planned or expected"
- :the occurrence of two or more things at the same time"
- Simple Definition of
- *:ransom:* money that is paid in order to free someone
- who has been captured or kidnapped"

Sorry. This is such a big deal? I don't want Obama to get away with lying about it and sloughing it away into never-never land.
Let's see. In the dead of night at precisely 1:00 am an Iranian plane carrying 4 hostages secretly arrived at an airport In Europe.
On the same night at precisely 1:00 am an unmarked plane carrying $400 million dollars in Swiss francs secretly arrived at the same airport.
Within minutes the $400 million in Swiss francs was transferred to the Iranian plane carrying the hostages and the hostages Were transferred to the unmarked plane.
Zoom. Both planes go on their merry way.
Would you call this a coincidental ransom, or
Would you call it a ransom coincidence?
No matter. The big question is:
Where did the $400 million come from?

Obama's slush fund?

Thought for today Aug. 10, 2016

Rigging, rigging, rigging.
A fact of election life.
Dead people with no voter ID, have won many elections.
Live (somewhat) people without voter ID, have won many elections.
Some election results are predetermined.
Berni Sanders thinks that is so.
Ballot boxes are stuffed.
Ballot boxes are lost.
Computer programs record YES votes as **NO** and **NO** as YES.
In the 2014 election electronic voting machines
switched votes from one party to the other in at least six different states.
Rigging, rigging, rigging.
PS: People who think Hillary would make a good president, also think Bruce Jenner is a woman and Obama is a Christian.

Our next 1st lady? NEVER!!!!

Donald, you got to really Sic 'em!!

Thought of the day Aug.12, 2016

Hillary Clinton big money contributors!
You really don't have to wonder why a "President" Hillary would be so valuable to these people IF they can "give" away this kind of money.

Hedge fund	George Soros	$7M
Hedge fund	Haim & Cheryl Saban	$10M
Hedge fund	James Simon	$7M
Hedge fund	Donald Sussman	$4M
Hedge fund	David E. Shaw	$2.5M
Venture Capitalist	JB Pritzker	$6.5M
Save & Loan	Herbert Sandler	$2.5M
Liberal	Laure Woods	$3.31M
"Dear friend Danny"	Daniel Abraham	$3M
Openly Gay	Fred Eychaner	$2M

(Fred gave $14M for Obama 2012 campaign)
Planned Parenthood,Marsha & Henry Laufer $2M

Environtalist	Jan Stryker	$1.5M
Liberal democrat	Pat Stryker	$1.5M
Socialist	Barbara Lee	$1.407M
Hollywood	Jeffery Katzen berg	$1M
Hollywood	Steven Spielberg	$1M
Hollywood	Thomas Tull	$1M
Trial lawyer	John Steven Mostyn	$1M
Investments	Bernard Schwartz	$1M
Neurology-Headaches?	Dr Silberstein	$800,000

She has sold her heart. mind and soul for
Money. money, money!
Donald Trump-a threat to their cookie jar.

Sic 'em Donald!

Thought for the day Aug. 13, 2016

Who would have thought?
Simone Biles at the 2016 Summer Olympics has just become the best gymnast of her generation, perhaps ever.
In a way you have seen a miracle.
Simone's birth mother was addicted to drugs and alcohol, and as such. was a prime candidate for the Planned Parenthood Butcher shop.
Simone could easily have been destroyed along with millions of aborted babies.
After her birth in 1997, her father, whoever he was, was never a part of her life. So, in 2002 her addicted mother lost custody of her 4 children and Simone was placed in foster care, eligible for adoption.
Fortunately, Simone's grandparents adopted her and became her legal mother (Mom) and father and the world has been blessed.
Today we have a GOLD medal winner, who, before her birth, was a perfect candidate to be thrown in the garbage dump.
Makes you wonder, Hillary
HOW MANY OTHER POTENTIAL GOLD MEDAL WINNERS HAS PLANNED PARENTHOOD DESTROYED?

Sic 'em Donald!

Thought for the day Aug. 14, 2014

Some of you who receive my "Thought for the Day" and do not know me probably wonder who this nut is.
SO............ I will tell you. I am really many things.
The Lord put my soul in a white body which makes me...
a racist.
I am a Christian which makes me
an infidel.
I am over 80 and retired which makes me
a useless old person.
I think and I reason which makes me anathema
to main stream media lies.
I appreciate the police and our legal system which makes me
a right-wing extremist.
I believe in hard work and fair pay for actual work done
which make me anti-socialist.
I am proud to be an American and proud of our culture
which make me a minority.
I acquired a college education without government loans
and had no debt which makes me a sucker.
I believe in a strong military for the defense and protection
of America which makes me a warmonger.
I was born with male hardware and I know
which rest room is mine!
So, this is who I am, and I am proud of it. I cannot be who I am not.

Sic 'em Donald!

Thought for the day Aug. 15, 2016

Two items worth noting.
Let me get this straight......
The DNC is mad at Russia because they "Think"
Russia is trying to manipulate our election
by exposing that the DNC is manipulating our election?

The death tax: Hillary just postulated that if Trump were dead,
The government would get $4 billion in Taxes, which would pay tuition for thousands of college kids, or provide medical care for millions of children.
THIS IS WHAT YOU CALL 'PLANTING A SEED IN THE MIND OF SOME DERANGED INDIVIDUAL'.
For the media this is a non-event.
When you realize how many dead bodies that have been left on the Clintons trail, is she making a threat?
If Trump HAD POSTULATED THIS about HILLARY,
the media would go into cardiac arrest!

Sic 'em Donald!

Thought for the day Aug. 16, 2016

The Clinton's· just released their income tax return for 2015.
Their gross income was $10.2 million.
Pretty good for two unemployed people.
Being big-hearted they contributed $1,042,000 to charity.
Out of the $1,042,000, $1, 000,000 went to the
Clinton Family Foundation.
How thoughtful. They tithed the standard 10% to .... themselves!!
The remaining $42.000 represents 0.41% given to real charities. (Maybe)
Whoopee! My cup of joy runneth over!

Sic 'em Donald!

Thought for the day Aug. 17, 2016

There is an old saying "you find what you look for"
This is true.
I got up this morning, a blessing in itself, looked in the mirror, realized I have one more day, and I said
"Thank you, Lord. Thank you very much"
My sweet wife is still sleeping peacefully and
I have a 10:08 tee time. I know the world sucks but
I choose to look for happiness today.
Bet I find it!!
Hope you have a happy day, too.

Sic 'em Donald!

Thought for the day Aug. 19, 2016

I am well aware that:

1. I have very strong opinions.
2. Some people I know are like minded.
3. Some, who are uninformed, disagree with my opinions.
4. Facts are not relevant to the uninformed.

So, with that said, I am not under an illusion that
everyone enjoys my thought for the day.
Some strongly disagree. Not my problem.
The Lord willing, in less than 2 months, I will have survived
91 years on this earth. For now, I live one day at a time.
I have bones that ache, a back that hurts,
and Arthritis lives with me 24 hours a day.
But I know I am one of the lucky ones.I have had a long life full of happiness. Some sadness sure. Life is what it is.
Many never get to my age.Most important. I have loved and been loved.
My mind is still good (I think). I am at peace with myself, and happy.
I look for things to laugh about and I laugh a lot.
So what do I think about people who disagree with me?
Nothing. Nah dah.
My final thought for today is I hope that even those
who disagree with me are smart enough to...................
NEVER VOTE FOR THAT LYING, CROOKED, HILLARY CLINTON.

Sic 'em Donald!

Thought for the day Aug. 20, 2016

This is for fun only.
I got to thinking about our English language and how strange it is.
Some words are spelled alike, but have different meanings.
Some words are spelled different, but pronounced the same. (cents, sense-sole, soul)
Then the word "up" hit me and I couldn't tum it loose so I started listing all the UP"S I could think of and I got this:
UP.
on the up and up, stickup, straight up, pickup, hang up,
step up, lay up (golf term), stay up, stand up, go up,
what's up, raise up, give up, true up, creep up,
crawl up on, sneak up on, call up, bring up, speed up
set up, get up, frame up, burn up, rake up, cut up
sun up, clean up, dirty up, walk up, dress up, fly up
caught up, dry up, rinse up, wash up polish up
make up, sweep up, stop up, plug up, c limb up,
mess up, fess up, grow up, scare up, gather up
pour up, throw up, broke up, right side up
left side up, this end up, leg up, light up, think up
grind up, up on, uptight, uptown, up yonder,
up above, up the creek, up to no good up late
up early, up yours, upside down, upset, up and at 'em
Enough. Now, pray tell me, what is the definition of UP?

Sic 'em Donald!

Thought for the day Aug. 21, 2016

Yesterday was not my best day.
I attended the funeral of a friend, a friend who worked with me years ago,
and a fellow Christian.
His name was Mike. Mike accomplished many things in his working life, made many friends, and enjoyed life to the fullest.
Mike was a happy person with a wonderful family,
and took advantage of the good things this world has to offer.
As I sat there listening to his good life being remembered by the preacher,
memories of my own life began to flash through my mind memories of myself as a boy, as a man, as a husband and father,
and as a Christian.
I couldn't keep my mind from asking
'What will the preacher, or whomever, say about my life when it is over?"
It has been said, and it is true, funerals are for the living, not the dead.
So, my worry today is not what will be said by loved ones and friends,
but what the LORD will say in the hereafter.
Will it be "Well done, good and faithful servant?"
So, today, as I sit in church, happy to have one more day,
I realize there is no need to worry.
At 90+years the die has been cast.
I am what I am. Good or bad, I have made my mark.
The Lord, not people, will be my judge.
Amen
Finally, for you and them and all of us I have to say

Sic 'em Donald!

Thought for the day Aug. 23, 2016

I don't know why but something triggered the term "Character flaws" in my mind.
Nobody is perfect, but most people try to minimize or at least subdue their flaws.
However. Hillary Clinton is not one of those people. If anything she amplifies her flaws, and laughs about them.
So, I thought it might be interesting to list her flaws, without comment.
Here goes: absentminded, forgetful, abusive, arrogant, audacious, bigmouth, bigot, racist, blunt, callous, cruel, deranged, disloyal, disturbed, Very egotistical, erratic, fierce, frail, gruff, hard hearted, incompetent, indecisive, indifferent, liar, liar, liar, untrustworthy, liar, liar, liar, megalomaniac, nervous, obsessed, pacifist, paranoid, pest, precarious, predictable, unjustly proud, rebellious, remorseless, seducer, approaching senility, scoundrel, selfish, self-righteous, temperamental, ugly, user (of People), vain, bobble headed, Fantasizer!!!!

Then there is Trump:
sensitive, mis-speaks, defensive

WOW! What a difference!

Sic 'em Donald!

Thought for the day Aug. 25, 2016

DEMOCRATS-WHERE DO THEY FIND THEM?
"We have to pass the bill so we will know what is in it..-Polosi
"We're going to take things away from you on behalf of the common good."
-Hillary Clinton
"At this point what difference does it make?"-Hillary
"Speaking from my own religious tradition in this Christmas season, 2,000 years ago a *homeless woman gave birth to a homeless child* in a manger because the inn was full." – Al Gore, 12122/1997 during a press conference on "homelessness"
"The southern border is more secure today than in the last 20 years"-Obama
"You can keep your doctor"·-Obama "I invented the internet"-Gore
"In 50 years we will not have a North Pole."-Gore
"The vast right-wing conspiracy has been after my husband since he announced for President"-Hillary "There is no terrorist threat"-Michael Moore. (Over 19.000 terrorist attacks have occurred since he made that statement)
"It is just a JV team"-Obama "AI QUADA IS ON THE RUN"-Obama
"I want to be as transparent as possible!"-Democrat *Hillary Clinton*
(THIS SPACE LEFT BLANK. PAUSE AND REFLECT)
I want the public to see my email, I asked State to release them. They will review them or release as soon as possible.- Clinton
(So, why did you erase them and why do they just keep coming?)
"I been in all 57 states"-Obama
"We have to spend more money, to keep from going broke."-Biden
"We can always print more money"-Obama
"Can you imagine someone like Donald Trump being COMMANDER-IN-CHIEF?"-Hillary (My comment-I CANNOT imagine Hillary with that job)
"I told the truth about my e-mails. "-Hillary
"It was that video that caused the Bengasi attack".-Hillary, Obama, Rice
"I stand here as a freed slave"-Shelia Jackson Lee

(Freed by President Lincoln 150 years ago.
The previous owners were not available for comment)
“Every month we do not have an economic recovery package
500 million Americans lose their jobs:-Nancy Pelosi
“All this country needs is a 3 letter word- .JOBS, .JOBS, .JOBS!”-BIDEN

Sic ’em Donald!

Thought for the day Aug. 26, 2016

A woman you know as lying, crooked, Hillary made a speech in Reno, NV yesterday.

She spent the whole of her speech casting supporters of Donald Trump, *such as me and you and America First, as racists.*

Personally, I felt insulted *until/ considered the source.*

The Alt-Right are America First patriots who, like me, believe in placing the needs of Americans above the needs of foreign countries, illegals, or refugees.

That's not RACIST, that's COMMON SENSE.

The term "Racist" is what Liberals and Progressives start yelling when they are losing an argument, and believe me, she is losing it, (perhaps in more ways than one), and the scandals on her back are getting heavier and heavier. The reason she only comes out of her hole every three-four days is---- she has to rest.

Meanwhile, she is married to a man constantly accused of rape and sexual assault, she takes MILLIONS from Middle East countries who abuse women and execute gays, and she also "made out" with a *KLU-KLUX-KLAN Grand Dragon,* who she and her husband proudly called "A FRIEND."

I am NOT a racist but she is a BIGOT!

Sic 'em Donald!

Thought for the day Aug. 29, 2016

Liberals hate the filthy rich.
Liberals hate white supremacist.
Liberals hate bigot Christians.
Liberals hate Wall Street corruption.
Liberals hate war.

Hillary is everything Liberals hate.

Yet, just mention her name and they pee down both legs.
Insane?

Sic 'em Donald!

Thought for the day Aug. 30, 2017

MY GOLDEN YEARS

1. I will enjoy the present moment. It is all I am guaranteed.
2. I don't worry. Worry makes you older, and I don't need any help to speed the process.
3. I exercise, eat TOO well, and get my naps nearly every day.
4. I enjoy my money and hope my children enjoy theirs.
5. I don't stress over the little things.
6. Love is not age related. Loving brings sed on acquired wisdom. Sometimes it is good. Sometimes it is worth about what it cost.
7. I know my time is now. As I write this I am still alive having fun and enjoying life.
8. The golden years of my life have been many and I savor each day as a reward for trying to live a good life.
9. As long as I have my senses I will not burden my children by living with them.
10. At this point in life I have hobbies to keep me active and alive-golf, bowling, this computer, and an intense patriotism for my country.
11. I get out of the house, and refuse to become a couch potato.
12. 1 try to speak softly and courteously.
13. I try not to complain or criticize, I Love my sweet wife, Clarene, life, my family, my neighbors where I live, and my country.
14. I am comfortable with myself, both inside and out.
15. My looks are what they are. They are part of who I am.
16. I obviously have an active email account and try to use it for good.
17. Sometimes I give advice about the current political situation, I get a poor grade here.
18. As I get older, pain, discomfort, and me are becoming close acquaintances. Not friends, just acquaintances.

19. Someone said" Holding a grudge is like taking poison and expecting the other person to die."" I try not to take that poison. Life is too short.
20. I laugh. I laugh a lot. I love to laugh. Silly things, funny things, dumb things. Anythings.
21. Finally, and firstly, I try to live true to my beliefs.

    I am a Christian. I believe in God, Jesus, heaven, and life in the hereafter.

    I am calm, comfortable, and serene trying to live by the Lord's commands.

    I am really a free spirit, at peace with the world, and happy as can be.

Amen

Thought for the day Aug. 31, 2016

Have you ever seen a Muslim do anything that contributes positively
to the betterment of mankind or to our American heritage?
I can think of one marginal contribution.
i.e. They minimally control population growth by cutting off heads.
On second thought this is offset by having 10 children
who are taught from birth how to cut off heads.
Has Obama the Muslim, made your life better? If so, How?
Would Hillary, with her Muslim adviser as Chief of Staff,
make your life better? If so, How?
If in doubt, you may want to cogitate on the subject.
If you come up with one (1) thing, please tell me.

Sic 'em Donald!

Thought for the day Sept. 1, 2016

Around Election Time we hear a lot about jobs, jobs, jobs. All the politicians tout their ability create jobs and put people back to work.
So, I have to ask you ''When is a Job a job'?
Below is a little lesson in Job Creation 101.
As President neither Hillary Clinton nor Donald Trump
will be able to create a single job.
Elected officials can't create jobs.
They can only hinder job growth through taxation and regulations.
True job growth comes from people who take risks with their own capital and skills and/or they pool their capital and skills with investors who contribute their own money and skills for a return on their investment.
The money that governments use to create a government "job" is stolen money. It's taken from people who earned it and given to people who have not earned it.
Electing people to steal money from some people so it can be given to other people is theft by proxy.
Wealth redistribution by majority vote is still theft.
Hillary and Bernie are both professional at redistributing your money.
In real life, Donald trump has created Thousands of REAL jobs.
For Hillary, Bernie, and Obama the number is ZERO, nah dah, none!

Sic 'em Donald!

Thought for the day Sept. 2, 2016

A little humor here.
On numerous occasions in the past I have felt compelled to write, fax or call my Representative or Senators.
This little story, supposed true, aptly represents the success of my attempts to initiate some action.

A female journalist heard about a very old Jewish man who had been going to the Western Wall to pray, twice a day, every day, for a long, long time. She went to check it out. She went to the Western Wall and there he was, walking s lowly up to the holy site.

She watched him pray and after about 45 minutes, when he turned to leave, using a cane and walking very slowly, she approached him for an interview.

"Pardon me, sir, I'm a reporter for World News. What is your name?"" He said, with a strong Jewish accent. *"Morris Feinberg"* •

"Sir, how long have you been coming to the Western Wall and praying?"

"*For about 60 years"'.*

"60 years! That's amazing! What do you pray for?"

"I pray for peace between the Christians, Jews, and the Muslims"
"I pray for all the wars and all the hatred to stop ..
"I pray for all our children to grow up in safety as
"responsible adults and to love their fellow man.'"
"I pray that politicians tell us the truth and
put the interest and needs of the people ahead of their own interests."
And finally,he said *"I pray that everyone will be happy.'"*

"How do you feel after doing this for 60 years?""

"Like I'm talking to a brick wall!'"

Sic 'em Donald!

Thought for the day Sept. 4, 2016

Tomorrow is Labor Day holiday, a misnomer since millions of people DO NOT labor but get paid anyway. People who have to labor are paid 1 1/2 times normal.

It has been celebrated as a national holiday in the United States and Canada since 1894.

As has been his custom Obama will give a Labor Day speech.

You won't like it. He continues his smooth-talking crusade to divide us.

And I can't help but wonder-what does this guy, who never had a real job know about labor? nuthin, really.

Hope you have a safe and sane holiday.

As for me, I may also take the day off, unless a thought for the day comes along that is earth shaking.

Sic 'em Donald!

Thought for the day Sept. 6, 2016

I told you twice.
This will be thrice!
The elites ($$$$), the press, and the media
Have already elected Hillary.
The uninformed Americans, those who always
vote democrat just because they always have,
and those who are riding the fence,
ARE DROWNING IN PROPAGANDA.
Propaganda of lies, told over and over,
to warp your thinking, put doubt in your mind.
Beware, be careful, analyze what you hear.
These people are professional at what they do,
So, it is easy to fall in the ditch.
The election is just for looks, unless, somehow
the sleeping giant of loyal Americans can be awakened.
I am trying to do my part and hope you will, too!!!

Sic 'em Donald!

Thought for the day Sept. 7, 2016

Can you possibly believe this is real?
IT IS!

Hillary Promises to Deliver Regular Press Conferences... On One Condition
As of today, it has been 274 (call it an absolute zero) days since Clinton's last formal press conference on December 4, 2015, something even the left-leaning WaPo and NYT have expressed outrage against.
Naturally, as questions mount if and when the Democratic Presidential candidate will finally speak to the press, overnight Clinton's press secretary, Brian Fallon, had some good news, when he assured an ABC News podcast that she will hold regular press conferences, but under one condition.

That she is president or as Nancy Pelosi might put it, "you have to elect her to ask her questions.

This is not a joke: this is how ABC put it,
''Clinton's lead press secretary, Brian Fallon, vowed that if elected, "Hillary Clinton will hold press conferences." And here we were worried that if elected, Hillary would serve Clinton Foundation Corporation and Middle Eastern donors for (at least) 4 years without speaking to the press at least once (an idea Trump may want to consider).

Fallon, seemingly unaware of how this statement sounded, added that "The amount of interaction can only go up," noting that the traveling press will soon be flying with Clinton on her new campaign plane.
It's just like Obamacare. You have to pass the bill (elect her) to find out what's in it.

Sic 'em Donald!

My second thought today Sept. 7, 2017

Sorry to burden you with my 2ND thought of the day, but it hit me like a ton of bricks and I have to share it now.

I have a Mexican man named Juan who mows my yard, fertilizes, trims my hedges, and does odd jobs for me. He is very good, reasonable, and dependable.

We have a Senora named Abby who comes to clean our house every 3 weeks. It takes about 3 hours and we pay her $60. That's $20/hr, but it is worth it for "old folks".

Today was her day. To get out of her way I took a cup of coffee and sat on the back porch. As I was sitting there I noticed by backdoor neighbor was getting a new roof. Two Mexican men were very busy removing the old shingles, and I got to wondering. "Were they legal, or illegal immigrants, maybe citizens, or what?" Then I remembered I recently got a new roof, which was put on by about 7 Mexican men. Today, also, my neighbor across the street is getting a new roof and I counted 5 Mexican men working there.

This led me to a different train of thought. Why were all of them Mexican? Why were there no whites or blacks? These are good paying jobs requiring mainly a strong back and a willingness to work up a sweat. So, it just seems like some strong, but unemployed white or black men would try to get a job roofing. Or is this beneath their dignity? Maybe they don't know where to find these jobs? Hogwash, my favorite expression. These Mexicans found these jobs because THEY WANTED TO WORK AND MAKE MONEY! The next time you eat out, check the employees. Who is working? Who is cooking? Who I cleaning? Everywhere you go, check out who is working.

So, like it or not, you have to realize that if we rounded up all the good, hardworking illegal immigrants and shipped them back to Mexico, the economy would come to a complete standstill!

It can't happen. It won't happen. BUT-the bad ones have got to go and future immigrants have to be legal!!

Sic 'em Donald!

Thought for the day Sept. 8, 2016

Why am I confused?
In an editorial titled "Donald Trump is no Republican," the Dallas News rebuked the GOP hopeful, advising Texas voters that Trump is "not qualified to serve as president and does not deserve your vote." (So, you are saying that Obama with no experience of ANY kind, was Qualified?) Hypocrites!
They argue that Trump "inexplicably" won the primary despite being "the one who thumbed his nose at conservative orthodoxy altogether. Trump is - or has been - at odds with nearly every GOP ideal that this newspaper holds dear."'(that *makes you right'!)* they wrote.
"Donald Trump is no Republican and certainly no conservative."
(So if Hillary is a conservative Republican, -bad joke-the News must be communist!*) (might be!* (And you are saying the millions of people who voted for Donald were just STUPID unwashed peons and you are genius?)
(You also are also saying Hillary is more conservative and more nearly Republican than Donald?) Stupid!
In late July, another prominent Texas newspaper with a history of conservative political endorsements - the Houston Chronicle -
also made headlines when it endorsed Clinton and
labeled Trump a "danger to the Republican Party in an op-ed.
(So Hillary is NOT a danger to the Republican Party?) asinine!
I am really not confused, the Dallas News is, and lost in the forest.

Sic 'em Donald!

Thought for the day Sept. 9, 2016

“Yesterday Is History, Tomorrow Is a Mystery,
but Today Is a Gift. That Is Why It Is Called the Present”: Anon.

Don’t waste it!
This is

A wealthy, old white woman who sees you............

merely......

as a means to her enrichment and greater power.

Think about it.

Sic ’em Donald!

Thought for the day Sept. 10, 2016

President Obama turned a Laos press conference into a platform for_ Dragging America in the dirt on Thursday,
Telling reporters that Donald Trump was not ready to assume the responsibilities of the Oval Office.
"I don't think the guy is qualified to be president of the United States," Obama said.
"And every time he speaks, that opinion is confirmed.
"Obama, an expert on what it means to be unqualified for the presidency, said that he was still certain that the American people would ultimately reject Trump.
On the eve of 9/11 I wonder:
Would Trump pay IRAN $400,000,000 ransom for 4 Iranian prisoners and claim coincidence not ransom?
Would Trump promote a health system based on deception and lies?
Would Trump negotiate a treaty with terrorist nation Iran giving them fast track to a nuclear bomb and give them $150 BILLION to SPEED UP the process?
Would Trump draw a RED LINE in the sand, and then erase it saying "Excuse me!..?
Would Trump fly all over the world telling nations we are not a Christian nation?
Would Trump fly all over the world telling nations that Americans are lazy, complacent and ignorant?
Would Trump spend billions of dollars to resettle Thousands of un-vetted Muslims in America, some of which are ISIS terrorists?
Would Trump put up a Holiday tree at Christmas or a Christmas tree?
Would Trump substitute "I'll want to teach the world to sing" for our national anthem?
.Would Trump keep the flood gates open for illegal immigrants?
Would Trump take the side of criminals instead of the police?
Would Trump favor the Palestinians and shun Israel?
Would Trump hire Muslims for all the important positions in the White House?

Would Trump view Americans as stupid, unwashed peasants?
Would Trump be a slip-slop coward when negotiating with other nations?
Would Trump tell a business man .. You didn't build that! .. ?
Would Trump call ISIS just a JV team?
Would Trump say... Global Warming.. or ""Climate change .. is the greatest threat to National Security?
Would Trump bow to the king of Saudi Arabia?
Would Trump bow to anyone?
Finally, would Trump forced cohabitation of sexes in the military and expect ""Hands Off. Don't touch! .. ?
If you answered .. NO! .. to each of these you see the gross incompetence of the thing we have now!
Think about it!

Sic 'em Donald!

Thought for the day Sept. 11, 2016

Sometimes in my thoughts for the day, I think I may be talking to myself.

But that's Ok. Sometimes I probably need talking to. I can always use a little advice, and who better to talk to?

TODAY AS I WAS WATCHING REMEMBRANCES OF 9/11/2001, AND SAW WHAT OBAMA'S MUSLIM FRIENDS DID,

I GAVE MYSELF A STERN TALKING TO. AND NOW I AM MORE RESOLVED THAN EVER TO DO EVERYTHING I CAN TO MAKE SURE WE DON'T END UP WITH A LYING CLINTON IN THE WHITE HOUSE!!!!!!!!!!!!!!

Sic 'em Donald!

Thought for the day Sept. 12, 2016

Man's best friend.
As far as I know yesterday, 9/11, passed without a major incident. Not so September 11, 2001. As the horror and destruction was unfolding there were simultaneous acts of heroism taking place. People helping people to live, and, sadly, rescuers dying in their efforts to save others. There are thousands of untold stories that will never be told.

But there is one story not too well known and it is about dogs, not people. You may like dogs. You may not.
But dogs truly are man's best friend. People being intelligent, smart, and rulers of the world would never consider dogs as people.
And that is true. We smart people know that.
But dogs don't know that-they think they are people. Treat them as you will they will love you, guard you, hunt for you, always be loyal, and never ever voluntarily leave you. If you scold them, beat them, starve them, they still love you, and given the least opportunity will give you a big kiss.

Hundreds of people were buried in the rubble, many still alive.
Hundreds of Search and Rescue dogs were brought in help search for survivors in the rubble. Dogs have a keen sense of smell and hearing, and they had the ability to go where humans could not.
Time was so critical. Tirelessly for 24 hours a day for days they searched, finding many still alive who were saved.
They also found the remains of many, giving some comfort to their survivors.
Their reward? A pat on the head, a hug, a kind word, water, something to eat, and a little rest.
God made dogs for many reasons.
THIS WAS ONE!
Think about it.

Sic 'em Donald!

Thought for the day Sept. 14, 2016

As we all know Hillary has pneumonia, among other things.
Sunday, she went to the 9/11 memorial in 77 degree weather.
Due to the “”heat” she became dehydrated and nearly collapsed in the street.
Serious matter.
Yesterday our comic President, and he is a comic, was on the campaign trail promoting Hillary. During his speech he paused and said
Oh there is a lady about to faint. It is really hot in here.
Somebody help her.
Then with a little grinning smirk, thinking he has made a “funny, he continued spewing out his garbage.
This is the President the world sees, the world that does laugh at our comic, not because he is funny, but because he himself is the joke!

Sic ’em Donald!

Thought for the day Sept. 15, 2016

<u>What you have to look forward to as you grow old.</u>

At 90, nearly 91, and sane of mind (so far), but with a body beginning to creak, bringing forth an occasional OH! I am noticing how old people are perceived by others. Others being the very young, the young, middle-aged married and unmarried, young seniors, old seniors, and those also encumbered.

Some treat me with respect, courtesy, and appreciation. They hold the door, make room on elevators, offer me their seat, smile speak, ask about my well-being, and are just plain nice. Some are just plain rude. They can't wait for me to get out of the way, and barge in front. They see me driving a car and say with surprise "Are you still driving?"!! Some just ignore me as though I don't exist. Some say "How old are you anyway"? "Really?" "You don't look that old."

Being old really hit me in the face last Tuesday. I am having extreme pain in my back. Excruciating is the word. Six weeks ago I called this surgeon who did work on my back in 2005. Tuesday September 13, six weeks later, was the first opening he had. I was glad Tuesday finally arrived, thinking relief was on the way.

Wrong! After valet parking and walking a good distance to his office on the 5th floor, I hurt really bad, am bent over to try for some relief, so I look and act like my age. The receptionist looked at me with that look that says "Boy have we got an old geezer today" and says "you haven't been here in a while (under statement) so we need for you to fill out some papers and I need your insurance papers and driver's license-IF you have one." Ouch!

I took the 10 sheets of paper and filled them out even though some questions were a little too personal, like 'Are you pregnant?' Shortly, believe it or not, a very nice young man came after me for x-rays. He treated like maybe his own father or grandfather and made me feel good. Then a nurse took me to one of those isolation rooms and closed the door. She began to fool around with the computer which had a picture of my backbone and seemed nervous. She took my vitals TWICE and spending time with an old cripple was not where she wanted to be. Sensing this I asked he if she were having a good day. She lied to me and said she was having a great day, without even a hint of a smile. She did her thing and left, never to be seen again.

So, I sit in my isolation room and wait. And wait. FINALLY, my doctor shows up and I am so happy to see him. He gives me a cursory exam, says my back is a mess, and had me set up for injections by another doctor. All this in 5 minutes. I waited six weeks and saw him for 5 minutes. There was no chit-chat, no "where do you hurt", no emotional involvement. I am sad again and feel that he thinks I am old and not worth spending much time with.

I left with the other Doctor's name, address, telephone #, and the name of Gladys who will call me and set up an appointment. Today is Thursday, 2 days later. Gladys has not called. I called the number for Gladys yesterday and got a recording, press 1 for, press 2 for, etc, and found no way to talk to a live person.

It is as though they think "if we stall long enough, his pain will go away" and when you think about it that is true, but I would enjoy some relief while I am still here. The system is rigged against me and Donald.

Sic 'em Donald!

Thought for the day Sept. 16, 2016

"You can put half of Trump supporters into what I call the basket of deplorable racist, sexist, homophobic, xenophobic, Islamophobic, you name it."

-Hillary Clinton at New York City Fund Raiser, Friday, September 9, 2016

I didn't know I was one of these.
But if Hillary says so, it must be true.
She never lies! Make you feel good?
Made me think of an old yell the pep squad had for our football team:
Two bits
Four bits
Six bits
A dollar
All for Trump
Stand up and holler!

Sic 'em Donald!

Thought for the day Sept. 17, 2016

This is just a non-serious day. Relax and be glad in it.

We went to a fast food restaurant last week.
Normally I am a mild mannered, patient person, but sometimes *my other self* shows up.
This was one of those times.

One of my pet peeves is waiters in restaurants, especially fast food places.
The waiter's job is to get you seated, serve you, get your money, and get you out as quickly as possible.
I know that.
I don't always know what I want until I read the menu, and depending on the complexity of the menu, this can take a while.
This was a new menu.
Apparently, I took too long to decide. I noticed the waiter standing there shifting his weight from one foot to the other, waiting for this old man to decide.
So, I decide to oblige him and started a conversation.
"What is your name? Have you worked here long?
What is the house specialty?
What is your favorite?
Can I have baked potato instead of fries?"
By this time, he was really getting nervous and the pen in hand is wiggling.
And I know what he is thinking "Hurry up and order, old man. You are costing me money."
Obviously, I am getting sensitive to this kind of thinking.
So, to make my day, not the waiter's,
I said "I don't see anything I like. I will just have coffee and water.
'"Make the coffee half decaf and half regular.
‥I would like at least 3 creamers and I like real cane sugar. Do you have that?""

“”Oh, and I need a straw and a napkin.”
and lemon for my water””.
Kinda mean I guess, but I said it all graciously!
My other self-felt really good.
But Clarene was embarrassed. We won’t go there again.
(Being big hearted I tipped him 40%)

PS: Not true! This is just a fantasy I created about something I have wanted to do many times. Hillary taught me how to do it.

Sic ’em Donald!

Thought for the day Sept. 19, 2016

Why does Hillary wear these?

Life with Zeiss Z1 F133 protective lenses

A testimonial (NOT BY ME)

The Zeiss F133 lenses are a deep cobalt blue. They filter out a lot of light, and block out the color red, the most seizure provoking color. I promised to share information about my daughter's experience with the blue Zeiss Z1 F133 lenses that I've written about previously Here's what I can tell you:

They absolutely do prevent seizures while Alice watches TV!

They also prevent the seizures that happen when she reads uninterrupted for very long periods.

And they're handy for unexpected events out in the community emergency lights, flash photography, and flickering fluorescent bulbs.

Sic 'em Donald!

Thought for the day Sept. 22, 2016

Think about this.
White police officer kills white man. Non event.
Black police officer kills white man. non event
Black men shoot black men, women and children in Chicago. non event.
White police officer kills black man. riot

Black police officer who reports to black police chief shoots black man Common denominator: black man is shot, no matter why or by whom= RIOT.

Reason #1: Political correctness, permissiveness, people like Obama, Clinton, Sharpton

Real reason #1: For decades, starting with Lyndon Johnson's "War on Poverty", the Democrats have dangled the carrot before black people, promising more and better things, but never delivering anything, Except welfare checks, aid to 'dependent children', and free phones.

Slowly the plight of black people has deteriorated.

Poor schools, children born out wedlock, no father, becoming more and more dependent on welfare checks, no job skills, AND LIVING WITH THE LIE THAT IF YOU DON'T VOTE DEMOCRAT. REPUBLICANS WILL CANCEL YOUR WELFARE.

Republicans fought the Civil War to free blacks from the plantation, and Democrats have fought ever since to "keep blacks on the plantation" and have succeeded very well.

For the most part blacks are dependent on their Democrat masters for the food they eat, the clothes they wear, and the shacks they live in.

It is disgraceful and undoing the damage will take years, BUT IT WILL TAKE FOREVER IF NO ONE IS WILLING TO SINCERELY TAKE THE PROBLEM ON AND BEGIN TO FIX IT.

It is obvious by what happened in Charlotte last night, blacks are desperate.

They have reached the panic stage. Riots are nothing but screams for help.

Obama could have helped the blacks, but for 8 years he has chosen to ignore their plight, and by his actions even made it worse.

Hillary panders to the blacks knowing if they escape the plantation, her dream of power is doomed, so she is not an option for improving anything.

My first reaction was- Law and order-LOCK 'EM UP!!! <u>But that is not the solution.</u>

<u>I think Donald Trump is sincere in his desire to dramatically improve the lives of black Americans</u>.

With Trump they have a chance. The process has to begin.

Sorry this is so long. Then again, I am really not. It needs to be said.

Sic 'em Donald!

Thought for tomorrow Sept. 23, 2016

From the beginning of slavery in America until today, Democrats have considered themselves as MASTERS of the black race, and have subjected them to cruel and inhuman treatment. BETWEEN 1882-1964 THE DEMOCRAT KU KLUX KLAN LYNCHED 3446 BLACK PEOPLE!!!!!!!!!!

So, it is an enigma, despite the debasement of blacks by Democrats, they still, like a dog, lick the boots of their Masters and refuse to leave the “plantation”.

They tum their backs on Republicans, who, since Lincoln, have fought for the equality of races and for the GOD given rights of all.

The time is now. right now. to begin destroying the Plantation once and for all.

It must be done or America will self-destruct.

Trump is our hope. our ONLY hope.

Hillary, the Democrat, is an elitist who, along with other elitist Democrats, will on continue

to keep their foot on the necks of blacks.

African American? Their own ancestors in Africa sold their great, great grandparents intoslavery. How can they be proud of that? The blacks today were born in America. They are American citizens entitled to the rights of all citizens. It is time to salute the flag, stand tall, and proclaim “I am an American”>

Blacks must rise up and destroy the Plantation, and save America For everyone!

Sic ’em Donald!

Thought for the day Sept. 24, 2016

There are different ways of getting rich.

1. Be smart. work hard, save your money.
2. Win a lottery
3. Dumb luck
4. Be a successful actor
5. Smart investing in stocks
6. Strike oil

Having a lot of money affects people in different ways.
Some continue to work, creating jobs and wealth for others.
i.e. Donald Trump
With some it scrambles their brains and they become 'wise' beyond their years. Some, unaccustomed to having money, can't spend it fast enough-houses, yachts, cars, girlfriends, etc. A fool and his money... Tiger Woods!
Some set up benevolent charities, to reduce income taxes,
and just rest on their laurels'. Bill Gates
Then there are the obnoxious ones. They tum into clowns and buffoons. They can say stupid things. do stupid things, make total fools of themselves."so what?" they say. "It is my money"".
Here we have Mark Cuban,
You be the judge.

Mark Cuban says he plans to watch closely as Hillary Clinton
tries to "overwhelm" Donald Trump.
Mark Cuban takes front-row seat for presidential debate

Sic 'em Donald!

Thought for today Sept. 25, 2016

"Friends f o r E V E R !.. Please note!
September 18th, 2008<<<<<<<<<<<<<<
8 years ago<<<<<<<<<<<<<<
Trump endorses McCain

Trump also said Alaska Gov. Sarah Palin
had rejuvenated the Republican Party.
Real estate mogul Donald Trump
is endorsing Sen. John McCain:"
I've known him. I like him. I respect him.
He's a smart guy and
I think he's going to be a great president,"
Trump said Wednesday night on CNN! fs Larry King Live.
"I endorse him."
Trump also had praise for McCain's decision
to pick Alaska Gov. Sarah Palin as his running mate.
"I think she's made a tremendous impact.
The impact that she has had on rejuvenating
almost the Republican Party, it's been unbelievable."
FRIENDS FOREVER?
(McCain is so grateful, he refuses to endorse Trump!)

Sic 'em Donald!

2nd Thought for today Sept. 25, 2016

“Friends f o r E V E R! ‘”Trump endorses Romney
Fri February 3. 2012<<<<<<<<<<<<< 4 years ago<<<

Trump to Romney:
Go get “em
Celebrity business magnate Donald Trump endorsed
Mitt Romney for president Thursday, telling reporters
he will not mount an independent campaign
if Romney is the Republican nominee.
“It’s my honor, real honor, to endorse Mitt Romney,”
Trump said, with Romney and his wife standing nearby.
Calling Romney “tough” and “smart; Trump said,
“he’s not going to continue to allow bad things
to happen to this country.”
Romney responded by praising Trump for “an extraordinary ability to understand how our economy works and to create jobs” and for being “one of the few who has stood up to say China is cheating” in international trade.
McCain 8 years later. Bragging on Trump? Not Hardly. Where is he?
Romney 4 years later. Bragging on Trump? not hardly.
Here’s what Romney says about Trump in 2016<<<<<<<<<<
If we Republicans choose Donald Trump as our nominee.
the prospects for a safe and prosperous future are greatly diminished ....
If Donald Trump’s plans were ever implemented,
the country would sink into prolonged recession ....
Donald Trump is a phony. a fraud.

His promises are as worthless as a degree from Trump University.
Life comes at you fast sometimes.
With friends like McCain and Romney
You don't need any enemies!

Sic 'em Donald!

Thought for the day Sept. 26, 2016

The sun rose slowly this morning over America,
trying to see what we had in store for it today.
Everybody is talking about the BIG Debate on TV, radio, Facebook, twitter, etc.
"What time will it be?" said the sun.
8 o'clock.
"How disappointing! I will be in bed then!""
Sun ""Anything else happening today?"
"Nope. absolutely nuthin will happen today until 8 o'clock. and then we are really gonna rumble. Sorry you will miss it."
Sun "Me, too. Seems like all the fun happens at night when I am sleeping,
i.e. riots, shoot 'em up, dancing, drinking, stealing, hanky-panky, all that stuff."
"I am really bored. Same thing day after day after day.
See you tomorrow. Same time, same place."

Sic 'em Donald!

Thought for the day Sept. 27,2016

IT is over.
The first debate before 100,000,000 people
Reminded me of a

About all I remember is Hillary teeth and right hand.

Sic 'em Donald!

Thought for the day Sept. 29, 2016

Rigging, Alive and well. Ask Bernie.
Rigging: the act of arranging *dishonestlv for* a desired result

Imagination is funny.
For example: Imagine you are sitting at home watching Hillary on TV. Imagine it is 10 pm. Now imagine the doorbell rings and you go to the door.
You hesitate. Who could it be this late?
"You say who is it"? Imagine your shock when a voice says:
''This is Hillary Clinton. I have come to spend the night with you."
Imagine you open the door and there she is smiling, teeth hanging out and her right-hand waving in the air. She has 4 huge bodyguards each carrying 2 suitcases. Imagine there are 4 black limousines parked in front of your house, and all your neighbors are standing in their yards! Of course, there is Bill standing to the side with his glasses hanging on the end of his nose, and grinning.
Your mind starts racing. Imagine the thoughts that run through your mind.
'I don't have clean sheets on the guest bed. Where will these men sleep?
The bathroom can't handle all these people, and Bill. Bill has that you know look in his eye. Imagine you are home alone!
Imagine panic sets in. They can't stay here!!!
How do I get rid of them?

?
?
?
Easy. stop imagining.
Now, Imagine you just had a little thrill.

Sic 'em Donald!

Thought for the day Sept. 30, 2016

THIS IS REALLY "FOOD" FOR TODAY, TOMORROW, AND DAYS TO COME.

Do you know which cities in the US are the most distressed, have financial problems, have the highest unemployment, and have serious racial problems?
You don't?
My research list the following:
Washington, DC
Baltimore
Detroit
St. Louis
New .Jersey
Chicago
Milwaukee
Atlanta
Any idea how long the Democrat mafia has controlled these cities?
You don't?
Here is the answer in years:

Washington, DC	43
Baltimore	49
Detroit	55
St. Louis	65
Newark	81
Chicago	85
Milwaukee	106
Atlanta	137

Now you smart.
Next question: Do we need another Democrat, to succeed a Democrat, who will continue down the road of making the
whole of America like these Democrat cities?

We don’t?
After careful deliberation, me and my house have concluded
WE DON’T!
Surprised?

Sic ’em Donald!

Thought for the day Oct .1, 2016

Yikes! It is October already. Today my thought was like a bomb exploding! I have many intelligent reasons *for not wanting Hillary to be my grandchildren's President.*
My main reason is: SHE IS A LIBERAL, SOCIALIST, PROGRESSIVE, POWER HUNGARY, LYING, CROOKED, DECEITFUL, PERSON.
But. SHE IS experienced you say? 30 years on the public payroll! Wow. Let"s see if we can identify her experiences.

1. She is a magician.
   40+ people who crossed her path died mysteriously.
   One cell phone turned in to 13, some of which were attacked and destroyed by a hammer. She once dodged imaginary bullets in Europe.
   She made $200,000 worth of silverware disappear from the White House.
2. She might be a good Travel Agent.
   As Secretary of State she traveled the world at taxpayer expense.
   She knows the best palaces in which to stay.
   She is on a first name basis with MOST of the world's dictators.
3. She is an Orator. She has made millions speaking to groups like AFL-CIO, Goldman Sachs, MOVIE STARS
4. She has many "friends"
   For being a friend, many have thanked her by giving her $millions. All they expected in return was a "favor". No problem.
5. She is (along with Bill) a good negotiator. She lied to Congress and the FBI-and you- No problem. She violated her oath as Sec. of State. She destroyed her illegal e-mail system. No problem.
   Lied about Benghazi. No problem.
   Committed many FELONIES worthy of prison. No problem.
   Husband Bill negotiated a GET-OUT-OF JAIL PASS deal With Loretta Lynn,
6. She has kissed Obama's dirty butt for the last 8 years.

She can lie with a straight face an unlimited number of times
Both have committed acts that border on treason and gotten away Scott free.
Butt kissing is SOP for Democrats. You kiss mine, I will kiss yours.

7. She is good at deTAIL.
   She hired private detectives to dig up dirt on Bill's girlfriends.
   She was unrelenting until his girl friends were destroyed.
   She loves women! Yes, one woman. Herself.
   Her research uncovered an event that happened to Donald 20 years ago.
   She destroyed thousands of incriminating e-mails just in time.
   As she said about Benghazi and 4 men slaughtered
   "At this point, what difference does it make"". "lets move on".
8. She keeps a clean house Sweeps all her dirt under the rug.

Sic 'em Donald!

Thought for the day Oct. 2, 2016

When I was a boy in the 1930"s Sunday was STOP day. The only things open were churches, the hospital and the jail. The only work done was milking our Jersey cow.
People rested.
In the book of Genesis we learn the GOD made everything in 6 days. On the seventh he rested.
God knows everything. In his wisdom He set aside one day a week to rest.
If God thought it was smart, I certainly agree.
This is Sunday, and I am resting.
AMEN

Sic 'em Donald!

Thought for the day Oct. 3, 2016

If it sounds like I am yelling, I am!

SOME OF YOU HAVE NOT BEEN PAYING ATTENTION AND NEED TO GO BACK TO OCT. 1ST THOUGHT. LET IT SOAK IN. TRY TO IMAGINE THIS "THING" AS YOUR PRESIDENT.

Sic 'em Donald!

Thought for the day Oct. 4, 2016

"STOP TRUMP" "DUMP TRUMP" is alive but sick.

1. Resurrect an obese beauty queen from 20 years ago. Make BIG deal.
2. Illegally release "partial" Trump tax return from 20 years ago. Make a BIG deal.
3. Unauthorized release of a person's tax return is a FELONY. Somebody should be in jail.
4. Trump lost over $990 Million in 1995. REALLY. REALLY BIG. BIG DEAL
5. In 2005 General Motors lost $51.1 Billion. Equals $51.100 Million Tax credit. NADA!
6. In 2012 General Motors lost $30.26 Billion. Equals $30,260 Million Tax credit. NADA!
7. IRS rules allow individuals, businesses, corporations to carry losses forward as partial credit against future income. (In my case as an individual, I am carrying forward mucho stock market losses. IRS allows me to deduct up to $3000 each year from taxable income, until I use up my credit)
8. We have depressions, regression, good times and bad. "Fair" tax laws make allowance for the good and the bad.
9. Donald Trump has paid all the taxes he owes every year!
10. The Clintons LAST YEAR gave $1.030.000 to charity, $30,000 to a legimate charity, and $1 000,000 to the Clinton Foundation. In other words, they gave a $1,000 000 to themselves TAX FREE!

Summary: It is a steep, lonely hill Donald has to climb.
especially with all the rocks being thrown at him.
Believers have to push and push. Faint hearts never won anything.

Sic ’em Donald!

Thought for the day Oct. 5, 2016

America's inheritance

In 1918 America went to war in Europe to save Europe.

In 1942 America went to war in Europe to save Europe again.

In 1953 America went to war in Asia to save S. Korea from N. Korea.

In 1966 America went to war in Asia to save S. Vietnam from N. Vietnam

In 1990 America went to war in the Middle East to save Kuwait from Iraq.

In 2003 America went to war in the Middle East to save Iraq from its self.

In 2016 we are at war with ISIS in America, Europe, and the Middle East, but NOBODY KNOWS IT.

Today we have peacekeeping military in Europe, Asia, and the Middle east, costing billions.

Makes you wonder-How did we inherit the role of babysitters of the world?

In 2017, if Trump is elected President, we will destroy ISIS.

In 2017, if Hillary is elected President, we will just surrender. Goodbye America.

Sic 'em Donald!

PS: Last night I saw Tim Kaine for what he is: a rude obnoxious lying HICK! Easy to see why Hillary picked him—Birds of a feather... etc.

Thought for the day Oct. 7, 2016

Corruption in our Federal Government is rampant, lawless, kaput. Laws apply to most people. Laws do not apply to some people. Think about these one at a time:

1. Oval Office
2. Attorney General
3. FBI
4. RS
5. State Department
6. EPA
7. Supreme Court & Federal Justice system.
8. Our 'beloved' Congress

THINK ON THIS- ON NOVEMBER 8, 2016
Millions know this. Millions will vote for Donald Trump.
Other millions know it, and they will
look this corruption right in the eye, shrug their shoulders,
and vote for continuing the corruption and lawlessness.
Other millions, Don't know it, Don't care, and Don't vote.
Sad.
If Hillary wins, it will speak to WHO we as a people are becoming,
and the picture is not pretty.

NOW #9. The media: biased, misinform-er, uninformer, non-informer, partial informer, selective informer, and professional propagandist!

Will Anderson Cooper, the moderator Sunday night, make an effort to be unbiased, or make an attack similar to the following?
We will see.

Sic 'em Donald!

Thought for the day Oct. 8, 2016

Sense: perceive, become aware of, come to one·s senses

Make sense: meet with approval, I agree

Nonsense: baloney, bull, hogwash, hooey, poppycock, rot, hot air

Good sense: sound practical judgment; “”he hasn’t got the sense God gave little green apples”;

Horse sense: farsightedness, judgement, matter, intelligence, practicality

No sense: Are you crazy, who told you that, go away you bother me.

Common sense: sound and prudent judgement, don’t argue with a woman, good sense, horse sense, don’t stir a crusted cow pie, don’t eat dog poo, don’t shoot yourself in the foot, don’t take Ex-lax at bedtime, Come to one’s senses: VOTE FOR DONALD TRUMP, Makes sense.

Sic ’em Donald!

Thought for the day Oct. 9, 2016

The Zodiac sign for people born in October is Libra, symbolized by balanced scales.
There is much evil in this world. A Libra assumes the job of trying to find enough good to keep Evil from unbalancing the scale.
This election has got this Libra working 24/7.
This is Sunday my day of rest.
BUT I can't rest. My world is trying to tum upside down.
My dream of a Constitutional Supreme Court, stopping terrorism, and MAKING AMERICA GREAT AGAIN, borders on being a nightmare.
Must wake up before it is too late.
Tonight, Donald must rise to the top and show America what Hillary really is: a pompous, conceited, self-centered, hypocrite!
This Libra needs help!

Sic 'em Donald!

Thought for the day Oct. 1 0, 2016

The 2nd debate was last night. I have a comment
on that but first I have to say this.

For years I have known that all politicians were crooked.
There has never been any doubt that Democrats
have sold their soul to the devil, but I have clung
hopefully to my bible, guns and Republican beliefs.
Naively, while I know nobody is perfect, I have thought Republicans
were much less crooked than Democrats.
When Hillary dug up Donald's latest boo boo, something
from 11 years ago, I discovered how naive I really am.
I know you may not believe it, and I find it hard to believe myself,
but my Republican congressmen are not crooked at all.
They actually are angels. Angels can't be crooked and they sure
can't be associated with someone like Donald.
So.......... what did they do? They hung Donald out to dry, grabbed
their Halos, flapped their wings and flew off into the sunset!
Bunch of cowardly hypocrites, masquerading as saints.
Jerk is a kind word for them.
On the debate, Donald did himself proud Last night, and Hillary
showed she has the ability to form partial sentences out words.
It did not matter if there were no Substance to words.
But she won't give up. The game is to keep your attention focused on
Donald miscues, so that you don't think about her greater miscues.
Like I said,
IT IS A GAME. THERE WILL BE MORE STUFF.
COUNT ON IT, BUT.......... DON'T FORGET..........
THE FUTURE OF AMERICA HANGS IN THE
BALANCE. SO PLEASE, DO NOT WAVER.

Sic 'em Donald!

PS: Happy Birthday to me!

Thought for the day Oct. 11, 2016

The mystery of Hillary's "coronation".
I am flabbergasted almost beyond words.
When you look at the repeat failures, errors,
and crooked deals in Hillary's life, from defending
the thug who raped a 12-year-old girl, to Benghazi,
to the wiped out incriminating e-mails, to lie after lie after lie,
it makes you stop and think:
"Why would anyone believe she has "earned" the right
to be President" ????
This little song paints a picture of the REAL Hillary!
You can sing along and enjoy the learning experience.
Liar, liar, pants on fire
Your nose is longer than a telephone wire

Sic 'em Donald!

Thought for the day Oct. 12, 2016

A true story about the real “people loving’ Hillary.

Former military K9 handler Eric Bonner says an encounter

with then-Secretary of State Hillary Clinton

led him to never support her for president.

“It has nothing to do with her views,” Bonner posted on Facebook.

“It really doesn’t even matter about all the laws she broke.

“It’s because She actually talked to me once. Almost a sentence.” he wrote.

“Being a K9 handler in the Military

I got to do a few details involving Distinguished Visitors.

Mostly Generals, DOD Officials, and Secretaries of Defense,” Bonner explained.

One of my Last details was for Hillary when she was Secretary of State.

She was in Turkey for whatever reason.

I helped with sweeps of her OV Quarters and staH vehicles.

Her words to me? “Get that F king dog away from me.,

Then she turns to her Security Detail

and berates them up and down

about why that animal was in her quarters.

For the next 20 minutes while I sit there waiting to be released

she lays into her detail. slamming the door in their faces when she’s done.

The Detail lead walks over apologizes and releases me.

I apologize to him for getting him in trouble.

His words “Happens every day Brother”.

And she, along with, some women,

Paul Ryan, and some Republican ‘saints’

were appalled by Trumps locker room talk.!!!!!!!

Give me a break!

Sic ’em Donald!

PS: It gets worse, much worse.

Watch for tomorrow’s people loving thought.

Thought of the day Oct. 13, 2016

First, I want you to know None of the words below are mine.
They are exclusively Hillary 'Filthy Mouth' Clinton's.

I apologize if this offends you, but this is what you will get,
if Hillary is elected President.
Hillary Clinton's Vulgar Mouth

This is from a post in a forum at *GOPUSA.*

Read it, then ask yourself if you want this kind of a woman as your leader.

I am sorry. I originally had Quotes of Hillary cursing here

But as I read them And re-read them

I felt they are so coarse And distasteful And the profanity so vulgar,

I have deleted them. Your eyes don't need

to start the day Looking at something So gross.

It turns my stomach to think such a detestable

Human .. being could be our president.

You can use your imagination And visualize how bad it was.}

I saved the following non-cursing quotes for you.

They are little examples of how Hillary thinks of all you "Deplorables".

“"You know, I'm going to start thanking the woman who cleans the restroom in the building I work in.

I"m going to start thinking of her as a human being?" .. - Hillary Clinton

"We just can't trust the American people to make those types of choices.

Government has to make those choices for people."

(Even with all the bad words,

the one I highlighted is, to me, the most serious/dangerous.)

Sic 'em Donald!

Thought for the day Oct. 14, 2016

With all the supposed confessions coming out about Donald Trump, I was reminded of an event in my life that I have never told anyone about before.

Now that I am old, grey and harmless, I think you might be amused with my story.

This was in 1965 when I was a 40-year-old man, still in the prime of life.

Actually it was on a Monday, July 19. I remember it well. It was etched in my mind.

I was flying from Dallas to Chicago on a Braniff 707.

We always rode first class, wore suits and ties, and on this flight, (I know you won't believe it,)

I found myself sitting beside Marilyn Monroe!!!

Well, I was flabbergasted and speechless. What does a hick from the backwoods of East Texas say to a beautiful famous woman like Marilyn?

Fortunately, or maybe unfortunately, Marilyn was a talker.

So, a conversation began. You know, like who am I, where am I going? Am I married? Then, am I happily married, etc. Then she told me what good friends she and Robert F. Kennedy were.

From there it seemed like really liked me, and I began to get nervous.

About half way through the flight, she reached over and put her hand on my leg. Words cannot describe what went through my mind, or the exhilaration I felt.

I began sweating like a stuck pig and my mind was racing a mile a minute.

Like I said I was just a 40-year-old man, married, with children, and I didn't need this kind of temptation!!!

I didn't want to make a scene. I didn't want to hurt her feelings by telling her to get her hand off my leg. (besides I guess I was flattered).

We landed in Chicago. When we got up from our seats she kissed me on the mouth.

I must have turned 10 shades of red and the other passengers started whooping, laughing and clapping their hands. We walked arm in arm as we got off the plane.

I start sweating again, profusely, and I am thinking
“How am I going to get out of this?’”
The Lord said I would not be tempted beyond what I can stand and I am thinking “Lord, where are you?’” As we walked into the terminal, lo and behold, there was her sometimes boyfriend, Bobby Kennedy, and she left me standing there. I never saw her again.
The Lord did not forsake me. Now you can see why I never told anybody. Nobody would believe me anyway, and neither should you. This was all a fantasy,
just like that 74 year old grandmother that accused Donald of molesting her on an airplane while she was sitting in a first class seat 30 years ago.
Marilyn died in 1962.

Sic ’em Donald!

Thought for the day Oct. 15, 2016

Propaganda

is alive but sick with an airborne virus.
The virus is very contagious and is spread
unceasingly 24/7 by radio, TV, social media, newspapers,
magazines, etc.
Once it enters your system, it warps your
brain, destroying your common sense,
crippling your thought processing,
and turns you into a babbling Bimbo,
unable to distinguish the difference
between truth, lies and fiction
when you hear it.
Propaganda has then done its job, and Democrats go happily
on their way, giggling and laughing.
A vaccination with real true knowledge will
prevent the virus from entering your system.
It ain't over! We have to win! Stand firm!
Don't forget. Hillary, Obama, political correctness,
and do-nothing Republicans created Donald Trump and
energized his millions of *deplorable* followers.
This election is kinda like rolling the dice
And we have to pray we don't roll snake eyes!

Think About it.

Sic 'em Donald!

Thought for the day Oct. 16, 2016

Years ago when Hillary was younger,
someone wrote this song-
♫You can't hide your lyin' eyes
And your smile is a thin disguise
I thought by now you'd realize ♫

It is so appropriate today!
Surely you have noticed!

Sic 'em Donald!

Thought for the day Oct. 17, 2016

This thought is for:
all those goody goody, faint of heart,
people who wear their feelings on their sleeves,
those holier than thou 'pretend' Christians,
and for those who have never heard profanity, and never cursed themselves.
It is also for those offended by sexual references,
or "unforgivable" sexual behavior, the lily whites of this world,
and for those who will not admit that sex has been a powerful force in determining what they are, who they are,
and how they think.
It is also for those without sin.
I will be glad to furnish rocks for you to throw.
SO... HERE GOES.
God's 9th commandment is: You shall not give false testimony
For those of you unfamiliar with this commandment, let me explain.
It means you shall not lie. All those not guilty. raise your hand!
There are white lies, bold-faced lies, lies to cover for lies, malicious lies.
There are compulsive liars, pathological liars, sociopathic liars, and chronic liars.
Hillary is a proven sociopathic Liar. We all know this.

Definition: A sociopath is typically defined as someone who lies incessantly to get their way and does so with little concern for others.
A sociopath is often goal-oriented (i.e., lying is focused it *is done to get what they want. -love, Power. revenge, money, wealth)*
Sociopaths have little regard or respect for the rights and feelings of others.
Sociopaths have no conscience. Curing a sociopath is nearly impossible.

HILLARY'S ONLY GOAL IS SATISFYING HILLARY AND SHE WILL CRUCIFY ANYONE WHO GETS IN HER WA ~ DO ANYTHING, AND SAY ANYTHING TO SATISFY HER LUST FOR POWER!!!

Believe me, Hillary is a sick woman and will be a disaster if elected President!

Donald is a man and by definition will color the truth, lie by omission, and has lied by mistake. Donald is not perfect, But he is not sick.

He is a patriotic American who believes, as I do, that America is on the verge of disappearing as a nation of free people, most of whom still believe in God.

He wants to make America strong, safe and proud, once again.

DONALD IS FOR ALL OF US. HILLARY IS FOR HILLARY!

Donald has spent millions of his own money trying to defeat a socialist, power hungry, sociopath who is spending millions of other people's money to satisfy her lust for what would be destructive power.

Sic 'em Donald!

Thought for the day Oct. 19, 2016

Tonight, in the "debate" when you see one of these faces you will know she is lying.

Sic HER Donald!

Thought for the day Oct. 20, 2016

The debate. If you saw it, you saw it.
Was there a winner? Was there a loser?
You decide.

Only one thing stuck with me and that was the question
to Donald:
''Mr. Trump, you have talked about rigged elections.Historically, transition of power in our Presidential elections has been smooth and without incident. My question to you is
"IF YOU LOSE, WILL YOU GRACEFULLY ACCEPT THE RESULTS OF THE ELECTION?''
To me this was a very stupid question.
Donald said "I CAN'T SAY NOW. I will wait until after the election."
It has already been demonstrated that the Democrats will do
ANYTHING legal or illegal to win this election,
SO WHY SHOULD HE ANSWER IN THE AFFIRMATIVE?
HILLARY WAS NOT ASKED THE SAME QUESTION. WONDER WHY? NOW I WONDER WHAT HER ANSWER WOULD BE. Will she accept Trump if he wins?
No, we will have another Al Gore fiasco.
With all the rigging the DNC did to guarantee the nomination for Hillary, and all the dirty tricks Hillary's democrat friends have pulled
to disrupt Donald's rallies, plus the paid fantasy confessions of
women, supposedly from Donald's past----Who knows what is coming next?
The aim of all this is, is to keep attention on Donald's 'short comings. and off of Hillary's gross misconduct. lies. and utter stupidity.

You say you can't vote for Trump because of the -women~
but you can vote for Clinton knowing she is a crooked, lying,
political machine hostile to Christian values?
To me that is a pretty high price to pay to
-send the Republican party a message~
Why not vote to defeat Clinton and tell the whole nation

that an immoral, deceitful person like Clinton is totally unacceptable!! We have a much better chance of having good government under Trump than Clinton.

One last thought:
Last night Hillary wore her “angel white “pants suit.
The only thing missing was her broom.
She discarded her halo years ago.

Sic ’em Donald!

Thought for the day Oct. 21, 2016

There are many reasons I like Trump.

Here are six.

1. He will not travel the world apologizing for America.
2. He believes in America first.
3. I hate what Hillary does and says -more than what Donald says.
4. He hates Political correctness. A thug is a thug.
5. He earned his money working, not through bribes.
6. SO IMPORTANT>>He believes in the sanctity of life!!

Sic 'em Donald!

Thought for the day Oct. 22, 2016

GUN CONTROL

The Australian-style gun control plan confiscated between 650,000 and 1 million guns.
This was about 1/5 of the guns in the country.
Hillary. being anti-gun to the core,
speaks lovingly of this plan to reduce gun violence in America.
Hitler and Fidel Castro also loved this type of plan.
So, let's think about applying this plan to the United States.
There are currently over 300,000,000 guns owned by over 125,000,000 people.
Confiscating 1/5 of those would be over 60,000,000 guns.
How would this be accomplished?
Would loyal red-blooded gun loving Americans come to Hillary's rescue and just tum them in? I don't think so.
Let there be no doubt.
Gun confiscation would have to be administered by force of arms.
I do not expect that those who dismissed their fellow citizens
for clinging bitterly to their guns are so naive that they imagine
these people will suddenly cease their bitter clinging
when some nice young man knocks on their door and says,
"Hello, I'm from the government and I'm here to take your guns."
The purpose of the Second Amendment is
to allow citizens to resist government oppression and tyranny.
Would people be so naive they would not use the Second Amendment to resist what they see as government oppression and tyranny?
I don't think so.
Only some militarized police could enforce an Australian gun-control scheme in the United States.
To take arms from men requires men with arms. There's no other way to do it.
Does anyone honestly believe this country has the will or resources to seize 60 to 100 million firearms from 125 million Americans?

I don't think so, BUT..........

Believe me, if Hillary is elected president and grasps the POWER of the Presidency,

she will void the 2nd Amendment and do everything she can to disarm Americans.

Chaos will result.

In so many ways this evil woman would be a total disaster.

Sic 'em Donald!

Thought for the day Oct. 24, 2016

This is a continuation of the thought FROM Oct. 23.
If you have not read that, please do.

Hillary is proud to be what is called "Progressive".
So, what is a progressive?
Turns out there "Progressive Christians" and "Progressive Politicians".
Progressive Christians say they believe in God and on a Sunday (not every Sunday) they meet in church and perform the ritual of worshiping God, (just in case there is a God).
At all other times, their religion is what, in their eyes, feels good.
Another name for them could be Chameleon Christians.
Their color (religion) changes to blend in with any situation.
HILLARY IS A CHAMELEON CHRISTIAN.

Progressive Politicians basically are atheists. They think simple people need a Godto give them hope. Progressives need no God, because they consider themselves "god", and are totally self-sufficient. Their role on earth is to take care of simple. deplorable, people.
HILLARY IS A PROGRESSIVE POLITICIAN.

It is difficult to be both a "Progressive Christian" and "Progressive Politician." But Hillary is both. She is a good actress, and after 30 years of practice, she can quickly change her "colors" and be anything she wants to be:-angel, Florence Nightingale, caring mother, liar, doting wife, friend, INNOCENT, enemy, liar, emotional, deceptive, scrupulous, mean, hateful, loving, an orator (for pay), shifty, dishonest, gender biased, but always pro-abortion! Kill dim babies!

There is an ad on TV of people, or who look like people, selling something.
A runner at the bottom of the screen says:
THESE ARE ACTORS, NOT REAL PEOPLE.
Hillary is an actor.

Sic 'em Donald!

Thought for the day Oct. 26, 2016

Some of you suggest that I calm down.
I can't calm down. This election is so important
and there are only 13 days left 'til we come to the Fork in the road.
Which road will we take?
To the left leads to the abyss with no turning back.
To the right leads to a chance to drain the swamp.
To those of you who are still sitting on your holier-than-thou
high horse, it is time drop the goody-goody facade and
realize we have only one choice
IF WE WANT A COUNTRY WE CAN BE PROUD OF AGAIN!
And that choice is "less than perfect•• (like the rest of us)
Donald Trump!!!

Sic 'em Donald!

Thought for the day Oct. 27, 2016

One of these will be your First Lady of the United States for at least four years. Choose wisely, my friends.

Sic 'em Donald!

Thought for the day Oct. 29, 2016

The world is full of enigmas.
Example: Pillows have been around since the stone ages.
So how does a guy invent “My Pillow” and make millions?

Example: Mattresses have been around since the stone ages.
There must be at least a thousand types of mattresses, and they all claim to deliver the ultimate in comfort.
So how does a guy invent the “Casper”” mattress and make millions.

One of my biggest enigmas is this:

> No one has invented a mattress and pillow combination that can compete with my recliner.
> Whoever invents one will make billions.
> Sleeping pills will become obsolete.
> 5 minutes in my recliner and I am unconscious.
>
> My really biggest, most flabbergasting, discombobulating, Enigma is this:

Why is Hillary not in jail?

Sic ’em Donald!

Thought for the day Oct. 30, 2016

You may have just witnessed the most brilliant
piece of Propaganda ever.
Follow me.
In .July the FBI declared Hillary guilty of several
illegal acts. If convicted, she would be a felon and in jail.
BUT............ the FBI and Attorney General declined to indict her.
NOW............ With polling tightening and foretelling a possible
Hillary defeat, out of the blue on Friday Oct. 28,
12 days before the Election. comes a letter fro the FBI
to Congress indicating more damaging information about Hillary.
BUT............ not revealing any detailed information.
Donald jumps on it with both feet saying
“”Hillary is a crooked liar”! “I told you so”!
BUT.......... Hillary goes about her business,
laughing and poo-pooing the whole thing, as if it is
a NOTHING thing. IT IS AS IF SHE KNOWS SOMETHING.
In the meantime many of Hillary’s voters are getting tired
of the whole mess and threaten to vote for Trump.
Follow me.
At this writing, there are nine days to Election Day.
It seems as if Poor Pitiful Pearl may at last be headed to .Jail.
BUT.......... WHAT if--lo and behold, two or three days before
Election Day The new information is declared worthless
and Hillary screams “”Free at last. I told you so!”
Hillary’s fans are exhilarated and on Election day
over 100,000,000 votes will be cast.
If Hillary wins, you can give credit to the
Democratic Propaganda Machine. Brilliant!

Print this and pin it to your frig.
I HOPE I AM WRONG!

Sic ’em Donald!

Thought for the day Oct. 31, 2016

Sorry Hillary

♫I beg your pardon,♫

♫we never promised you a Rose Garden♫

Sic 'em Donald!

Thought for the day Nov. 1, 2016

The web they spin.

- Marc Mezvinsky, Son of Edward Mezvinsky,
- (who was Convicted of fraud and sentenced to 80 months in jail),
- (also the nephew of George Crook Soros,)

- and Chelsea Clinton,
- daughter of Bill & Hillary Clinton,

- were married in a multi-million-dollar wedding
- at the MANSION of George Soros.

- They are in their early thirties and purchased a
- 10.5 million-dollar NYC apartment.
- Think about this.
- The monthly payment on a loan of $10.5 mil,
- at ZERO interest, for 30 years,
- would be $29200. THAT'S PER MONTH!
- With an annual salary of $350,000,
- That leaves nothing for groceries, cell phone, I pads, or Blue Bell Ice cream. Pity the filthy rich.
- Now you can understand why Hillary thinks"little" People are deplorable.
- not worthy to eat the crumbs that fall from her table.

Sic 'em Donald!

Thought for the day Nov. 2, 2016

Said the spider to the fly

Come hither, hither, pretty fly,
with the pearl and silver wing:
Your robes are green and purple;
there's a crest upon your head;
Your eyes are like the diamond bright,
but mine are dull as lead."
Alas, alas!
how very soon this silly little fly,
Hearing his wily flattering words,
came slowly flitting by.
With buzzing wings she hung aloft,
then near and nearer drew
Thinking only of her brilliant eyes,
and green and purple hue;
Thinking only of her crested head -
poor foolish thing!
At last, Up jumped the cunning spider,
and fiercely held her fast.
He dragged her up his winding stair,
into his dismal den, Within his little parlor;
but she ne'er came out again!
And now, *dear little* children~
who may this story read~
To idle, silly, flattering words,
I pray you never *give heed;*
Unto an evil counselor
close your heart *and* ear, *and* eye,
And take a Lesson
from this tale of the Spider and the Fly.
And the moral is: We have a spider like
running for President.
Don't be beguiled like the fly.

Sic 'em Donald!

Thought for the day Nov. 3, 2016

EQUAL JUSTICE UNDER LAW

This is the west Portico of the
US Supreme Court building.
Reading this makes you wonder
<u>when did the Supreme Court lose its way?</u>

Sic 'em Donald!
Bring back law & order

Thought for the day Nov. 4, 2016

From one American to another. Be proud.

Sic 'em Donald!

Thought for the day Nov. 5, 2016

Last night JAY Z had a concert in Cleveland promoting Hillary.
It was aimed at black voters in Ohio prior to Election Day.
Jay Z and his wife, Beyonce, of Superbowl Shame,
have always been fairly close with Barack Obama,
and now have endorsed Hillary.
Hillary, the "champion" of young people and women.
Hillary, of the white pants suit with halo
Hillary, *who revels in the gutter language of this "role" model*
for young people, and boast how she is for women.
And there Hillary was in all her "glory"
with these gutter people.

I apologize for the JayZ song below. and it may shock you, it did me, but it is necessary to show you the filth Hillary approves of, and promotes.

1. PIMPING
   Uh, uh uh uh
   It's big pimpin baby
   It's big pimpin, spending's
   Feel me uh-huh uhh, uh-huh
   Ge-ge-geyeah,geyeah
   Ge-ge-geyeah,geyea
   I changed my mind. This language is so bad

2. it does not belong in my Thoughts.
3. It just goes on and on, and this language is tame,
4. compared to some of Hillary's tirades.

<u>And you took offense to some of Donald's language?</u>
<u>Give me a break!</u>

Sic 'em Donald!

Thought for the day Nov. 6, 2016

3 days til the election.
In 4 days, will we have ....

Or will we have ....

TREAT 'EM ROUGH
—Morris for the George Matthew Adams Syndicate.

It will be a test of how civil we are.

Sic 'em Donald!

Thought for the day Nov. 7, 2016

Daylight and Dark

<u>DARK</u>
Did you notice at a Trump rally last
Saturday in Reno, Nevada
A Democrat Hillary supporter was on the
front row directly in front of Donald.
As Donald was talking the dimocrat
started heckling Donald and threatened bodily
harm. He was quickly subdued and arrested.

<u>DAYLIGHT</u>
At an Obama rally for Clinton Saturday a veteran for Trump,
in partial uniform and medals showing, stood up holding his
Trump-Pence sign. The crowd was more interested
in the veteran and Obama lost the crowd and panicked.
The vet was quietly ushered out, having made his point.
No problem

<u>Notice the difference?</u>

Sic 'em Donald!

Thought for the day Nov. 8, 2016

The DAY is finally here.
Am I nervous? Yes
If we win, will I accept graciously? Yes

If we lose, will I accept graciously? No
I am a very poor loser, and proud of it!

Picture of real loser!

Sic 'em Donald!

Chapter III

President-Elect

NOVEMBER 9, 2016 TO JANUARY 19, 2017

Thought for the day Nov. 10, 2016

Giving birth............

America just went through a very long and difficult pregnancy trying to give birth to a new President.

The labor pains along to the way were intense and agonizing.

But finally, on November 8, the baby was delivered pretty much without incident.

However, to the surprise and shock of many, the girl many were expecting turned to be a BOY!

Instead of America giving birth to the reincarnation of Al Capone in pantsuit, she got a rough and tumble BOY. There was both rejoicing and disappointment.

Sadly, one day later, the after birth is beginning to stench.

There are protest in the streets of New York, Chicago, and LA, so it appears the "smooth transition" of power will be a bumpy road.

The "tolerant" socialist Democrats are showing their intolerant self when things don't go the way they planned.

I thank the Lord I won't have to look at that pantsuit for another 4 years, or listen to that shrieking lying voice.

Our BOY will need the patience of Job, the wisdom of Solomon, the strength of Samson, and the endurance, and the endurance of marathon winner.

The "tolerant" Democrats will pull no stops to destroy him, and he can't turn his back on his Republican "friends."

Progress will be slow and difficult. The after birth stench will hand around for a lone time!!

So I ask my many friends to remain patient and understanding.

Don't fag out!

This mess was not made in a day and draining the swamp will take a while.

To our BOY Donald I say.

Stay Calm, Donald!

Thought for the day Nov. 11, 2016

♫It is crying time again♫

We just had and election. We elected a president.
Like it or not, he will be president of everybody.
You can say "He is not my President."
You can protest a legitimate election.
You can crawl out of your lofts, penthouse apartments,
Your holes in the ground, your basements, where ever, and march in the streets, find ways to make yourself into ignorant fools, and YOU CAN CRY.
You won't change anything. "It is what it its"!
Donald Trump is you President-elect. Live with it.
Let's move on.

Thought for the day Nov. 13, 2016

We got a mess. The communist left, funded by the devil, George Soros, is responsible.
Hoodlums, paid by a Soros Organization, Whip the dissatisfied, mostly the Young Gimme Gimme people, into protesting and marching. Professionally made signs start appearing, not just homemade.
Soon they have numbers and there is feeling of strength in numbers.
Now they get brave, followed by a feeling of invincibility.
All the while there is cursing and yelling and, with bravado, the destruction begins.
The enigma of it all is the signs.
My favourite is:

LOVE
NOT
HATE

And all you see is HATE.
Gives a whole new meaning to LOVE.

Stay Calm, Donald!

Thought for the day Nov. 14, 2016,

Donald Trump won.

The Dallas Cowboys won.

Mark Cuban and Hillary lost.
Life is good.

♫ God bless America.♫

Stay Calm, Donald!

Thought for the day Nov. 15, 2016

This is brilliant. Author unknown.
Enjoy.

Dear Hollywood celebrities,
You exist for my entertainment.
Some of you can deliver a line with such conviction that you bring tears to my eyes.
Some of you can scare the crap out of me.
Others make me laugh.
But you all have one thing in common, you only have a place in my world of entertain me.
That's it.
You make your living pretending to be someone else.
Playing dress up like a 6 years old.
You live in a make believe world in front of a camera.
And often when you are away from one too,
Your entire existence depends on my patronage.
Like a monkey, I'll crank the organ grinder; you dance.
I don't really care where you stand on issues.
Honestly, your stance matters far less to me than that of my neighbour.
You see, actors are not real people.
I turned off my TV or shut down my computer and cease to exist in my world.
Once I am done with you, I can put you back in your little box until I want you to entertain me again.
I don't care that you don't like Mr.Trump.
Get back into your make believe world.
Ill let you know when I'm in the mood for something blue and shiny.
And I'm also supposed to care that you will leave this great country when Trump becomes president? Ha.
Goodbye. Please don't forget to close the door behind you.
We'd like to reserve your seat for someone who loves this country and really wants to be here.

Make me laugh, or cry. Scare me.
But realize that the only words that the only words of yours that matter are scripted.
In my world, you exist solely for my entertainment.
So, shut your mouth and dance, Monkeys.
You are not real anyway.

Stay Calm, Donald!

Thought for the day Nov. 16, 2016

What has Trump done?? Part 1 of 8 parts

The press and Obama keep saying

Donald Trump won't make a good president;

He is bash, he is racist, he is a loudmouth;

You know, the normal things people learn to recite
after being programmed by television news.
"Trump is so arrogant, so braggadocios" you say.
Besides talking his Papa's money and becoming a billionaire.
WHAT HAS TRUMP DONE?
Well, let's see.

In June of last year, Trump entered the race for president.

In just a little over a year,
Trump single handedly, against all odds,
Defeated the Republican party.
In fact, he did so in such a resounding way that the Republican Party now suffers from an identity crisis.

What is a Republican, really?

He literary dismantled the party.

Trump even dismantled and dismissed the brand and value of the Bush family.

Thought for the day Nov. 17, 2016

What has Trump done?? Part 2 of 8 parts

Obama is petrified that Trump will cancel programs
That were not legally and properly installed.
AND HE WILL! The unaffordable Obama care
Will be one of the first to be replaced.
One of the things I like best about Trump—
He has single handedly debunked and discredited
Any value of the news media as we knew it.
And it is suffering an all time low of distrust
And respect. They really have no respect.
Today, excuses for Hillary's loss are on the front
pages. Dhe won the popular vote. She would have won
the election except for that
outmoded old Electoral Vote thingy
that has been determining our President
from the beginning.
There is no mention of the fact Trump
Won 32 of the 50 states.

Stay Calm, Donald!

Thought for the day Nov. 18, 2016

What has Trump done?? Part 3 of 8 parts

World leaders are talking about him.
World leaders are talking to him.
World leaders are coming to visit him.
Some like. Some don't. it really does not matter.
In this world today being liked is inconsequential, but respect is vital.
Donald is slowly building respect.
Powerful men who have been president before weren't liked by the global community.
It is doubtful that Mikhail Gorbachev liked Reagan when Reagan said, "Mr.Gorbachev, Tear donw this wall,"
He did not like him but he respected him.
Trump exposed the scan the Progressive left (democrats) has, for years, been selling the coronation of Hillary Clinton to America.
Before the election, Hillary was the winner.
A shew in.
No doubt about it.
High above the podium where Hillary was to give her acceptance speech was a glass ceiling.
I assume, somehow, during the speech she was going to symbolically break through the glass ceiling.
But the silent majority of "deplorables" were awakened and Hillary went sobbing to her room.
Like Cinderella's mean sisters,
The glass shoe just did not fit.

Stay Calm, Donald!

Thought for the day Nov. 19, 2016

What has trump done?? Part 4 of 8 parts

The press accused Trump of being a house of cards, but the press is the real house of cards.
From the beginning the so called "establishment" was in pure panic mode.
And they poured $millions into the "Stop Trump", "Dump Trump" Campaigns.
He exposed them for, not only who they are, but worse, what they are.
Trump's podium drew thousands of hours of FREE live news coverage long before he appeared.
Donald broke the news media propaganda machine, but they won't give up. They hobble along looking for bits and pieces of "news" they can use to continue their crusade of Trump Destruction. It ain't gonna work.
The "Deplorables" are not buying their lies.
They did accomplish one thing, however, to the detriment of America.
They, along with Hillary and Obama, are directly responsible for the brain-dead teenagers marching in the streets cursing, rioting, destroying property, and crying.
They have bought the garbage that Hillary should have won.
A generation of children are being raised to hate America.
Sadly, these "children" are being raised to hate America.
We old fogies will soon be gone,
Make you wonder "What will America be like in 20-30 years?"

Stay Calm, Donald!

Thought for the day Nov. 20, 2016

What has Trump done?? Part 5 Of 8 parts

For decades the Democrats Party has kept the African community on the "Plantation"
Better things tomorrow, but "tomorrow" never comes.
After all these years of promising, promising, and NO progress, Trump had the gall to ask them for their vote. And he asked them "At this point, WHAT DO YOU HAVE LOSE?"
"We have mass shootings, riots in our streets, ambushed cops, double digit inflation, bombs blowing up in our cities, targeted police both black and white, a skyrocketing jobless rate, no economic growth, privately owned land being seized by the federal government, the worst racial tension ever, no God in schools, more abortions that ever, illegal aliens pouring into our country, sick veterans receiving no care, and debt that doubled in seven to $19 trillion.
Are you really happy with the condition of the current system?"
"I want to make America great again for all Americans. I need your vote."
The above represents a boat load of things to fix now that Donald is elected.
He made us a promise and spent much of his own money because he believes, As many millions believe, that America is going in the wrong direction.
I believe, as many "deplorables" believe,
That with our help
He can begin the process of making America great again!

Stay Calm, Donald!

Thought for the day Nov. 21, 2016

What has trump done?? Part 6 of 8 parts

Millions of us think Trump will be a great President!
Some of you may think Trump will be lousy president.
That's your misinformed right.
But you cannot say he's ineffective.
He took on 16 Republican candidates,
The Republican party,
The Washington elites,
The billionaire CEO's
Megan Kelly, Fox News, CNN, MSNBC, Washington post, Rachel Maddow, the Huffington post, the New York times, raleigh's News and Observer, the AP, Don Lemon, Jake Tapper, the DNC, Obama's ranting and raving,
And Hillary's lying machine.
Collectively, their propaganda campaign told lie after lie, and degraded his character,
Trying to convince America that with his temperament and knowledge, he was unfit to be President.
He BEAT THEM ALL!
Collectively they failed and failed miserably to accomplish his demise.
Today he is President-elect and moving forward!

Stay Calm, Donald!

Thought for the day Nov. 22, 2016

What has Trump done?? Part 7 of 8 parts

For the last 8 years we have listened to Obama downgrade America. He has travelled the world apologizing for our past "wrongs", saying we are not a Christian nation, bragging on Muslim minimal contributions to humanity, down playing our moral values, creating racial tension and lying through his teeth at every opportunity, which were many since he is so enamored with hearing himself talk.

Today professional millionaire football and basketball players kneel for the national anthem, instead of showing respect.

We have little children aping their role models, brain dead teenagers marching in the streets, immigrants burning our flag and carrying foreign flags.

Many inhabitants of my America, (I hesitate to call them Americans), have no respect for America.

Respect for our heritage is gone.

Respect for our flag is gone.

Respect for GOD and our moral values is gone.

Respect for America by millions of "Progressive" Americans is gone.

Respect for America's blood bought hard earned freedom is gone.

But WITH Donald there is hope.

The fact that Donald beat Hillary, against seemingly insurmountable odds, makes me believe God has sent us a champion.

Thought for the day Nov. 23, 2016

What has Trump done?? Part 8 of 8 parts

So we come to the end of my dissertation and none too soon.
The silent majority is no longer silent.
Donald Trump has changed us, almost single-handedly in little more than a year.
We are speaking loud and clear.
Donald Trump is my President!
WE WANT OUR COUNTRY BACK AND WE WANT TO MAKE AMERICA GREAT AGAIN!
Long live the "deplorables"!

SLEEP WELL MY FRIENDS!

Stay Calm, Donald!

Thought for the day Nov. 24, 2016

For the first time in 10 years
Thanksgiving Day is truly a day for giving thanks!

My personal list of God's blessings is long.
At the top of my 'Thank You list' is Clarene, family, my faith, and health, followed by President-elect Donald Trump.
My prayer today (and tomorrow) is:
"God please give Donald Trump the wisdom and knowledge to restore America to its former glory.
Protect him from his enemies and his "friends".
Give him good health, patience, and strength.
And, God, bless all of America and let the healing begin."
Amen

Stay Calm, Donald! MAGA!!!

Thought for the day Nov. 26, 2016

Some days I like my computer. Some days I despise it.

This is a despise day. My server, ATT, is really messed up.

I put all my eggs in one basket, trusting ATT with my internet, my TV, house and 3 mobile phones. Mistake.

When I call about service I get a robot. I have to listen to his recorded message. Eventually IT transfers me to another robot.

Finally I get a live person, I think, who cannot help me, but agrees to find a technician.

Initially, and at each transfer, I have give name, rank, and serial #, and explain my problem.

Yesterday when I called because my TV is crazy, I got Betty.

After talking about Thanksgiving, her "boy friend" and children, she went through her checking procedure, which involved shutting down my computer, then back on.

This is where it gets funny.

She asks if my internet is working and I said "Yes".

And she said "What else can I do for You?"

And I said "What do you mean? I called about my TV not my internet!"

And she said "OH, do you have TV service with ATT also?"

And I said "Forget it!"

And hung up.

I still have serious TV and internet problems.

I try to stay calm like I tell Donald

Stay Calm, Donald! MAGA!

BUT IS DIFFICULT!

ps: my internet ain't fixed.

Thought for the day Nov. 27, 2016

Today is Sunday, the beginning of a new week.
In Cuba, Fidel Castro, the one who was guilty of murdering and enslaving thousands of people, is dead.
Goodbye Fidel. Good riddance.
Hopefully, this will bring a new beginning for the Cuban people.
There is an old saying

"Time wounds all heels"

Take note GEORGE SOROS.

Stay Calm, Donald! MAGA!

Thought for the day Nov. 28, 2016

Actually, I had this thought yesterday.
We went to church, had a good worship service and I came home feeling at peace with the world.
I turned on my computer and got a note "No service available".
I checked my modem and no lights were on.
My peace was destroyed.
I called ATT and got the robot. The robot kept telling me IT understands complete sentences and I could ask for a live agent at any time.
I did that and did that, etc five times.
Finally, I got a live person.
LIVE PERSON heard my ranting and finally said he would connect me with someone who could help me.
I GOT ANOTHER ROBOT!
Eventually, I got another semi-live person who spoke very broken English.
She talked and talked and I kept saying "What did you say" over and over.
My normally calm self began to get nervous and my voice went up several decibels.
Actually, I was yelling!
In the end, I think a technician is coming to my house this morning.
I can't help but wonder why a monster company like ATT can't hire people who speak fluent English. Sure makes me hesitate to call until I really, really need help. Maybe this is part of their plan.
What is really sad is I HAVE NO BETTER CHOICE

Stay Calm, Donald! MAGA!

Thought for the day Nov. 29, 2016

The ATT technician showed up yesterday.
I have to say I have never had a more pleasant experience with a service man.
He called ahead to tell me when he would be at my house.
And there he was. A nice looking young man named JOSH with a smile on his face and he spoke perfect English.
I explained the problem and he went to work.

In 45 minutes everything was working perfectly.
He carefully explained everything he did and gave me a good education on Wi-Fi, routers, modems, etc.
Josh left with a smile and he left me with a smile, and a warm feeling.
Thanks Josh. I needed a pep me up day!

Stay Calm, Donald! MAGA!

Thought for the day Nov. 30, 2016

Some of you have expressed concern about the Secretary of State show.
Don't get excited. Sit back, relax, watch, and enjoy the Puppet show.
Notice who is pulling the strings.

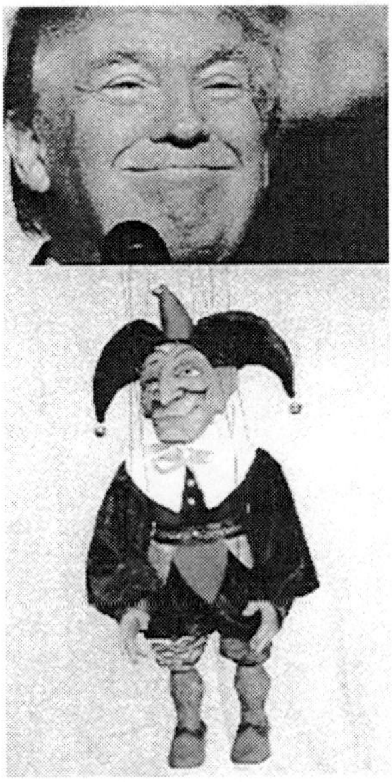

Stay Calm, Donald! MAGA!!!

Thought for the day Dec. 1, 2016

Well, this is just a trivia trash day.
Donald made no noise yesterday.
I didn't either.
Michelle Obama will be moving out of the house that "Slaves" built in January.
And............a legal immigrant will be moving in.
Think about it.
Jill Stein raised $3.5 million for her Presidential campaign.
She raised $7 million for a recount of 3 states.
Think about it.
My back surgery is scheduled for Dec. 19. Can't come too soon.
Have you given any thought about what America would be like
IF Hillary had won?
With Trump we have

With Hillary we would have

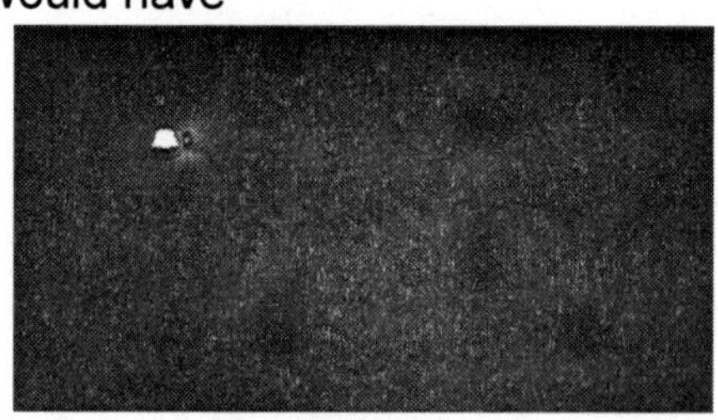

Think about it.

Stay Calm, Donald! MAGA!

Thought for the day Dec. 2, 2016

GET OUT OF JAIL CARD

Up until I was about 35 we played games to amuse ourselves.
We played canasta, bridge, monopoly, checkers, and dominoes.
We got television in 1995 and our lives changed forever.
We were glued to it and still are.
Canasta was an emotional game and I remember cards flying all over the room when someone lost. Some times that happened with bridge.
Monopoly was a thinking man's game, and by being smart, you could become very rich, on paper.
The thing I remember about Monopoly is one corner of the board, if you landed on it, it said GO TO JAIL.
The only way to get out of jail was to pull a GET OUT OF JAIL card when is was your turn. If you pulled one and were not in jail, you were very careful with it. Sooner or later you would be in jail.
During the Presidential campaign Donald threatened to throw the book at Hillary. However, she made such a magnanimous concession speech, the Donald softened and indicated he felt sorrow for her.
At that point he may have just given her a GET OUT OF JAIL card.
But she may have just spent her card foolishly by joining Jill Stein in her nonsensical, no win, recount.
Twitter notes indicate Donald's soft heart may not be so soft.
STUPID IS AS STUPID DOES.

Stay Calm, Donald! MAGA!

Thought for the day Dec. 3, 2016

The brain is a muscle.
Like any other muscle, if it is not exercised, it becomes useless.
So I read a lot, think about things, and try to find reasons why God put people on this beautiful earth.
Since God knows everything, he must have known they would mess it up.
My guess is HE got bored creating the universe.
You know, it was the same thing, day after day, creating a star here, some planets there.
Boring.
So, for His amusement, he created man.
Now every day he gets His laughs from the stupid, crazy things man does.
This Presidential election is a case in point.
The party that preached Love not Hate, Tolerance, and Save the planet, LOST.
Now that same party hates everything, is intolerant of everything, and is destroying everything they can.
Crazy has no limits!
Hypocrites!
How great this world would be, if every one would really be WHAT THEY PRETEND TO BE.
Think about it.

Stay Calm, Donald! MAGA!

Thought for the day Dec. 5, 2016

This is the day I think our new Secretary of State will be named.
This came in the mail yesterday.
Seems worthy to pass along.

Not a fan of anyone from the power-hungry elite, but this meme certainly rings true.

Stay Calm, Donald! MAGA!

Thought for the day Dec. 6, 2016

This page left blank because there was no blanket blank news yesterday worth thinking about.

Except: Romney for Secretary of State XXXX
You know he is a snake before you let him in.

Stay Calm, Donald! MAGA!

Thought for the day Dec. 7, 2016

On this day in 1941, I was barely 16 years old, a country boy living in Merkel, Texas, and pretty ignorant about the world outside of West Texas.

This was a Sunday morning and as usual we were in church.

Life was good. We had just finished a great football season.

I had a sweetheart named Clarene, who, 56 years later would be my bride.

We were still in the Great Depression, but to us young people, life was normal.

Shortly after church we learned the Japanese had bombed Pearl Harbor (where ever that was).

It was just before 8AM Pearl Harbor time, when waves of Japanese bombers started the attack. In one day over 3500 soldiers and sailors were killed, 1100 injured, ships and airplanes were destroyed. We were at war. The "Day of infamy" was born.

On December 11, 1941 Germany and Italy declared war on the United States.

Instantly, the world changed.

The Greatest Generation came out of the shadows.

They joined the army, navy, marines, coast guard, and with a patriotism and determination they defeated the enemy.

Thousands more would die. But we were a proud people, people who believed in freedom for all people, and we hated evil. We sang our National Anthem with a tear in our eye, and saluted our flag.

It was the worst of times. It was the best of times.

Fast forward to Today. Japan, Germany, and Italy are allies.

Yesterday, a Japanese billionaire told Donald Trump He was going to build a company in the USA which would employ 50,000 people. That is a good thing.

But somewhere along the way since the glorious victory of WWII, the world has changed again, and not for the better.

Patriotism is dying. There is flag burning, not saluting.

There is kneeling for the Anthem, not standing alert with hand over heart.
And we are at war, but a different kind of war.
During WWII everybody worn the uniform of their country.
You knew who the enemy was.
In today's war, the good guys wear uniforms, but the bad guys do not.
They walk among us, looking like ordinarily people.
Suddenly, without warning, they attack, doing their damage.
Don't forget the second "Day of infamy"
September 11, 2011, when 3000 died in a sneak attack.
I dread to think what a 3rd "Day of infamy" would be like.

Stay Calm, Donald! MAGA!

Thought for the day Dec. 9, 2016

We have talked several times about being alert for Propaganda,
and being careful that it doesn't cloud our thinking processes.
Rest assured that while the election is 'basically' over,
the propaganda machine is running a full speed.
Ironically, the politically correct people are now referring to their propaganda
as "fake news".
The New York Times, the Dallas News, other newspapers, and some TV networks, have been, and still are, feeding us Fake News and make no apology for it.
You can count on this:
The anti-Trump people are gearing up to feed you poison,
and to interrupt, or delay........the transition for our new President.
It will not be smooth.
Like somebody said "If you don't read the paper, you are uninformed.
If you do, you are misinformed."
So, stay alert for Fake News.

Thought for the day Dec. 10, 2016

"It's not my fault!"
"I didn't do it!"
"Donald did it!"
"Don't blame me!"
You have probably never heard these excuses before, much less used them yourself.

"He said with tongue in cheek."
Yesterday I saw Hillary on TV explaining why she lost the election, and she used all of these excuses, and more.
I kinda felt sorry for her. She looked old.
The sparkle is gone out of her eyes, and the cackling laugh is missing.
She dreamed this beautiful dream every day for years, and, suddenly, in one day it was only an illusion, a nightmare.
She had plenty of blame to go around but basically what she said was "IT WAS NOT MY FAULT"!

Stay Calm, Donald! MAGA!

Thought for the day Dec. 11, 2016

Ever thought about "happy"?
What is "happy" anyway?
What is "look" happy? Can you "be" happy and not "look" happy?
Can you "feel' happy and look happy?
Can you fake happy?
Are you always happy?
What makes you happy?
As human we have emotions: glad, sad, happy, angry, hate, love
The bible tells us the greatest of these is LOVE.
But life is trickly. Bad things happen.
Sad thing happen. Love becomes difficult.
Being angry and hateful becomes easy.
But as for me, God has blessed me abundantly.
when I do not feel happy, I try to figuratively slap myself in the dace and say "whoa"
"Look at what you got, BOY! Be grateful!"
happiness is a mind thing.
First you have to want to be happy.
Second, like anything worthwhile, it requires work.
When all else fails, I EAT A BOWL OF BLUBELL ICE CREAM.
CAN'T BE UNHAPPY EATING HOMEMADE VANILLA.

Stay Calm, Donald! MAGA!

Thought for the day Dec. 12, 2016

Yesterday December 11, 1941
Germany and Italy declared war on the United States.
US won.
Yesterday December 11,2016
The New York Giants declared war on the Dallas Cowboys.
Cowboys lost, made me sad.
Ate a bowl of bluebell Homemade Vanilla.
Got over it.
slept like a log.

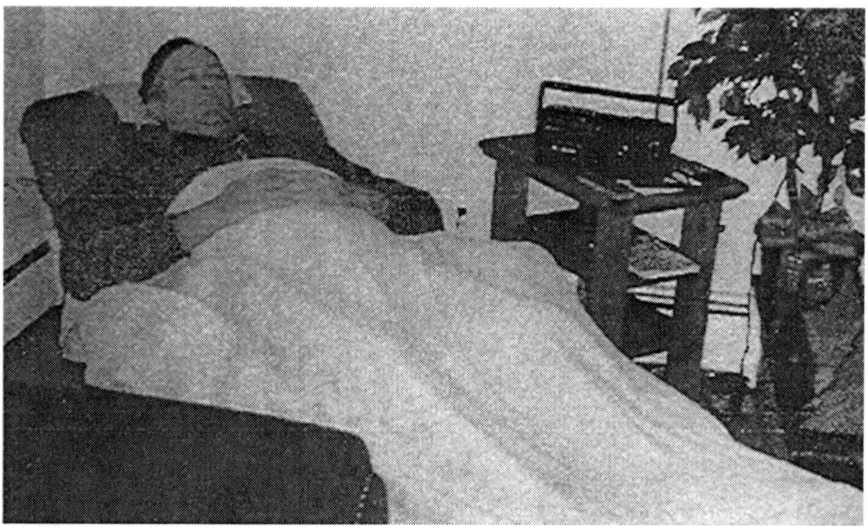

Stay Calm, Donald! MAGA!

Thought for the day dec.17, 2016

You may have thought,
Since you haven't been getting my Thought for the day, that this old fellow just quit thinking.
Far from true.
Since this computer bombed out last Tuesday,my thoughts have been very negative and not worth publishing.
It now is about half recovered and I can send and receive e-mails.
My back surgery is scheduled 10:30 AM Monday.
Surgery of any kind is serious business and much more so when you are 91.
In my discussion with my doctor I told him:
"I know I am 91 years old and could die tomorrow, but I am in good health with no serious problems except this pain in my back.
I could live to be a 100. But whatever time I have left
I would like to live it with some quality of life.
So I want you, as soon as possible, to make this pain go goodbye, adios, so long"
After today I am taking a sabbatical until next year.
Tomorrow is pre-op prep day. you know-laxative, fasting, and praying.
Finally, if you are so inclined I would appreciate it if would offer up a prayer for me, my surgeon, and Clarene.
The lord willing, we will talk next year.
Merry Christmas to all of you.

Stay Calm, Donald! MAGA!

Thought for the day January 1,2017

HAPPY NEW YEAR TO YOU, ME ALL THE DEPLORABLES. I AM HOME AND DOING WELL.
The 8 inch scar I received for Christmas was a blessing.
The doctor said he removed the PAIN and put it in the garbage, and not the recycle bin. Bye Pain.
So we are starting 2017 on a very high note. Great things are already happening and, I think we can look forward to many more.
Life is good!

Stay Calm, Donald! MAGA!

Thought for the day January 2,2017

I don't know about you, but my mind is a strange thing.
What a great day!
I sit here thinking about writing something positive.
Then a little pain hits my back and I think negative,
And rambling begins. ALL SORTS OF STUFF.
Then the biggan hits Taxes are due!!!! Have to write checks. Wow!
They take most of my income for the month. Add discover. ATT, Oncor electric, City, and some groceries
and things really turn negative.☹
But wait. I just had successful back surgery and I am looking forward to a quality of life I have not had recently.
I will be able to play golf, bowl and travel.
My cup overflows. The lord has walked beside me every step of the way. I have family, many friends and best of all
I have Clarene, my fantastic, loving, sweetheart, THE LOVE OF MY LIFE.
My life is like a rose bush with no thorns.
So I have made the circle. I AM NOW DELIRIOUSLY HAPPY.☺
Hope you have as great a day as I am.

KEEP CALM DONALD! MAGA!

Thought for the day January 3, 2017

Poor Russia.
Do you Remember when Hilary, as Secretary of state and as Russia's good friend, practically gave away 20% of our uranium to Russia for a contribution to the Clinton slush fund?
Less than two months ago she was guarantees to be elected the first "FEMALE" president of the United States.
Now Putin, a dear friend "supposedly" betrayed her. how could that be?
"Supposedly: Russia hacked Hillary's and DNC private e-mail and released their content, exposing the REAL Hillary as the lying, conniving, person she is.
Now Russia is to blame for cracking Her façade.
Poor Russia.
Our thanks to Putin, or whoever really did it.
It is unfortunate that Obama had to really get tough with Putin.
Pow! Take that Putin. Get all your ambassadors out of America..
That will teach Putin not to mess with Obama!
Poor Russia

Stay Calm, Donald! MAGA!

Thought for the day January 4, 2017

We got him elected and we are well on our way to great things.
My thought for the day, every day, revolves around my thanks to the Lord for all his blessings, and hope for a better tomorrow.
I am now in the re-hab business trying to rejuvenate this old body.
SO I AM PUTTING MY THOUGHT ON HOLD.
IT HAS BEEN FUN.
MUCH GOOD DONE.
DONALD SIC-EM DONAL LICK EM.
WE ON OUR WAY TO A BETTER DAY.
BURMA SHAVE

Stay Calm, Donald! MAGA!

Thought for the day January 5,2017

Sorry. I can't help it. Here is another thought,
During the campaign Donald had pet names for his opponents.

One by one they fell by the wayside.
there was:
Crooked Hillary
Little Rubio
Low Energy Jeb
Lying Ted
Crazie Bernie
Truly Weird Rand Paul
Pocahontas
"Spoiled brat" Mitt Romney
Now we have Chuck Schumer's clowns.
Wonder how many "clowns" Chuck will
sacrifice before he gives up?

Stay Calm, Donald! MAGA!

Thought for the January 6, 2017

February 13,1633
On this day, in 1633 Galileo was convicted of heresy and imprisoned for professing he believed
the earth revolved around the sun.
So I ask you, when does a fact become a fact?
Obviously, in the real world, what we believe vs reality is irrelevant.
Yesterday, January6, 2017, Donald Trump was officially declared.
the next President of the United State of America.
Believe it or not. Hillary, IT IS A FACT!
IT'S OVER!

Stay Calm, Donald! MAGA!

Thought for the day January 9, 2017

Well...

I thought I could give politics a rest for a while, but it aint gonna happen.
There is too much of the stuff floating around.
In fact, we are going to drown in it if we don't fight back.
Examples:
Kellyanne Conway was asked to come to the NBC studio and gave a 10 minutes interview for Sunday's meet the press. 'When 'Meet the press' aired Sunday, they had edited the interview down
TO ONE MINUTE,
Trump twittered angrily.
So did Kellyanne.
Kellyanne had dressed, caught a cab, had 10-minute interview, caught a cab home, turned on this TV to watch her 10 minutes interview reduced to 1 minute of NBC selected sound bites.
Rigging is their game.
Media is their game.
DON'T CALL AGAIN 'MEET THE PRESS'!

Stay Calm, Donald! MAGA!

Thought for the day January 10, 2017

Since I am convalescing from my back surgery, I am house bound. And at my age, very few entertainment options are available to me. But the LORD has hearing started on Jeff Sessions, The nominee to be the United State Attomey General.
Republicans and democrats take turns praising him and trying to shoot holes in his qualifications.
The question fall into a number of categories.

1. Intelligent
2. Ignorant
3. Facetious (on purpose)
4. Facetious (ignorantly)
5. Sincerely
6. Put down
7. Utterly stupid
8. Al Franken

Al is the Jr. senator from Minnesota.
He says he is not a lawyer, just a layman.
Previously he was a bad comedian.
He's still a comedian. Now his repertoire include being a bad senator.
His line of questioning was juvenile, and senile, but good for laughs and some snickers.
Not a poster child for America, but he is a good example of why the Democrats chose the jackass as their national symbol.

Stay Calm, Donald! MAGA!

Thought for the day January 13, 2017

SCRATCH MY BACK

Yesterday Obama gave Vice President Joe Biden
the Medal of Freedom "for helping make me who I am."
Last week Obama, A medal, FOR NO REASON AT ALL".

President Obama Awards Himself

Distinguished Public Service Medal

Stay Calm, Donald! MAGA!

Thought for the day January 15, 2017

As I have grown older, it seems like time files by.
I bet you have noticed that, also.
However, today old Father time is just shuffling hit feet.
Jan, 20 is just 5 days away, but I am so anxious for Donald to take over, each day seems like a week.
Next Friday, the Lord willing, we will finally have a President who believes in the Christian values America was found on.
AND a President who believes in me.

MAGA!!!!

Thought for the day Jan 16, 2017

In 2009 no Republicans skipped Obama's inauguration.
In 2017, 30 'so-called' Democrats plan to skip Trump's inauguration.
The intolerance of the tolerant, those so pure they can "caste the first stone"
lost the election.
You don't have to think twice to know why.
Will anybody miss them?
Words have meanings, actions have consequences.

MAGA!!!!

Thought for the day Jan. 17, 2017

The cap

Politics 101: "Hats don't look Presidential" for years it has been an accepted rule that president don't wear hats.

Apparently it is thought by the snobs that it is demeaning and undignified.

In 2015, early in the Presidential campaign. Trump flew into south Texas to check on immigration.

As the plane door opened out walked Donald wearing his red cap with slogan "Make America Great Again"

Immediately his campaign was reduced to JOKE status. And the "Insiders" wrote him off.

Maybe it was his hair, maybe something else.

But as the campaign continued, In all outdoor events, he wore his cap, sometimes red, sometimes white.

Soon hats by the thousands began appearing at all of his events. outdoors or indoors.

In retrospect, looking back, then looking forward to November 9th,

is it conceivable that The HAT WON THE ELECTION FOR TRUMP?

Frank Luntz, through out the campaign, brought together groups of people with mixed political views to get their opinions about candidates and topics.

In one group a lady apparently nailed it.

She said; "We know his goal is to make America great again."

"it's on his hat. And we see it every time it's on TV.

Everything that he's doing, there's no doubt why he is doing it:

IT'S TO MAKE AMERICA GREAT AGAIN."

You decide.

MAGA!!!!

Thought for the day Jan. 18, 2017

Enigma. A mystery.
Rep. John Lewis, a black man from Atlanta, Georgia, by all accounts is an American hero.
If you read his history, you would have to agree.
His role model was Martin Louis King, JR.
He marched peacefully advocating for equal right for "his" people.
He was nearly killed by police on orders from Democrats governor of Georgia while leading a group of protesters.
However, he was tenacious in his fight for equal rights.
At the same time, Democrats controlled the south and were determined to keep blacks "on the plantation".
He was beaten and arrested. He was jailed at least 24 times.
Once he was beaten and left in the street to die.
But he never lost sight of his fight for equal rights, voting rights, Desegregation of schools, and the demeaning "back of the bus".
In 1986 he was elected to the US Congress as a Democrat representing the Atlanta, Georgia area and holds that office today.
Therein lies the enigma.
His life at the hands of Democrats and the Klu Klux Klan up until 1986 was pure torture, a hell on earth.
As a Representative he was now able to join Republicans, who have, since Lincoln, fought for equal rights of black people.
He was now in a position to help make real equality possible.
What does he do? He joins the part of Liberal, Socialist Democrats, the party that tortured him for 25 years, the party that is determined to keep blacks on the plantation.
He rejects the hand of Trump who wants to be President of ALL the people.
Why?
It is a mystery.

Thought for the day Jan 19, 2017

I was happy to receive my official invitation to the "Welcome Celebration" today at the Lincoln Memorial. It is printed and hanging on the wall. What a thrill it would be to be in the crowd and experience the excitement, patriotism, and thankfulness for our new leader.
But this old back is not up to the trip.

Sic 'em Donald! Stay calm Donald!

One more day!

The 58th Presidential Inauguration

BJ Melton,
You are cordially invited to attend the "Make America Great again Welcome Celebration" on the Eastern front of the Lincoln Memorial on January, 19th 2017.

Chapter IV

President Donald J. Trump

JANUARY 20,2017 TO JULY 31,2017

My thought for today Jan. 20, 2017

What is a fool?

Well, mainly fools just appear without notice in the eye of the beholder. You can't describe them. He, She, is just there. You recognize one right off and you say "You fool". I look at the Democrats refusing to attend the awesome event of crowning out 45th President. i recognize them immediately, I say "you fools". In the history of man, this is a momentous occasion.

But, in the history of man, there have been millions of momentous occasions.

Do you remember any of them? Probably not.

So, in the reality of the real world, does anything matter? People are born to die. The sun has, for eons, risen in the east and will continue to do so. All rivers run to the ocean. The ocean is never full and the rivers are never dry. The wind blows this way and will continue to do so. None of those Democrats above know me, but if they ever see me, they will probably say "You are fool". Finally, if you really think about it—There is nothing new under the sun. life is just a circle-no beginning, no end. I am grateful the Lord has given me one more day. So, for me and my American generation we will rejoice and be glad in this momentous occasion!

Amen

This is the day!
MAGA!

2nd Thought for to January 20, 2017

For the last 18 months there has been joy, anxiety, fear apprehension, elation, deflation, worry, and now outright exhilaration!

IT IS OVER, NOW THE REVIVAL BEGIN!

Thank you, Donald for being you.
And GOD, welcome back to the White House.
Please, make yourself right at home.

My thought for today Jan. 21, 2017

DAY 1

The war has begun.

Inauguration day was all fluff and circumstance and make believe. Reality returns today. And Reality reminds me of my Childhood dog, Rex. I used to tease him with a bone. As long as I held the bone, we were best friends. He would and beg, and fo little tricks on command until.......... He got the bone. Immediately our relationship changed. If I tried to take the bone away, he would fight me, bite me, or run away.

For years the Washington Establishment (dog) has been collecting bones and we the people have gotten the short stick.

In the quotation below from Donald's speech he is essentially saying "We are coming after your bones" and for the "Dogs" on Washington that means War!

So reality begins today. There will be many battles, some wins, some losses. Draining the swamp won't be easy, but it is necessary to MAKE AMERICA GREAT AGAIN. "The establishment protected itself, but not the citizens of our country. Their victories have not been your victories. Their triumphs have not been your triumphs," Trump said. "And while they celebrated in our nation's capital, there was little to celebrate for struggling families all across our land."

Sic 'em Donald!

Thought for to January 23, 2017

The First Amendments

Right to Peaceful Assembly: United States

The First Amendment to the United States Constitution prohibits the United States Congress from enacting legislation that would abridge the right of the people to assemble peaceably.

The Fourteenth Amendment to the United States Constitution makes this prohibition application to state governments.

The First Amendment does not provide the right to conduct an assembly at which there is a clear and present danger of riot, disorder, or interference with traffic on public streets, or other immediate threat to public safety or order.

The protest we saw Friday during the Inauguration were nothing short of anarchy. Makes you feel proud of the Democrats who so graciously lost the election, doesn't it?

DON'T WAVER, DONALD! MAGA!

Thought for to January 24, 2017

I guess it is natural to occasionally think about the road you have traveled and the memories you have accumulated to get to this point in your life. And me-I got lot of memories and one came up this morning that I think is kinda funny.

Years ago my wife and I drove all over this country. When CB radios were invented, we got one. All the truckers had one. So did the police and emergency centers. As we traveled, if I needed help for some reason, I could sign on and someone would talk to me. The funny thing was sign-on names. Everybody had they're on unique name.

Mine was Chicken Turner.

Why? Well when I was a boy of 7-8 we lived on a farm. We had a water well from which we got our drinking water, one bucket full as a time. The well had a brick wall around it about 4 ft. tall. We also had chickens. At night they liked to roost on the rim of the well, and they were stubborn about it. My job every night was to turn every one of them face in to the well, for obvious reasons. So, I adopted "Chicken Turner" as my CB sign-on.

Made sense to me.

DON'T WAVER, DONALD! MAGA!

Thought for the day Jan. 26, 2017

This is the sixth day of Donald's Presidency. I have watched with awe as he has been full filling the promises he has made. It makes me thankful, and gives me a feeling of pride that in a way, a very small way I know, that I helped get him elected. He really is going to make America Great Again.

What will Day 6 bring us???

DON'T WAVER, DONALD! MAGA!

Thought for the day Jan. 27, 2017

The "Back Nine."

I started playing golf when I was eleven years old. Bought my first set of clubs st Montgomery Ward AND CHARGE THEM! Paid them off with money I made from my paper route. I read this story someone wrote about The Back Nine And I got to thinking.

I know I am on the back nine, but were?

I think, with this back problem, I may be on the 17th hole in a sand trap, plugged, with a downhill lie.

If you play golf, you know this is the hardest shot in golf to execute successfully. Chances are your next shot will also be from the sand trap. So, I look at where I am in life and give thanks. I will just take my shots. I don't know how many strokes it will take to reach the 18th hole, but I will make it.

Eventually,........ everybody does.

DON'T WAVER, DONALD! MAGA!

Thought for the day Jan. 28, 2017

TO: ******* *******

Writer for the Socialist Dallas News.

I read your column occasionally and most times I am tempted to rebut your irrational thinking, but don't. However, your Jan. 27 writing pulled my string, so here goes.

I think you mentioned a husband one time so I assume you are married. Do you have children? Just wondering what kind of person, you really are. Your defense of the Women's pro-abortion march is indefensible. I watched as they marched carrying their vulgar signs and listened as they made their nasty, profanity laced speeches. I saw one woman with two small children holding a sign that said "F--- Trump". What a blessing to have such a caring mother. You have to wonder how those two children escaped the womb alive! You talked about the crude jokes resulting from the march, and they were crude, but there was much material for has been known since the beginning of man. Having children has been God's plan to populate the earth. But these women believe it is their right to have their baby, made by God, ripped from their womb, have its head smashed, valuable parts removed, and the remained trashed.

For a few minutes, or maybe just seconds of ecstasy nine month before, a living human being pays a terrible price.

When I was boy and had reached the age of temptation and desire, I heard a joke that might have saved me from being a father at the sweet young age of 17-18.

"Young girl calls up her boyfriend and says she is pregnant. His reply was 'Hey girl, I wasn't serious. I just poking fun'" And he disappears.

And this reminds me of Simone Biles, Olympic all- around champion.

Simone was born to a drug alcohol addicted woman with 3 other children, a perfect candidate for abortion. Her husband was also an alcoholic who abandoned them and she never knew him. Unable to care for Simone she was place in foster care. Somehow, this "perfect" candidate for abortion fought her way and though much grit and determination became Simone Biles, Olympic all-around champion. So, I ask you, in the massacre of 55,000,000 children since RoeVSWade, how many Simone were wasted?

So finally I have to ask you, could you perform an abortion, smashing a child's head, and killing? Probably not. Then what kind of animal can do this over and over, with impunity? Is this what civilized people are supposed to do? I think not.

God bless Donald Trump and the PRO-LIFE Republican Party!

Thought for the day Jan. 30, 2017

When the funny is not funny because
it gets too personal.
You know when you are getting old,
when you can't pass a bathroom without thinking
"I might as well pee while I am here."

It is called "Plan Ahead"

Don't waver Donald! MAGA!!!

Thought for the day Jan. 31, 2017

This is one of those days I know what I want to say, but I don't know how to say it. Donald seems to have himself in a mess with this immigration thing. But does he? This is something he has been saying he would do for 15 months, and when he does it it is so awful, so inhumane, so un-American.

The bleeding-heart liberals are shrieking, ACLU is filling law suits. Chief Clown Chuck Schumer is shedding tears he is overwrought. In fact, this morning he is right in the middle of the protesters, egging them on.

Then there is Obama, the Community organizer, doing what he does best, spreading his dividing poison.

This is so unbelievable. They are so wrong!!

The sky is falling! Could we be witnessing Treason? Just asking. Our constitution does not say we should rescue everyone who unfortunately was born in another part of the world and is being victimized. People who declare themselves a REFUGEE and deserve a chance for a better life in America. Being a compassion people, thousands of immigrants are admitted legally to The United State every year. Mostly these are people who assimilate with their community, many becoming American citizens.

So what is the problem?

At home it is the Socialist liberals, our home-grown barbarians funded by George Soros, who lost the election, and are determined to destroy America at any cost. In the Muslim world it is also Barbarism. Animal dedicated to the killing of Americans and Christians everywhere. Donald has promised to protect America from these animals, by destroying them where they hide, and minimize the chances of them entering America with one intent: TO KILL AS MANY AS THEY CAN.

The inconvenience of instituting the Ban immediately, without notice, was unfortunate, but necessary. The problems will be rectified, and the possibility a terrorist not property vetted and planning on infiltrating America were at least put on hold 120 days.

DON'T WAVER, DONALD! MAGA!

Thought for the day Feb. 1, 2017

Things that require a valid ID

Driving Boarding a plane
Doctor's office hospital
Applying for a job
Buy a firearm
Donate blood
Social Security Services
Pharmacy
Bank transaction
Pawn shops
Writing a check
Using a credit card
Applying to a School
Buying car insurance
Applying for store credit
Car registration
Buying a car
Medicare Medicaid
Buy a house
And would believe
The simple thing of
CHECKING A BOOK OUT OF A LIBRARY

DON'T WAVER, DONALD! MAGA!

Thought for the day Feb. 2, 2017

GATES AND LOCKS

When I was a boy of 7 or 8 we had a Jersey cow named Bessie which gave us milk which my Mother turned into butter, buttermilk and some into clabber. Bessie stayed pinned up because she had a frees spirit and would love to roam the neighborhood if she could. There was this gate that was designed to keep Bessie in the corral, so to speak.

One day, for whatever reason, I left the gate open, and before I knew it Bessie was headed down the road. Papa was not happy and herding a stubborn old cow is not easy. I said all that to say this, gates are designed to keep livestock in, locks and moats are designed to keep the unwanted out. So every evening we lock and double lock our house.

And for good reason.

The world is what it is and there are people out there who, given a chance, would do me harm or steal from me. If someone knocks on my door wanting in, and I don't know for sure they are a friend.

THEY don't get in.

I bet you are the same way, aren't you? It only makes sense. Then pray tell why do we Americans, knowing there are people out there somewhere who want to do us harm. Leave the door wide open, literally inviting them into our house?

Why, Why, Why?

There is no sensible excuse, just simple stupidity! So Donald lock the door for 90 days in order to develop a system designed to let friends into our house, and eliminate those who would do us harm. Makes sense, but there is walling gnashing of teeth in the streets.

Stupid!

DON'T WAVER, DONALD! MAGA!

Thought for the day Feb. 3, 2017

Food for your thought.

Every year we take in about 1,000,000 immigrants. Mostly these are unprivileged, or persecuted people wanting a better life. This is our humanitarian attempt to help solved the world's poverty problem.

The soft-hearted do goaders feel warm and cozy. Don't get me wrong. We have done a good deed. But while we are taking in a million, elsewhere in the world the population is increasing by 20 million or more. So our effort to solve the world's poverty is like whistling in the wind. Maybe there is a way to help people where they live or May it is like the Bible says "The poor you have with you always".

Think about how fortune you are!

DON'T WAVER, DONALD! MAGA!

Thought for the day Feb. 5, 2017

This is Super bowl Sunday, Hurrah.

The Cowboys, like me, are watching at home, a long with 100,000,000 other people. Thousands will pay $$thousand$$ to spend a night or two in New Orleans, then sit in the stadium with thousands of others who did the same.

There will shouting and moaning.
There will be spills and thrills.
There will be a winner and a loser.
But think about it.
It is really just another day, just another game.
No matter who wins.
Tomorrow will be Monday.
Today will be history.
Life goes on.

Just for fun I pick the Falcons.

STAY CALM, DONALD! MAGA!

Thought for the day Feb. 9, 2017

Racism

What is racism, really?

Today, the world is thrown around all the time by people of color and whites alike. Use of the term "racism" has become so popular that it's spun off related terms such as "reverse racism," "horizontal racism" and "internalized racism."

Racism is nothing more than Human nature vocalized and/or visualized. If I think I am better than you, for any reason, i.e.: color, position, wealth, physically that's racism on my part. If you sense that I think I am better than you, if you, that's racism on your part. In reality, in God's eyes, I am not better than anybody, unless "good" or "evil" is involved. In earthly terms I may be better OFF 'materially' than you, but not better than you. This is where the mind gets warped. If you and I are not morally corrupt, we are equals. If you are morally corrupt, and I think I am not, then I think I am better than you. Like beauty is in the eye of the beholder, Racism is in the mind of the beholder. Sadly we have had racism forever, and will always have it.

We CAN fix ourselves, but not others.

Think about it.

STAY CALM, DONALD! MAGA!

Thought for the day Feb. 10, 2017

Let's see. We have a Presidential branch, A legislative branch, and A judicial branch.

The legislative branch is primarily responsible for budgets and making new laws.

The judicial branch is responsible for enforcing the constitution as written, and laws passed by the legislature.

The President, as a Commander-in-chief, is responsible for security and safety of American citizens, and Legal immigrants. HE IS NOT RESPONSIBLE FOR ILLEGAL IMMIGRANTS, OR ANYONE IN FOREIGN COUNTRIES WHO IS NOT A US CITIZEN.

The duties of each branch are clearly defined in our constitution.

A wall exist between each branch and is not to be breached.

So I ask you,

HOW CAN AN INSIGNIFICANT FEDERAL JUDGE CLIMB THE WALL, ASSUME THE DUTIES OF THE PRESIDENT, MAKE LAW CONGRESS, AND GET AWAY WITH IT???

STAY CALM, DONALD! MAGA!

Thought for the day Feb. 11, 2017

NEW FLASH!

February 10 AUSTIN, TEXAS

The NFL sharpened its warning to Texas on Friday about a "bathroom bill" targeting transgender people, suggesting for the first time that the football-crazed state could miss out on hosting another Super Bowl if the proposal is enacted.

"If a proposal that is discriminatory or inconsistent with our values were to become law there, that would certainly be a factor considered when thinking about awarding future events," league spokesman Brian McCarthy said in response to an email question about the Texas bill.

Transgender population in USA

An earlier report published in April 2011 by the Williams Institute estimated that 3.8 percent of Americans identified as a gay/lesbian, bisexual, or transgender: 1.7 percent as lesbian or gay, 1.8 percent as bisexual and 0.3 percent as transgender.

Now consider this. Can 0.3% of the people force stadiums, arenas, grocery stores, department stores, small business, to spend millions of dollars to accommodate a momentary "inconvenience".

What have these people been doing for eons?

STAY CALM, DONALD! MAGA!

Thought for the day Feb. 12, 2017

I don't know where they find these people but these people deserve a lot of credit.

Year after year they have hoodwinked their constituents into thinking they are for them!

While enjoying the good life, being over paid with a nice fat expensive account, somehow become millionaires. (Guess how.)

They are not dumb, just con artists and leaches.

Nancy Pelosi,
#1 Clown Schumer,
Richard Blumenthal,
Feinstein, Dianne,
Kaine, Timothy
Elijah Cummings,
John Lewis,
Bill de Blasio,
Rahm Emanuel,
Elizabeth Warren,
Bernie Sanders,
Richard Durbin,
Leahy, Patrick,
Franken, Al,
Maxine Water,
Sheila Jackson Lee,
Reverend Jesse Jackson,
Al Sharpton

If you will take careful notice, you will see they are all democrats, and anti Trump!

STAY CALM, DONALD! MAGA!

Thought for the day Feb. 13, 2017

Yesterday Jordan Spieth won the Pebble Beach Golf tournament.

He is a fine young man, and my favorite golfer.

Made me feel so good yesterday, and the feeling is hanging over today.

……to each his own…..

As for me I will have a happy day.

Hope you do, too.

STAY CALM, DONALD! MAGA!

Thought for the day Feb, 14, 2017

~~I started to write about politics today~~
But I changed my mind.
Thought of something more important.
Today is Valentine's Day.
This morning I awoke and got to thinking.
There beside me was MY VALENTINE the person I love very much and I realized she is mine, all mine.
Happiness is my sweet Clarene.
I am so fortunate.
Great are my blessings.

Hope you have a happy Valentine's day, too!

Thought for the day Feb. 15, 2017

Believe this!

Barack Obama, your ex-President and America destroyer is back where he started as Community Organizer. ONLY ON A MUCH LARGER SCALE-all of America.

You wonder where all the protesters come from?
You wonder why Trump has so much resistance in draining the swamp?
You wonder why there are so many “LEAKS” of security information?
You wonder why his cabinet is not intact?
Well--- Welcome to the Office of Barack and Michelle Obama

We love you Back

His new origination, Organizing for Action, is training the next generation of progressive organizers.

He is following the rules of his favorite Communist Saul Alinsky
Two of Saul’s favourites are:

5. Ridicule is man’s most potent weapon
12. Pick the target, freeze it, personalize it, and polarize it.
    (See what happened to Michael T. Flynn)

YOU CAN SEE THEM IN ACTION TODAY!! Obama’s basic agenda besides promoting

1. Save Obamacare
2. Save the Iran treaty.
3. Destroy Donald trump.
4. The total destruction of our moral fiber.

BELIEVE IT. WATCH IT UNFOLD!

Thought for the day Feb. 16, 2017

MSNBC, the ultra-liberal TV networks that specializes in "Fake news" half-truths, ridicule, and 'on-the-edge' slander, announced yesterday that:

"Morning Joes" bans Trump aide Kellyanne Conway."

What a blessing. Say "Thanks" Kellyanne, and be happy to oblige him.

Joe Scarborough's main talents are character assignation, some days good things happen.

Watch your back Donald! MAGA!

Thought for the day Feb. 18, 2017

FAKE NEWS

Nordstrom drops Ivanka Trump clothes line.
Sales Jump!

(off the cliff)

Credits cards

Watch your back Donald! MAGA!

Thought for the day Feb. 19, 2017

FAKE NEWS

"PUTIN HELPS TRUMP GET ELECTED"

Sharing a joke among friends.

US President Barack Obama with Putin before the first session of the G20 Summit in Los Cabos in June 2012

Watch your back Donald! MAGA!

Thought for the day Feb. 20, 2017

FAKE NEWS

DID YOU KNOW THERE NOW IS A WEB SITE FAKENEWS.NEWS?

Fake news has become so common, the media, like the Times and Washington Post, seem to be competing for the best Fake News story.

Here is a simple Fake News story:

> Donald Trump refuses to take a question from CNN's Senior White House Correspondent @Acosta
>
> (Trump gave him about 10 minutes in his press conference last week)

Fakenews.news has not verified the fakeness of the story linked above.
They add—Any story linked here may contain real news and be 100% true.
Proceed with caution.

Watch your back Donald! MAGA!

Thought for the day Feb. 24, 2017

It is time for re-dedication.

Obama and his 'hoods', the media, and late night? Comedians? have become unmerciful.

Trump and Flynn are being crucified, not because Flynn was a bad pick for NSA, not because Flynn was doing his job, but because Flynn, for some strange reason, lied to VP Pence, violating a trust.

TRUMP MADE A MISTAKE!

Federal judge made law by ruling Trump could not do what the constitution authorizes him to do about immigration.

TRUMP MADE A MISTAKE!

Town hall meeting have become useless because of Obama paid hoodlums causing chaos, rendering such meetings totally unproductive.

Propaganda by the media, and micro analyzing Trumps every word and action, are all part of the Liberal process in their unrelenting efforts to destroy what could be the greatest President ever.

Don't waver. Don't start second guessing.

Keep the faith. Recognize the enemy for what they are-scumbags!

Fake news is fake news.

Watch your back Donald! MAGA!

Thought for the day Feb. 27, 2017

I did not watch the Oscar last night.
Did I miss something?
The paper says a "comedian" named Kimmel, or something like that, was host.
Apparently, the joke, if any, was on him.
How come we don't produce any BOB HOPES anymore?
We do have some politicians that are Jokes.
Like Kimmel, they are not funny either.

Watch your back Donald! MAGA!

Thought for the day March 1, 2017

I watched Donald's speech last night.
He proposed a number of things to make America better.
Democrats sat on their rumps.
Does this mean Democrats do not want America better?
That's the way I read it.
They seem to spit in the faces of the American people in an attempt to keep Republicans from getting credit for anything.
Low life.

Watch your back Donald! MAGA!

Thought for the day March 3, 2017

There are few things more irritating than a leaking faucet.

It is drip,drip, night and day.

Finally, you will take desperate measures, even call a plumber ($80 just to cross the threshold of your door).

Trump has faucet leak. It is leaking information, some of which is highly personal, and some which endangers national security.

It is apparent, no obvious, that Obama left moles in various department who are intent on embarrassing and harassing Trump.

The leak to the Washington Post about so-called secret meetings Sessions had with Russian Diplomats, is a case in point.

The leaking faucet has to be fixed!

What ever it takes!

Seriously, Donald, you really have to

Watch your back Donald! MAGA!

2nd thought for the day March 3, 2017

Today I find I am capable of having more than one thought a day.

Chief clown Schumer, the democrats, and some RINO Republicans have gone absolutely ballistic about Sessions "doing his job as a senator".

Ranting and raving against everything good for America has become their MO.

You have to wonder where were these voices when Clinton met secretly with AG Lynch to plan for the election of another President Clinton?

Where wre they when Hillary, Obama, and Rice lied about Benghazi, or the IRS scandal?

How many thoughts is that?

Well, I got more but I will sum them up by saying "anybody against MAKING AMERICA GREAT AGAIN to save their own hide, is a Scumbar to me!"

There! I've said it and proud of it!

Donald, the swamp is full of alligators and now they have added piranha.

Watch your step! MAGA!

Thought for the day March 4, 2017

Every President (43 of 'em) before Obama, after completion of their term, Clinton went to his mansion in New York, the bushes went to Texas, Reagan went back to California, and Carter went to his peanut farm In Georgia.

Supposedly, Obama has a million $$+ mansion in Chicago.

So why is he staying in Washington, DC, renting an 8200 sq ft walled mansion?

How can he afford to pay $10,000 to $15,000 month rent?

To be continued..........

Watch your back Donald! MAGA!

Thought for the day march 5, 2017

Obama's new residence continued.........
This walled mansion is valued at $6 million +.
Who owns it?
As it turns out the owner, Joe Lockhart, is an interesting, and close associate of both the Obamas and Clintons.
So.. who is Joe Lockhart?
He served as press secretary and adviser during the Bill Clinton administration.
He was strategist for John Kerry's Presidential campaign.
During Hillary's term as Secretary of State, Joe founded a PR firm, Glover Park Group, working for better relations between the U.S. and the egyptian government.
It is known Joe received well over $5,000,000, for his work.
(It is not known how much Egypt contributed to the Clinton Foundation)
Maybe it is coincidental but in 2016 Obama approved the shipment of weapons and fighter jets to Egypt.
Question : How did Joe Lockhart go from press Secretary for Bill Clinton to be the owner of a $6.5 million house for lease?
How much did the Clintons & Obama put in Joe's pocket?
Maybe the house Is rent free for favors'?
Obama's new residence continued........

Watch your back Donald! MAGA!

Thought for the day March 7, 2016

Obama's new residence continued.......
The questions keep coming.
Obama still owns his house in Chicago, making approximately $7500/month payments.
It is guarded by Secret Service and Chicago police around the clock, but he never expects to live there again.
So when you add the payments of his rent house in Washington, DC (aslo guarded 24/7)
You are talking about real money, as much $20,000 monthly purchased a house in California and one in Hawaii.
As President he was paid a salary of $400,000/yr plus $50,000 expense account.
He is living a very rich man.
Makes me wonder how he got so rich.
Tomorrow: "Organizing for Actrion"=OFA

Sic 'em Donald!

Thought for the day March 8, 2016

Obama's new residence continued.......

You may not believe what I am about to tell you. Unfortunately, most of us live in a cocoon and care content to just let the world go by.

Barack Obama was and still is a left wing community organizer with a goal of destroying the foundations of the American Enterprise System, and replacing it with Marxist Socialism.

So it was not by accident Michelle Obama legally founded "Organizing for Action", OFA, January 2013.

It is a pollical organization, a shadow government, so to speak, for the explicit purpose of sabotaging his successor---who, as it turns out is our duly elected President Donald Trump.

OFA combines agitation and propaganda.

You can see it every day in the anti-Trump marches, isolated protest, interrupting town hall meetings, shutting down airports, drumming down conservative speakers on college campuses, leaks about General Fynn, and sessions. And OFA has money. Lots of money. In the first two years it took in over $40 million and by now has over $100 million in it coffers.

OFA is anti-American. OFA is organized to trian more organizers. OFA has a big web site promoting itself, recruiting "members" and accepting donations. And Obama sits the wheel, 1000 ft from the largest mosque in Washington, DC, guiding the progressive Socialist agenda.

This gets really dirty.

Obama's new residence continued......

Watch your back Donald! MAGA!

Thought for the day March 9, 2017

Obama's new residence continued.....

The following is copied from OFA's web site. What this tells you is they are creating 1000's of little Obama organizers to create havoc in an attempt to destroy President Trump and his plan to make America Great again.

And Obama sits in his new residence guiding the whole thing.
If this is not treason, then we need to redefine what Treason means.
"Growing the progressive movement is one of OFA's top priorities."

We're dedicated to creating high-quality talent at every level-from recruiting and training activists to become skilled organizers to developing the skills of mid-and senior-level staff throughout the progressive community.

OFA is strengthening the pipeline of talent throughout the country with leadership development and training programs.

OFA FELLOWSHIP PROGRAM Organizing for Action's elite fellowship program in designed to train the next generation of progressive leaders and issue advocates. Fellow emerge from this intensive six-week program highly skilled in the tool community organizers use every day to create change (HAVOC) in their communities. Working in one of three tracks (basic, intermediate, or advanced), fellows develop skills in areas such as community engagement, digital organizing, and digital content production. All OFA fellowship tracks involve either working alongside veteran chapter leads include direct instruction from experts of OFA headquarters in Chicago. Each track will involve work on important issues such as climate change, health care, and women's right, so fellows can apply their new skills immediately.

Find out more about how to apply—sign and we'll let you know as soon as thhe application opens.

Sign

DONALD, THIS GUY IS SPENDING MILLIONS
TO DESTROY YOU!

Watch your back Donald! MAGA!

Thought for the day March 10, 2017

Yesterday was my oldest daughter's birthday.
She would have been 67. Her name was Pam.
Unfortunately, she died in 2002 of ovarian cancer.
I have so many memories.
I want to tell you about one special memory.
One day when she was about 5 years old she did something she should not have done, and she knew it.
When I called her to me she walked up to me and suddenly grabbed me by the leg and said "Daddy, I love you!"
It melted my heart.
Love is an many splendored thing.

Watch your back Donald! MAGA!
Some people don't love you!

Thought for the day March 11, 2017

THIEVES
This is just a little information for filing.

Official copy of the Bill, Hillary and Chelsea Foundation for the tax year 2014.

Total revenue (line 12)..................................$177,804,612.00
Total grants to charity (line 13)..............................$5,160,385.00
Total expenses of $91,281,145.00

Expenses include: salaries (line 15) $34,839,106.00
Fund raising fees (line 16a).....................................$850,803.00
Other expenses (line 17)..$50,431,851.00

They list 486 employees (line 5)
So it took 486 people
Who are paid $34.8 million ($71,800 per person ave.) out of $91.3 million in 'expenses'
To give away $5.1 MILLION- WHICH IS LESS THAN 3% OF TOTAL REVENUES!
Please note: $86 million left over went to the Foundation slush fund NO TAX PAID!

Watch your back Donald! MAGA!

Thought for the day March 12, 2017

This is self explanatory.
These people are out there in numbers and Obama is nourishing the whole disgusting bunch!

Watch your back Donald! MAGA!
NOT EVERYBODY LOVES YOU!

Thought for the day March 14, 2017

Little bug here, little bug there, here a bug, there a bug, every where a bug!
Old Obama had a bug.(or two or three, or more) E I E I O.

Watch your back, front, and sideways, Donald! MAGA!

Bugs bite!

Thought for the day March 15, 2017

Trump's tax return

I find it interesting for several reasons.

1. Who leaked the 2 page summary of his 2005 return?
2. As a % he paid more that Warren Buffet.
3. As a % he paid more than Obama.
4. As a % he paid nearly twice as much as Bernie, the tax-the-rich guy.
5. As a % he even paid more than poor Warren Buffet's secretary, who paid a bigger % than Buffet himself!
6. The New York times claimed Trump paid no Taxes for 20 years. Where is the retraction?
7. Finally, you don't have to look far to find a bunch of despicable scumbags in this country.

NO need to name any of them. They self recognize and proclaim what they are every day.

Hang tough, Donald! MAGA!!

There are a lot of alligators in the swamp!

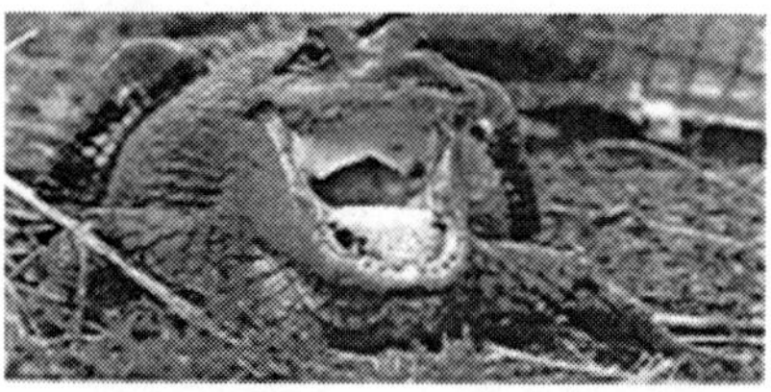

Thought for the day March 16, 2017

It seems to me there is a whole lot of "nonsense" going on.

Definition of nonsense:
"words or language having no meaning or conveying no intelligible ideas.

Actions, Language, Conduct, or an idea that is absurd or contrary to good sense."

Examples:
Democrat Congressmen and Congresswomen and Republican RINOS.
Why did Valerie Jarrett move in to Obama and Michelle's mansion? Concubime?
Putin threw the election to Trump.
A federal Judge telling President Trump he can't do his job.
Refugees deserve to be in America.
Islam is a religion of peace.
Obama stayed in DC, paying $15,000 monthly rent, so daughter can finish school.
Democrats eager to help Trump MAKE AMERICA GREAT AGAIN. (their way)
Trump should have appointed poor people to his cabinet, not successful billionaires.
Hillary should be President

The alligators are real, Donald. I wish you well in. MAKING AMERICA GREAT AGAIN!

2nd thought of the day March 16, 2017

Sorry, this won't wait.

NEW FLASH WEDNESDAY MARCH 15, 2017

"U. S . District judge Derrick Watson in HAWAII put on hold President Trump's revised travel ban just hours before it was to go into effect."

Add background info:

Barrack Obama is in Hawaii.

Obama and Watson attended Harvard together.

Watson was appointed Judge by Obama.

Want to guess what Dirt bag Obama and Watson discussed?

You know, if George Bush (instead of keeping his stupid mouth shut) had scuttled Obama the way Obama is determined to scuttle Trump, we would have endured Obama for only 4 years, instead of 8!

Obama is not your Friend, Donald.

Stop pretending and being nice to him, if you really want to

MAKE AMERICA GREAT AGAIN!!!

Thought for the day March 17, 2017

Today I woke with warm fuzzy feeling, and came to full realization of how fortunate I am, and America is, to have Donald Trump as our President.
God works in mysterious ways.
I am going to rejoice and be glad for this day AMEN

Stay strong, Donald,
and keep the faith! MAGA!!

Thought for the day March 18, 2017

Angela Merkel, the Head of State of Germany, came to town yesterday.
She came, she saw, she left, no better than before.
The socialist Dallas News had a small article on page 4 of today's paper.

Some things you may not know.
The United States has kept thousands of troops in Germany since the end of WWII.
As a result Germany has not been in a war for over 70 years, the longest period in their history.
The thousands of troops (currently 37,000+) have added billions to the Germany economy.
Did Angela say "Thank you?" No.
The NATO Alliance agreement specified how the members would share the expenses of NATO.
Has Germany paid their part? No.
Did Angela agree to fix it? No.
Will Donald Trump force a fix? I believe he will.
What's fair is fair.

Time to sic 'em, Donald! MAGA!!

Thought for the day March 20, 2017

Is inflation a good thing?
I retired in 1987 with a pension and Social Security.
It was a good deal at the time.
But I haven't had a raise in 30 years and I am beginning to really feel the pinch of 30 years of inflation.
So I ran some numbers to see how much money it takes today to buy what $100 would buy in 1987!
Shocking! No wonder I feel the pinch!!
It takes $210.19!
So my pension is buying less than half of what it bought in 1987.
I took it a step further.
I graduated from college in 1947. Today it takes $1123 to equal $100 in '47.
Graduated high school in 1942. Takes $1558.
If I live another 30 years, at this rate, ...
I don't want to think about it.
Inflation is a cruel thing.
It obviously explains why......
I am driving a 14 year old car!!!

We need help, Donald! MAGA!!

Thought for the day March 21, 2017

I understand this may be Fake News, but it is rumored the ASPCA has filed a cruetly to animals complaint against more that a dozen Democrat Congressman.

I watched as they spent all day yesterday beating a dead horse to death.

The stench has become suffocating. If they really find out Russia like Trump more than Clinton, is that a crime—

PUNISHABLE by what?

On my like-able scale, I always gave Trump a 10 and Hillary a zero, and I did everything I could to influence people to vote for Trump.

So did millions of others.

And we are guilty of what?

Watch your back Donald! MAGA!

Thought for the day March 22, 2017

What is blooming idiot?
Definition:
A "blooming idiot, is referred to as a foolish person who consistently makes mistakes or idiotic choices."
The word blooming is a British slang expression meaning to a great degree.
Question: Why do so many end up in Congress?
Their only talent is enunciating words.
I listened yesterday morning to part of RINO Lindsay Graham's rambling during the hearing for Supreme Court nominee Neil Gorsuch. For at least 5 minutes he enunciated, to a great degree, disjointed words clearly but they added up to nothing.
This sign reminded me of Lindsay.........

Drive thru buffet?

Stay strong, Donald! MAGA!

Thought for the day March 23, 2017

America is a country of laws, laws that agree with our constitution.
These are our laws, American laws.
There is room for no other.
Shariah law diabolically opposes American law.
Yesterday in London Shariah law was responsible for 4 deaths and many injured people.
There 82 Shariah law courts in England, that make rulings on Muslims that are contrary to British law.
In effect, a country has been created inside a country that has no allegiance to the mother country.
In America today we have millions of whom have formed little communities within a community.
They have not tried to assimilate or learn the English language, and attempts made been made to set up Shariah Law courts.
They are like cancer, procreating at a rapid rate, and fulfilling their mission to have Shariah law supersede our Constitution and Allah replace our God.
The bleeding heart liberals and Muslims sympathizers are determined to flood our country with more Muslims.
Some will be terrorist when they arrive.
Others will proselytized.
Like what happened in London yesterday, more Americans will be killed by terrorists, and their blood will be on whose hands?
Trump is trying to slow the process.
Trump needs help!!

Stay strong, Donald! MAGA!

Thought for the day march 24, 2017

Water. Ever think much about water?

It really is amazing stuff and we have all kinds.

There is ice water, hot water, fresh water, muddy water, still water, salt water, running water, and of course sweat water. Good old sweat.

There is sweat of the brow, fever sweat, and hard labor sweat. Sweating is healthy for the body, but sadly, after a while it begins to stink.

Sweat reminds me of politicians, especially our Congressmen. They have been sweating out this Health Care thing for months and now they STINK unbearably!

But back to water. Giant dams are built to store lots of water. Hydro-electric generators are placed at the bottom of the dam.

Measured water is released from the top and generates electricity, lots of it.

The power of water is incredible.

Just look at the Grand Canyon!

Donald Trump has been patiently storing up water, lots of water.

My guess is Donald is about to open the spigot and give these sweaty politicians a jolt of electricity and bath they won't forget.

Sic 'em Donald!

Thought for the day march 25, 2017

Old folks are sensitive and brittle.
Sometimes our body hurts.
Sometimes our feelings are hurt.
Sometimes we err.
Err requires a fix.
Yesterday morning I erred.
My feelings were hurt.
Now I know I erred.
They fixed it.
To err is human.
To forgive, divine.
I forgive me.

Stay strong, Donald!
We got a lot of work to do
TO MAKE AMERICA GREAT AGAIN!

Thought for the day March 26, 2017

Today is Sunday, my day of worship and rest.
But something is brewing for Monday.
Watch for it.

Thought for the day March 27, 2017

How could I be so naïve?

I think i think like Republican should think.

BUT IT JUST HIT ME IN THE FACE- THERE IS ONE DECMORAT PARTY BUT.........

There is note Republican party, but several groups that casually call themselves Republicans

1. Rinos who really are Democrats hiding behind the name
2. Social Republicans who blow with wind
3. Moderate Republications who mean well but have little guts
4. Then there is the Republican Caucus, presently made up of about 31 members.

They are so seat up with their power they are willing so sink the ship if the other 400 congressmen won't yield their demands. By refusing to join the other "Republicans" and vote FOR Obamacare repeal, they sided with Pelosi, in effect voting NO.

By voting as a block, they can pass or fail I don't know why this did not occur to me earlier.

We have a two-party system in our United States of America.

Republican and Socialist Democrat.

But NOT in Washington.

In Washington, we have a one-party system, or a Uni-party as some call it.

To surprise of EVERY body, America's Republicans elected Trump, but the SWAMP people, the Uni-part, won't accept it and are fighting back, giving no quarter.

"Destroy Trump" at any cost!

This, coupled with Obama's 30,000 thugs spread around the country causing havoc, may prevent Donald from draining the swap.

STAY STRONG, Donald!
You are our only chance

MAKE AMERICA GREAT AGAIN!!

Thought for the day March 28, 2017

The gimme, gimme, something for nothing generation, the degeneration of our moral coda, and devaluing human life through unfettered abortion, has become so pervasive in our country, there may be no turning back. Are we witnessing the end of the "second Roman Empire"?

I was hoping the various Republican "Party's" could unite with the Uni-party, and give Donald some support.

Unfortunately, Donald inherited a swam full of back stabbing, lying, vicious, two-faced thieves.

There are dedicated to making Donald fail.

Power, Greed, and $$$ are in control.

And when people like Schumer and Pelosi are allow to run wild, the end is no if, but when!

Donald is not playing the fiddle like Nero, and as he is fighting to put out the fire.

So, there is still faint hope.

We ain't giving up!

Hang strong, Donald!

We go to MAGA!!

Thought for the day March 29, 2017

Half full?
I know I put out some stuff that sounds negative. I do that because this old world is full of negative stuff.
Every since God created Adam and Eve, there has been negative stuff.
So, it is all man's fault.
I have a friend who thinks my glass is half empty.
But I disagree. I think my glass is full and running over.
See Psalm 23
I live in my world and I am happy in it.
I try to count my blessings every day, but I can't count them all.
So I tell GOD every day "Thank you for all you do".
At the same time I know about a lot of the bad stuff and I think if I preach about some of the bad stuff, and it changes someone for the better, hopefully, in a small way, I have made the world a little better.
Hope you have a happy day!

Stay strong, Donald!
You can make America better!
My Glass

Watch your back Donald! MAGA!

Thought for the day March 30, 2017

Nancy Pelosi 1955
Age 15

Nancy Pelosi 2017
Age 77

Things you may not know.

Nancy Pelosi: born March 26, 1940 elected to Congress 1987.

In 30 years in Congress she has become the become the richest Democrat in the House.

House Democratic leader Nancy Pelosi and her husband, Paul, have $42.4 million to $199.5 million in assets.

That includes commercial property in San Francisco, stock in Apple Inc. and Visa Inc., an interest in the Auberge du Soleil resort in Rutherford, California, and ownership stake lives in a multimillion-dollar Georgetown condo: she owns a 16 acre vineyard in Napa Valley and 3,700 square-foot house in San Francisco's tony Pacific Heights, valued at $5.8 million, according to here May 2015 financial disclosure statements.

No I have to ask you- HOW DID SHE, ON A SALARY AVERAGING ABOUT $180,000 PER YEAR, FOR 30 YEARS, BECOME A MULTI-MILLIONAIRE?

HOW?

Being neck deep in the SWAMP, that's how!

Nancy, you have come a long way, Babe, since being elected Miss Lube Rack!

Drain the swamp, Donald, one alligator at a time.

MAGA!!

Thought for the day March 31, 2017

A few of the swamp alligators in Washington, D C

All alligators look alike.

Thought for the day April 2, 2017

For obvious reasons there were no thoughts on April 1
I don't need no puns! But there were 2 thoughts on march 31.

Last year, quite innocently, my wife agreed to a magazine subscription at practically no cost.

Immediately we started getting magazines we never heard of and many we know about. We have been inundated with magazines. Really, practically every mail day we get a magazine sometimes 2 or 3.

Now we are getting duns to renew!

Friday this one came from Rolling Stone. I had never read this one, but the cover was rather clever and caught my attention. If you look closely, The Trump article was a book, but I read it all.

It was a masterpiece of Fake News, half-truths, and slander that bordered on the edge of libel.

Makes you wonder why anybody would want to babysit a world of crybabies.

Reminded me of this song.

♫You picked a fine time to leave me Lucille Hillary.
I'm sitting here contemplating the money I spent.
And wondering where it all went.

My heart is broken and I'm all alone today,
since you dun gone, and lost your way.♫

Be stroong like Samson, Donald! MAGA!!

Thought for the day April 3, 2017

Is there nothing real anymore?
This ad shows a giant termite taking down a house in one bite.
Gives me the shudders.

Last night I witnessed a commercial about roaches, those creepy, crawly things nobody like.
The ad show this roach heading for the sewer. Then the camera shows the roach, in "daylight" crawling through the pipes, up the walls, and out into the kitchen UGH!
And lo and behold, the moment he sticks his ugly head out, there is the Terminix man who zaps him to eternity.
Oh, I forgot to tell you. The ad shows the Terminix man chasing the roach from the instance he went into the sewer.
Poor roach never had a chance..
Just another Fake News story.
And the Democrats want us to believe the Russians elected Trump President when not one of them voted.
Is there nothing real anymore?

Some people are like roaches. I am not naming any names, but I know a few.

Sic 'em Donald! MAGA!!

Thought for the day April 4, 2017

Did you know.........

> As a Secretary of State Hillary made 4 trips to Moscow?
> As a Secretary of State Hillary met numerous time with the Russian Ambassador?
>
> When Hillary Secretary of state, Bill made 2 trips, and was paid $500.00 for one speech?
> Hillary gave 20% of our uranium resources to Russia?

More tomorrow on unbelievable stuff.

Sic 'em Donald! MAGA!!

Thought for the day April 5, 2017

Well, this is tomorrow. See below

Thought for the day April 4, 2017

Did you know................

As Secretary of State Hillary made 4 trips to Moscow?

As Secretary of State Hillary met numerous times with the Russian Ambassador?

When Hillary Secretary of State, Bill made 2 trips, and was paid $500,00 for one speech?

Hillary gave 20% of our uranium resources to Russia?

More tomorrow on unbelievable stuff

All this noise about Russia help get Trump elected is a façade to cover up what really happened.

Russia had a love affair with Obama and Hillary.

On April 8, 2010 this happened:

Prague, Czech Republic – President Obama and Russia President Dmitry Medvedev on Thursday signed a major nuclear arms control agreement that reduces the nuclear stockpiles of both nations.

Pray to this, in 2009, Hillary visited President Dmitry Medvedev in Moscow.

They discussed setting up a "Silicon Valley" in Skolkovo, a suburb of Moscow.

Hillary invited him to visit Silicon Valley and escorted him there, where he met numerous company officials.

Thank you Hillary.

Soon after dozens of U.S. Tech firms, such as Google, Intel, and Cisco ($1 bil)
Made major financial contributions to the Russian Silicon Valley project.
In May 2010, Hillary facilitated a visit to Moscow of 22 of the biggest names in U.S venture capital.
By 2012 the Russian Silicon Valley had assembled 28 Russians, Americans, and European "Key Partners".
Thank you, Hillary.
Surprisingly, I say with tongue in cheek of the 28 "partners", 17, made financial commitments to the CLINTON FOUNDATION totaling 10's of millions of dollars.
Hillary thanks you.
There was all this, and more, IN HERE JOB AS SECRETARY OF STATE.
So I asks you, why would Russia, which has benefited so much from Obama's presidency and Hillary as secretary of State, forsake Hillary in her time of need for someone unknown like Trump?
Behind the façade, Russia did not forsake Hillary.
The American people forsook Hillary.
And her excuse "it's not my fault. Russia did it!
Donald Trump is our President, Hillary! Get used to it!!!

Sic 'em Donald! MAGA!!

Thought for the day April 6, 2017

PRESIDENT ABDUL EL-SAYED?
Etch this man's face and name in your mind.
His name is Abdul El-Sayed.

He is 32 years old, born in the USA, and an extremely well educated Muslim Doctor in Detroit Michigan.
(education funded by George Soros)

He is handsome, articulate, charismatic (more so than Obama), and smart.

He is sympathetic of the Muslim Brotherhood, and is running for Governor of Michigan, which is Step 1 in his preparation to run for President of the United States.
He has the potential to be Obama #2, but far more openly Muslim.
In 2020 he will be eligible to run for President!
Democrats' mouths are watering anticipation and raising money.
Elizabeth Pocahontas warren is already campaigning for him.

Another Trojan Horse?????

Try harder, Donald!
You our only chance to MAGA!!!

Thought for the day April 7, 2017

Finally, a President with GUTS!

US Launches Dozens of Missiles into Syria Response to Chemical Attack

APR 06, 2017 // 9:19pm

The United States has launched 59 cruise missiles against a military airfield in Syria following a chemical weapons attack Tuesday that left nearly 70 dead.

Thank you, DONALD!! MAGA!!!

Thought for the day April 8, 2017

A week to remember!

To say I am fascinated by our President is an understatement.

1. Today we got the constitutional conservative approved that he nominated to the Supreme court.
2. This week he had constructive meetings with 3 heads of state, one being China. The China head XI, invited Trump to continue their discussions in China.
3. He ordered the military to launch 59 missiles on an airport in Syria where deadly chemicals are stored, In retaliation for Assad poisoning his own people.

Quite a week to remember.

Sic 'em Donald! MAGA!!

Thought for the day April 9, 2017

The lord said "Thou shall not bear false witness"
But it means nothing to lot of people.
Susan rice is one of those.
Susan rice lied about what caused the massacre in Benghazi over and over again.
Lying is her forte.
She is good at it.
She was in the news recently she lied about the unmasking of Trump's subordinates.
First, she said I know NOTHING about it.
Second, she DID know about it, and SHE DID IT for "security" reasons????
What security???
Third, she has now disappeared.
CNN, MSNBC, ABC, CBS, NCA, have not mentioned here for a week.
Where is Susan rice? Maybe in Tahiti with Obama?
I hope she is all right. We may need her to testify and see how well she lies under oath.

Sic 'em Donald! MAGA!!

Thought for the day April 10, 2017

Politics aint everything, and it sure aint the most important thing.
We went to lunch with some friends after church yesterday.
(Friends are important.)
As we were having lunch, the sun was shining on a car window outside (where else) and reflecting in to the eyes of a friend. She complained about it and thought occurred to me.
How lucky we are to have sunshine.
(Sunshine is important.)
Each little ray of sunshine took nearly ten minutes to traverse the 93,000,00 miles from the sun to give us light and heat, and it is always right on time.
What a miracle it is and how grateful we should be.
Yet we complain if it is too hot, or is not hot enough, or too bright.
WE complain about a lot of little things.
(Little things are important.)
Basically, we are just an ungrateful lot.
Think about it!

Sic 'em Donald! MAGA!!

Thought for the day April 11, 2017

To all who may be concerned, our unconcerned.
I am spending today, Wednesday, and Thursday reminiscing, and remembering the wonderful things that have happened to me in the last 20 years.
You see, April 13 will be 20 years since my beautiful wife, Clarene, and I said "I DO".
In 1941 and 1942 we were real sweethearts.
Following high school graduation our lives parted.
I went to college, then to service, and back to college.
My first job sent me far away from Merkel and Clarene.
Time passed. 50 years passed. I heard nothing about Clarene.
Finally, after our 50th High School reunion we made contract.
As I turned out, she married and had kids. I married and had kids.
Sadly, her husband died with prostate cancer, 5 years after our original contact, my wife died with liver cancer, leaving us both without mates.
55 years after 1942, the Lord provided a way for us to be reunited.
We were sweethearts again.
Now it is 20 more years later.
I can truthfully say, in my opinion, no two people have ever been more compatible or enjoyed life more abundantly than Clarene and BJ!

Happy Anniversary to US!

BM BJ Melton Reply |
Wed 4/12, 8:02 AM
You; Alvin Simek

Thought for the day April 12, 2017

On getting married.
We found out it doesn't take 6 months to plan a wedding.
We were engaged and had our rings, but had not set a wedding day.
On Thursday, April 10, we got our license at 4pm. (just in case)
In Texas, after getting your license, you have to then wait at least 72 hours, to get married.
We were at her house in Desdemona, Texas.
When we awakened Friday morning, the 11th, the desire was too great, and we decided to get married Sunday the 13th at 4p. (72 hours)
Suddenly, there were things to do.
Find the preacher (out of town)
Get a best man
Notify family and friends
Plan a reception
Get a punch bowl
Get a cake
Music for the wedding march.
Rehearse our wedding vows
Clothes to wear
Where to honeymoon.
Stay turned tomorrow, the 13th, for how it all worked out.

Thought for the day April 13, 2017

THE WEDDING!

Saturday morning, the 12th, things began to 'sorta' fall in place.
We found the preacher in Lubbock and told him he had a wedding to perform at 4pm Sunday.
I wanted my son to be best man and he was 250 miles away. He said he would try, but not sure. So I had to arrange for a substitute.
(Son Made it)
On Friday, we ordered a cake from the grocery store and picked it up today.
The reception was planned.
Friends and family invited.
I practices "I do", and got it down pat.
Arranged for a short honeymoon in a motel 50 miles away.
Finally, we decided on the wedding march.
Now it is Sunday, the big day.
We were to be married in Clarene's house and i am nervous, wanting everything to go right.
I called Clarene "My pretty Woman" because that was what she was, and still is!
4 PM. The wedding party is stationed in front of the fireplace.
Clarene's mother in on the couch facing me and not exactly smiling.
Her sister is standing against the back wall.
It is time.
Clarene's two sons marched her down the hall, and in to the den.
The wedding march started playing
♫Pretty woman, the kind I like to meet♫
Clarene's mother smiled.
Clarene's sister laughed out loud in our solemn ceremony.
We said our "I do's" and were shortly on our way, never dreaming that 20 years later I would be reminiscing like this.

Happy Anniversary to US!!

Thought for the day April 14, 2017

THE HONEY MOON

When I was about 50 I read about this old couple getting married and going on a Honeymoon, and I thought to myself, what would 70 year olds do on a Honeymoon?
Now, I know, and if it ever your lot in life to experience one, you will find out. You won't find out from me, because it is personal.
Curiosity got the best me so I had to look up "Honeymoon".
The term evolved from two similar words back in the 5th century AD.
Basically, it meant a short time of extreme bliss for a married couple, followed by warning of the bliss.
It is like a full moon. It is so pretty, but quickly fades away to a silver.
BUT IT DOES NOT HAVE TO BE THAT WAY, AND IN OUR CASE IT HAS NOT BEEN.
WE HAVE HAD MANY "SPECIAL" HONEYMOONS, BUT, IN REALITY, THE PAST 20 YEARS HAS JUST BEEN ONE SHORT HONEYMOON.
TODAY WE START ON OUR 21ST YEAR OF HONEYMOON.

Tomorrow I have to get back to saving America!

Sic 'em Donald! MAGA!!

Thought for the day April 17, 2017

This is the new Democrat donkey.
I am having trouble analyzing the significance of it.
It appears the hoofs and head are made of steel, or aluminum. Or maybe an iron head?
That fits. And a red eye???
Then there is an antenna sending out signals.
Most confusing are two wings and a jet engine blasting away.
Do we have a hardheaded flying jackass?
Can you help?

Sic 'em Donald! MAGA!!

Thought for the day April 18, 2017

Some days are different than others.
Yesterday was a down day, because it rained. We need rain, but rain limits what you can do.
I went to the bowling alley to bowl in my league and it was raining.
I got wet.
When I got inside, a friend bowler started singing ♫ For he's a jolly good fellow♫ to me.
Isn't it surprising how a song at the right time, can affect your feel good?
He made my day.

Sic 'em Donald! MAGA!!

Thought for the day April 19, 2017

Well, today I am back in the real world, which is a mess.
We have out of control Communist dictators, terrorists of all kinds, including the losing Progressive Democrats, "peaceful" Muslims who want Sharia law to replace our constitution.
We have Obama's shadow government sponsoring ugly protests and riots all over.
These are "people who did not get their way, and rather than working to make America better, have set out to destroy it.
Actually, we have a Communist revolution going on, and Bernie Sanders, the DNC, and Pocahontas are just feeding the fire.
We have an out-of-control judicial system that is usurping the power of the President AND Congress.
And where are the good guys? What are they doing?
Sadly, so far, most of them are just looking around, turning the other cheek, and wondering what is happening, while the back alley thugs are running amok.

Donald, pay attention!
You are our only chance to MAGA!!!

Thought for the day April 20, 2017

Please forward!
You think I am kidding about the Communist left?
Rioters wear masks. They are not Lone Rangers, just hired thugs!
Good guys don't need masks.
These pictures were taken at a Trump rally and are small sample of what is going on across America.
These "people" are vicious thugs!

Anti-fascist protesters using "black bloc" tactics – covering faces, dressing in black – arrive at the protest last week.

Donald, This is Obama's parting gift to you!

Sic 'em MAGA!!

Thought for the day April 22, 2017

Today is Science Day.
What is Science Day?
I don't know.
This guy must be a scientist!
I saw him in the parade.

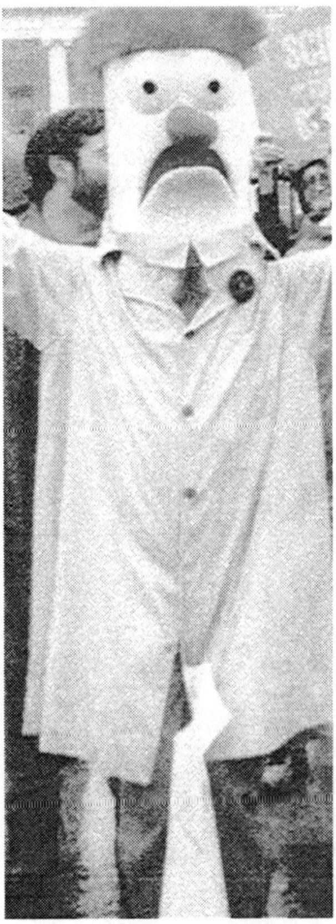

Sic 'em Donald! MAGA!!

Thought for the day April 23, 2017

Obama and Soros, the best of friends.

Together they hope to destroy America.
Obama with his shadow government
funded by Soros with his $$$,$$$,$$$.

WATCH your back, Donald!!! MAGA!!

Thought for the day April 24, 2017

Here is a breakdown of the air around us.
You hear a lot about the culprit $C0_2$ causing
"Disastrous" global warming.
Tomorrow, (Tuesday), I plan to present a Treatise on the subject your consideration.

Composition of Air

Component	Symbol	Volume
Nitrogen	N_2	78.084%
Oxygen	O_2	20.947%
	99.998%	
Argon	Ar	0.934%
Carbon Dioxide	CO_2	0.033%
Neon	Ne	18.2 parts per million
Helium	He	5.2 parts per million
Krypton	Kr	1.1 parts per million
Sulfur dioxide	SO_2	1.0 parts per million
Methane	CH_4	2.0 parts per million
Hydrogen	H_2	0.5 parts per million
Nitrous Oxide	N_2O	0.5 parts per million
Xenon	Xe	0.009 parts per million
Ozone	O_3	0.07 parts per million
Nitrogen Dioxide	NO_2	0.02 parts per million
Iodine	I_2	0.01 parts per million
Carbon Monoxide	CO	trace
Ammonia	NH_3	

Sic 'em Donald! MAGA!!

Thought for the day April 25, 2017

The air around us!

The air around us is complex and each component plays some part in maintaining life for every living thing on earth-plant, animals, birds, fish, and even insects. Not for a second do I think I can unwind the complexity of it all, so this will be simple.

But this much I know.

1. Without nitrogen, everything would die.
2. Without oxygen, everything would die.
3. Without carbon, everything would die.
4. Without hydrogen, everything would die.
5. Without water, everything would die.
6. Without carbon dioxide, everything would die.

All of these are used UP, but they are NOT used up, because GOD has provided for each to be recycled and REUSED. (Incidentally, the water you drink today has been drunk (drank) before, & recycled thousands of times)

Carbon dioxide, CO2, is not an evil creature. It is absolutely essential for:

1. All animas to live, grow, and to function,
2. Plants to grow and reproduce.

Now consider this. The population of earth increases by millions every year.

There is need for increased plant growth (food) every year.

Tests have shown that when plants are exposed to a slightly elevated CO2, they grow larger and faster.

So, if man made activity, as claimed by NUT Al Gore and his paid scientist hacks,

This may be GOD'S way of providing more foods for us animals.

(tomorrow-CO2 and global warming, if any)

Sic 'em Donald! MAGA!!!!

Thought for the day April 26, 2917

CO2 and global warming, if any.

In case you did not notice from yesterday's thought, Nothing new is made, and nothing destroyed.

As far back as man knows, (or thinks he knows), we had 5 "Ice" ages followed by 5 "warm" ages.

Supposedly, an age can be hundreds of thousands, or even millions of years long.

Burning of fossil fuels requires Carbon and oxygen, and the two combine to form carbon dioxide, CO2.

CO2 is vital for our survival. Any 'excess' is absorbed into the earth or water, or used by plants.

But there are other by-products of combustion, some of which are undesirable.

1. Benzene
2. Sulphur Dioxide
3. Nitrogen Oxides
4. Formaldehyde
5. Poly-cyclic Aromatic hydrocarbons
6. Mercury
7. Silicon Dust
8. Radon Gas
9. Hydrofluoric Acid

Most of these things come out the exhaust of your car when it is running, and you know-there are upteen millions of cars running all the time-and you are breathing the air.

Question: How come we ain't all dead?

The real question is:

How come the only product, necessary for our survival, CO_2, is portrayed as the villain?

It is a money thing. Somebody figured out a way to make money by trying to convince you that GOD'S PERPETUAL MOTION MACHINE IS BROKEN.

The earth will get so hot all the polar ice will melt, flooding the sea with so much water that thousands of acres of prime beach front property will be Inundated and destroyed. Can you visualize New York City under water?

Sic 'em Donald! MAGA!!!!

Thought for the day April 27, 2017

Today on a jet plane I fly away,
Up, Up and away they say
My bags are packed,
I am ready to go!
My great grand daughter will be
3 years old next Sundae.
So relief you will get
So relief you will get
From my Thought for the day.
In the meantime, thank you for the many comments on my thoughts, good or bad, and those you who thought enough of them to forward to your friends, a special THAN YOU! In the 2nd meantime………

Sic 'em Donald! MAGA!!!!

Thought for the day May 2, 2017

Well, I am back. I just spent 4 days in Colorado having a love affair with my 3 year old GREAT Granddaughter.

Things happened while I was gone. The biggest event had to be trumps' 100 day rally in Pennsylvania, where thousands hear Donald toasting Donald. And the least significant event was the White House Correspondents Dinner where hundred's heard liberal celebrities and the media roasting Donald. Then there was yesterday when Soros and Obama Fascist caused riots across the country.

Sick people.

HAPPY MAY-DAY COMMIE SNOWFLAKES

Sic 'em Donald! MAGA!!

Thought for the day May 3, 2017

I am becoming increasingly disturbed.
Yesterday's headlines were all about the May day riots with thugs smashing windows, destroying cars, property, and abusing legitimate protesters.
Today's headlines are about killing, murder, slaying, and stabbing.
Since Roe vs Wade and creation of planned abortion killing of babies, life has become so cheap.
Hollywood glamorizes all kinds of immoral behaviour.
I say immoral and then I realize "immoral" has become the new norm.
Having been here for many years and still in control of my facilities, I remember a different set of morals.
We once visualized ourselves as a "civilized" country and were a proud beacon to the world. No more.
We have an enigma.
Riot in the street-no problem.
Kill a newborn child-no problem.
Abuse a dog, or cow, or horse-go to jail.
Human life is cheap!
The dictionary defines "civil" as: "to bring out of a savage, uneducated, or rude state: make civil, elevate in social and private life: enlighten; refine:"
WE NEED A NEW DIFINITION!

Sic 'em Donald! MAGA!!

Thought for the day May 4, 2017

Sometime I get nostalgia in a negative way thinking about what might have been. But then I say "Whoa". Life is what it is and I thank the Lord for what is. As I look into these piercing eyes of Elli, my Great granddaughter, I am grateful she can see. As for myself, with cataracts and glasses, I, too, have perfect vision. Today I listened to a young lady sing 'How Great Thou Art' at the National prayer breakfast. It was beautiful! What I did now know at the time, THE YOUNG LADY HAS BEEN BLIND FROM BIRTH AND HAS CEREBRAL PALSY!!!

In spite of that, she has done what she can do with her life and her singing made thousands feel good. Nostalgia grabbed me. What if I had been born blind? What if Elli had been born blind? Then I say "Thank you Lord!" Elli and I can see. If you can read this, you, too, might want to pause and give thanks.

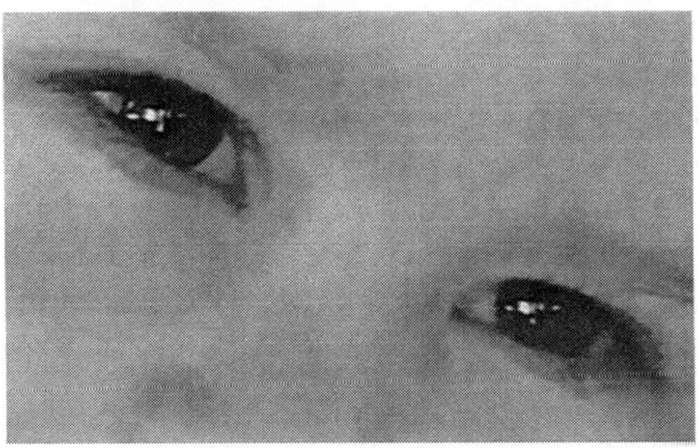

Sic 'em Donald! MAGA!!

Thought for the day May 5, 2017

Definition of hate

Intense hostility and aversion usually deriving form fear, anger, or sense of injury, extreme dislike or disgust: antipathy, loathing

I am not sure where this thought came from. Yesterday I watched the debates in Congress on Trump care.

I find some of them very offensive and would be easy to generate a "hate" feeling.

But when I consider their ignorance, sympathy is more appropriate, especially since Trump care passed. Last night I watched Trump honour 7 WWII heroes on board the USS intrepid and I had feeling of love and gratitude. I can appreciate them more than most because I am a veteran of WWII, but never had a chance to be a hero. I watched the Obama thugs rioting on May Day. They destroyed property, abused other people and physically demonstrated what hate can do. Then I wondered, was their hate and acquired 'talent' or That's it! Money! Money explains the contemptible actions of Congressmen and the Rioters. Obviously, money mixed with greed can buy hate. So I read the definition of "hate" again and I realize hating is not my thing. Hate is stressful and can't be good for the body or soul. I do dislike some things like broccoli, weeds in my flower bed, and back aches.

How About You?

Sic 'em Donald! MAGA!!

Thought for the day May 6, 2017

Sometimes my free spirit leads me off on a tangent like it did yesterday. But I had a warm forgiving feeling, very unlike the stressed out feeling I had a getting Trump elected. It now appears the Trump agenda is moving forward, slowly, but forward. Of course, the 'enemy' is continually saying Social Security is dead, millions and millions will not have insurance, and republicans are throwing me and grandma over the cliff without a parachute. The demons have played this tune for decades over and over again. It has quit working, but they are so antiquated and out of touch with real America, they don't have enough vision to even change the words. Demons! We don't want your socialism, communism or fascism. We refuse to be hand fed by ignorant bureaucrats. We refuse to be silenced by Gestapo tactics. You want to take our guns?

BETTER THING TWICE! The second amendment is here to stay. Believe it! Fake news is your game, just propaganda for the simple minded.

We like the way America used to be and gonna be after we MAGA!!

Sic 'em Donald! MAGA!!

Thought for the day May 7, 2017

The French are voting today and there are riots in the streets. The hoodies are out in force. Back In November we showed everybody how to hold a 'civil' election. It is so simple. Have riots. Burn buildings. Intimidate voters. Claim fraud. March in the streets. Carry nasty signs.

Plan ahead

Do riots professionally

Make a living at it.

Any day is a good

Day for a riot!

Isn't that right, Obama?!

Sic 'em Donald! MAGA!!

Thought for the day May 8, 2017

The Senate version of our "Healthcare Plan" is now in the works and here comes Sen. Schumer and the rest of the clowns. They will make every effort, and pull every trick they can think of, to make sure America DOES NOT get a workable healthcare plan. I find it idiotic, imbecilic, and even treasonous that Congress cannot work for a better America.

Sic 'em Donald! MAGA!!

THOUGHT FOR THE DAY MAY 9, 2017

WHEN I SAW THIS

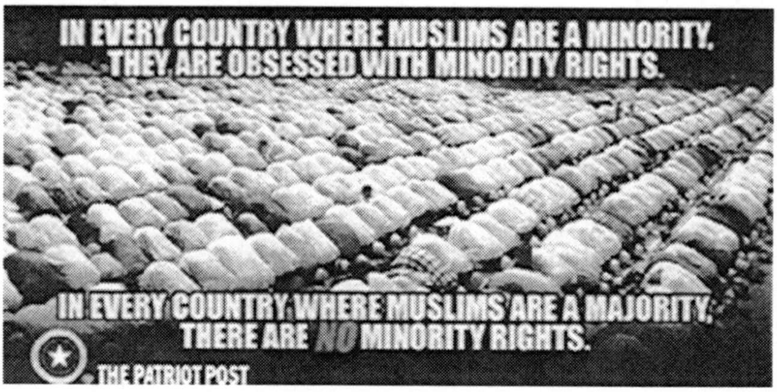

WHY DID I THINK OF THIS?

Sic 'em Donald! MAGA!!

Thought for the day May 10, 2017

Yesterday President Trump fired James Comey.
James Comey is 6'8 tall.
James Comey got too big for his bitches.
James Comey was appointed, not elected, Director of the FBI
James Comey was not everybody's boss.
James Comey made many serious mistakes.
James Comey gave Hilary a free pass.
James Comey said he could not be fired.
President Trump fired James Comey.
There is one less swamp critter.

Remember this prophecy?

Thought for the day May 11, 2017

WHAT IS A HYPOCRITE?

These are just some of the Democrats, who, as recently as last week, wanted to fire James Comey! Hilary blames him, (among the other things) for her loss!

Trump fired him Tuesday.

As of Wednesday, Comey has become a martyr.

The Demos are crying "Why did you fire our beloved Comey? What are you covering up? These people are hypocrites

Now you know.

Sic 'em Donald! MAGA!!

Thought for the day May 13, 2017

Newspaper headlines

JOHNSON DENIES BEATING HIS WIFE!
(if he denies it, he must beat her)
TRUMP DENIES PUTIN HELPED HIM!
(if he denies Putin helped, Putin must have helped)

Liberal Media Logic.

Almost every day I have to take inventory of myself. When I do, I find myself level headed, considerate, compassionate, well informed with common sense, and rational with red blood in my veins. Then, after I see the news, hear the news, witness the news, I can than only come to one conclusion. The news media, as a whole, is comprised of hate for Trump, hate for America. I am being pulled right and left by multiple polls showing Donald with negative numbers, by fake news, half truths, and political garbage. Every day we are being inundated with VICIOUS propaganda which has only one purpose:

THE WARPING OF OUR MIND AND THE DESTRUCTION OF DONALD TRUMP!

Stay strong. Stay alert! Consider the sources!

Sic 'em Donald! MAGA!!

Thought for the day May 14, 2017

Happy Mothers' Day to all you Mothers!

This is Joe Biden. He loves ice cream.

Recently at a dinner, dessert was pie and ice cream. Donald Trump got two dips. Everybody else got one. It was on the news. CNN devoted 3minutes to it. My question: Why was this news at all? I like ice cream. It soothes the soul, and calms the spirit. After my back operation, if I got to hurting too bad, I would eat a bowl of BLUE BELL Homemade vanilla. You can't hurt when you are eating Blue Bell ice cream.

Sic 'em Donald! MAGA!!
Eat more ice cream!

Thought for the day March 15, 2017

PRESIDENT TRUMP JUST SAID SOMETHING THAT MADE ME PROUD!

March 13, 2017
President Trump stood of THOUSANDS of student at Liberty University and dropped this truth-bomb on them. “IN AMERICA, WE DON’T WORKSHIP GOVERNMENT, WE WORSHIP GOD” Amen!

Trump Continue: “IT IS WHY OUR CURRENCY PROUDLY DECLARES, “IN GOD WE TRUST” AND IT IS WHY WE PROUDLY PROCLAIM THAT WE ARE ONE NATION, UNDER GOD, EVERY TIME WE SAY THE PLEDGE OF ALLEGIANCE”

And what did Muslim Obama say over and over?

“The sweetest sound I know is the Muslim call to prayer” “America is not a Christian nation”

Dear GOD, welcome back to the White House!

Sic ’em Donald! MAGA!!

Thought for the day March 18, 2017

You don't remember The Light Crust Doughboys from Burrus Mills. You don't remember W. Lee O' Daniels Governor of Texas, and later a Senator. You were not born yet. O' Daniels was an old fashioned conservative Democrat. My papa was an old fashioned conservative Democrat. They both believed in working for a living. O' Daniels created the Light Crust Doughboys band in 1993. He put them on the radio playing Hillbilly music, advertising his flour "Eat more bread". He wrote the song "Beautiful, beautiful Texas" a classic. But♫ pass the biscuits, Pappy♫ was his theme song. He took his band and they campaigned throughout the state, serving hot biscuits at every stop, and promising a chicken in every pot. The hot biscuits, paid for with his own money, bought him enough votes to defeats 12 other candidates with 51% of the votes. When I saw 12 years old I attended one of his rallies in Buffalo Gap. And ate on of his biscuits. They don't make democrats like "Pappy O' Daniels, or my Papa, anymore.

Shame.

Sic 'em Donald! MAGA!!

Thought for the day March 17, 2017

Yesterday was a great day. The stock market was up. I felt good. My beautiful granddaughter from New York is in town and we had a delightful dinner together. This morning I awoke to a beautiful day, sun shining, and feeling good. I got a cup of coffee and turned on the TV.

Mistake #1.

The market is way down. Fake news stories are dominating TV and the newspaper. The Democrats are playing their back alley game to the hilt-a literal avalanche of lie after lie after lie. I know they are lies, but they still put knot in my stomach. And I think HOW CAN "AMERICANS" BE SO HELL-BENT on DESTROYING MY COUNTRY?

Mistake#2 would be to swallow this filth,
BUT I AINT BUYING IT! HOPE YOU DON'T EITHER!

And Donald, Be calm and Be strong! MAGA!!

Thought for the day May 20,2017

When you woke up this morning President Trump was having a meeting with a Saudi prince. Saudi Arabia, you know, is a Muslim country. Women have no rights. Homosexuals have no right. Actually they are an abomination. We do business with the Saudis. Buy oil, sell guns, missiles, planes, and all kinds of stuff. American businesses make money by doing business with Saudi Arabia. In America businesses make money by doing business with Saudi Arabia. In America, in particular, North Carolina, people are asked to use the potty corresponding to their biological birth sex. If you pee standing up, try the potty marked "MEN". If you pee sitting down, try the potty marked "LADIES". Simple. Seems fair to me, BUT......... "Not fair!" the homosexuals cry and businesses and sports teams shun North Carolina like plague. See definition of 'Hypocrite'.

Sic 'em Donald! MAGA!!

Thought for the day May 21, 2017

Yesterday has to be a historic day. Trump and first lady Melania Trump were greeted in Saudi Arabia at the airport by 81-year king Salman, in a red carpet ceremony, which also included a military flyover in which several jets left red, white and blue streamers King Salman shook hands with President Trump and Melania!. There was no bowing and scraping. Just two leaders showing respect for each other. The first lady wore a black pantsuit with a golden belt and did not cover her head for the arrival, consistent with custom for foreign dignitaries visiting Saudi Arabia. Trump and Melania, along the welcome path, walked on 400 feet or RED carpet to the airport terminal, where they had coffee, before departing to their hotel.

MAGA!! DONALD!!

Thought for the day May 22,2017

President Trump was bestowed with Saudi Arabia's highest civilian honour. King Salman awarded Trump the gilded collar of Abdulaziz al Saud. Trump was honoured for "his quest to enhance security and peace... in the region and the world"

STOOP NOT BOW!

Sunday was the 'No holds barred' speech to 50 Muslim nations which made me proud. It was well received and welcomed world-wide. "Compliments" bombarded

Twitter.

Today it is on to Jerusalem.

Sic 'em Donald! MAGA!!

Thought for the today May 23, 2017

Yesterday I sat and watched as Donald walked up to the Wailing wall and put his hand on it. What was he thinking? Then I watched Melania walk up to the wall and put her hand on it. What was she thinking? It had to be a sobering time and humbling experience for all three. The wall was built before Jesus was born. The Jewish people consider it holy, but whether it is or isn't, really irrelevant. What is relevant is ones' thought process as they approach the wall and touch it.

You cannot help but think of GOD and be humbled as you say a little prayer. Then you begin to realize how really insignificant you are in the scheme of things. I know I did, just watching them.

Sic 'em Donald! MAGA!!

Thought for the day May 24, 2017

These are two pictures of the wall surrounding the Vatican. The Pope lives behind these walls, when he is in town. All entrances are guarded by Swiss police for maximum safety. Nobody gets in who aint approved. Today President Trump will sit down and talk to the Pope somewhere behind this wall. Trump wants to build a wall on our southern border to keep out unwanted immigrants. The Pope, as he hides behind this wall, says walls are anti-Christian and we should let anybody in to our country. The Pope is a hypocrite. The Pope believes in "Global Warming".

The Pope things CO^2 is a pollutant. The Pope is a sucker for a sad story. The Pope would be shocked and in utter disbelief if someone told him he is NOT all wise like Solomon. Let me say it: "The Pope is not all wise!" He should stick to helping Catholics be better Catholics.

AMEN!

Sic 'em Donald! MAGA!!

Thought for the day May 25, 2017

MANNERS

Notre Dame is a Catholic university where they teach Young men and women how to cope with this world while being good Christians. You know-love one another, etc. Seems like that would include Good Manners, doesn't it? Well, VP Mike pence was the keynote speaker at commencement on May 21. As he began to speak, about 150 out of 1500 or so, walked out. We saw bad manners in action.

Yesterday at the Vatican, the Citadel of Catholicism, President Trump and his entourage gave a classic example of what "Good Manners" is like. They were Dignified, courteous, used proper decorum, gracious, thoughtful, considerate, POLITE, and respectful. Simply said THEY WERE REGAL!

Made me proud.

Sic 'em Donald! MAGA!!

Thought for the day May 29, 2017

Today is Memorial day, a day to honour those who died for us, so that we could have a day to remember. My problem is I am old, BUT NOT SENILE. That would be a blessing. I do remember days when America was a much better place to live. I remember when people were honestly patriotic, believed in God, honoured the flag, and I felt proud and privileged to be an American. Today is not the America I once cherished. BELOW ARE SOME OF THE REASONS I DESPAIR ABOUT MY AMERICA TODAY. THIS MESSAGE IS IN RED LETTERS AND ALL CAPS BECAUSE I AM SCREAMING. AFTER YOU READ THIS I HOPE YOU WILL BE SCREAMING TOO, AND FORWARD THIS TO ALL YOUR FRIENDS. THIS IS NOT A 'CHICKEN LITTLE SKY-IS-FALLING' BECAUSE THE SKY REALLY IS FALLING. BEAR WITH ME!

1. OBAMA AND MICHELLE "COINCIDENTALLY" WERE IN ITALY GRABBING HEADLINES WHILE PRESIDENT TRUMP WAS VISITING WITH THE POPE.
2. WHEN TRUMP WAS MEETING WITH NATO, OBAMA WAS IN BERLIN GIVING A SPEECH TO GERMAN LIBERALS, KISSING ANGELA MERKEL'S BUTT. AND RIDICULING TRUMP'S WALL.
3. SIMULTANEOUSLY, HILLARY WAS GIVING A COMMENCEMENT ADDRESS TO 299 GRADUATES AT HER ALMA MATER, WESLEYAN UNIVERSITY, CALLING FOR TRUMP'S IMPEACHMENT, AND BRAGGING ON COMEY WHOM SHE HATED BEFORE HE WAS FIRED.
4. MEDIA MATTERS, ALONG WITH GEORGE SOROS AND OBAMA ARE RELENTLESS IN THEIR PROPAGANDA TO DESTROY THE TRUMP AGENDA. ANTI TRUMP HEADLINES ARE BEING CREATED OUT OF NOTHING!
5. COLLEGES ACROSS THE COUNTRY ARE BEING TAKEN OVERBY PROTESTING BRAIN WASHED COMMUNISTS STUDENT. SOME EXAMPLES: More than 100 students at the University of California, Santa Cruz took over an

administration building on Tuesday, calling school officials to meet demands on changes at the campus

6. WEAK KNEED, NO GUTS REPUBLICANS ARE RUNNING FOR COVER!
7. HATE FOR PRESIDENT TRUMP, BECAUSE OF HIS SUCCESS WORLD WIDE, HAS TURNED INTO GREEN-EYED JEALOUS MONSTER, MORE DETERMINDED THAN EVER TO DESTROY HIM AT ANY COST. IF THEY SUCCEED, IN TWO GENERATONS GOD WILL ONLY BE A DISTANT MEMORY FOR A FEW.
8. DEATH FROM DRUGS, DRIVE-BY SHOOTINGS, AND DESTRUCTION OF PROPERLY BY OBAMA PROTESTERS IS "JUST" ANOTHER DAY AT THE OFFICE. 10.THOSE WHO SHOUT "LOVE NOT HATE" ARE THE FILTHIEST MOUTHED HATERS OF ALL.

PS TO MAY 29 THOUGHT

LONG MAY IT WAVE!

Thought for the day May 30, 2017'

BM BJ Melton Reply |

Tue 5/30, 8:57 AM

You; Alvin Simek

I voted for Donald Trump because:
He says what he thinks.
He thinks like I do.
He doesn't like illegal immigrants.
He doesn't like terrorists.
He believes in America first.
He knows Washington is ruled by swamp critters.
He hates drug dealers and violent gangs.
He believes in our Christian God, not Allah.
He believes in honest pay for an HONEST day's work.
He thinks we have too much "GOVERNMENT" help.
He made his own money, lots of it.
He is bribe free.
He is anti-socialism and anti-communism.
America needed a saviour and he was our only choice.
He loves the military which Obama hates.
He salutes the flag. Obama would not.
He is a patriot.
He thinks like I do.
I like him!
Those who DID NOT vote for him and are
against him today are not my friends.

Sic 'em Donald! Drain the swamp!! MAGA!!

Thought for the day May 31, 2017

Warning this is gruesome, not fit for human eyes.

I apologize in advance.

This is Kathy Griffin, a so called comedian making a joke out of beheading Donald Trump.

She personifies the left at its best.

This is the kind of sick people in Washington Trump has to cope with every day to get anything done.

To get this slimy dirty, they have to swim in their cesspool every day!

Scroll down if you think you can handle it.

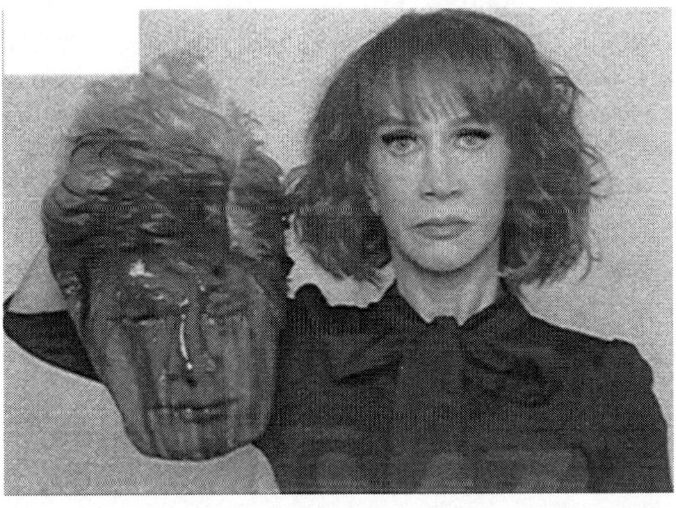

Sic ’em Donald! MAGA!!

Thought for the day June 1, 2017

Compared to other living things the human mind is a weird thing.
Think about it.
Chickens were born to lay eggs, and hatch eggs, make more chickens.
Roosters brag all day about their part in the process.
Birds build nests, lay eggs, hatch eggs, make more birds.
Fish swim around, lay eggs, make more fish.
Rabbits hop around, eat grass, make more rabbits.
Their life is simple. They love one another.
It is the same for cats, dogs, horses, apes, elephants, etc.

But humans love, hate, cry, laugh, envy, kill one another, insult, compliment, are jealous, connive, backbite, bully, are happy, sad, angry, get scared, suspicious, are morally good, morally bad, shy, extroverted, have passion, can be lustful, deceitful, irresponsible, nervous, heartbroken, hurt, furious, mad. Mix some of these together and you can get someone like Kathy Griffin, or Chuck Schumer, Donald Trump, Billy Graham, or Jesus Christ.

Living things, besides man, have no choice. They are what they are. God gave man the ability to think, to make choices.

The choices we choose make us what we are.

Think about it.

Sic 'em Donald! MAGA!!

Thought for the day June 2, 2017

Trump pulled out of the PARIS THING!!

Obama had signed on to it.

Like the Iran boondoggle, if Obama liked it you to know it was a bad deal for the United States.

Thanks Donald. Keep on doing good.

Sic ’em Donald! MAGA!!

Thought for the day June 3, 2017

Time

To

Build

The

Wall!

Sic 'em Donald! MAGA!!

Thought for the day June 4, 2017

Don’t have much today.

Thankful for 6.5 inches of rain the last two days. May get more today.

BUT Monday will be a different day.

A storm is brewing but thought hasn’t come together yet.

Intelligent Americans are proud of you, Donald.

The so called Paris Accord is a scam to make a few people filthy rich and we know it.

Thanks for saying NO!

Sic ’em Donald! MAGA!!

Thought for the day June 5, 2017

HOAX

What is hoax?

Definition: to trick into believing or accepting as genuine something false often preposterous."

P.T Barnum, the circus man, once said "There is a sucker born every minute" Nowhere is that more true than in America.

Eight years ago, "we", the suckers, elected a muslin President from Kenya and watched passively,

As he began the destruction of America.

Why we fell for this HOAX WILL FOREVER BE MYSTERY. Eight years later, America is having a hissy fit,

because we didn't elect a 'woman' who would continue the destruction.

A second hoax was almost perpetrated.

Fortunately, we elected a president dedicated to putting

"Humpty-Dumpty" back together again and the suckers are drowning in their tears.

All the while, the HOAX to shame all HOAX has consumed the world.

Think about this. How did Al Gore, the guy who 'invented' the internet, and came within a few votes of being President, convince enough billionaires that could make Billions more, if we could only make the suckers believe CO^2 is poison?

Don't know how, but he did. And it is a HOAX!! Big time!!

Millions are convinced that burning fossil fuels is causing an increase in carbon dioxide in the atmosphere which is increase the earth's temperature.

In the "Paris accord" 193 countries believe in 'global warming'

And they are having 'hissy fits' because Trump decided we will no longer be the Sugar Daddy for the world.

They are so concerned with this “Sky is falling” hoax, the most pressing world problem. TERRORISM, is being ignored

If 194 nations dedicated themselves to eliminating terrorism, it would be gone overnight!

Think about that!

Sic ’em Donald! MAGA!!

Thought for the day June 6, 2017

If you read about, or thought about, or heard about GLOBAL WARMING AND CARBON DIOXIDE, this will interest you.
There are 270,000,000 cars in the USA.
At least half fuel and producing carbon dioxide.
No complaints about cars.
There are 140,000,000 trucks in the USA.
At least half of them are running at any one time, burning fossil fuel and producing carbon dioxide.
No complaints about planes.
So...... what is the problem?
The one thing that provides you with a wonderful life.
ELECTRICITY!!!!
THIS HOW IT IS GENARATED:

FUEL	PLANTS	%
GAS	1793	34
COAL	400	30
OIL	1076	0.5
NUCLEAR	61	20
HYDROELECTRIC	1444	7
WIND	999	6
SOLAR	1721	1

Fossil fuels produce 65% and emit carbon dioxide.
A Hah! We find the source of 'Global Warming'.
Shut down these plants and problem solved if.....
We built 60 more nuclear plants, or
16,000 wind farms, or
172,000 solar plants.
In the meantime, your cost of electricity, if you have any, goes through the roof,
And your quality of life goes poof.
Global warming scare is a farce, designed to make a few people rich-At YOUR EXPENSE!

Sic 'em Donald! MAGA!!

Thought for the day June 7, 2017

Here is Michael Moore, the armpit of ultra liberal

Hollywood. Moore is the ultimate capitalist, and has made millions with sicko films and documentaries. He was a close friend of dictator Fidel Castro, buddies in fact.

He hates what America stands for, while wallowing in its wealth.

He hates President Trump.

He loves the Muslim Socialist Obama.

He loves progressive Socialist Hillary.

He hates President Trump.

He is very bitter because Trump won.

You might say He hates President Trump.

Yesterday he announced his Trump leaks campaign after the leaker Miss Winner was arrested. He set up a web site encouraging anonymous leakers, with information that might be damaging to the Trump administration, to send it to him.

He will then disseminate it to the world.

This is treason, and he knows it, but the Armpit has money and one objective-DESTROY TRUMP!

Sic 'em Donald! MAGA!!

Thought for the day June 8, 2017

I get up thinking about food.

I go to bed thinking about food.

I really like food.

Ran across this on Facebook.

Looks wonderful!

I think it would kill anybody's appetite.

I wonder if Jack-in-the-box would make one for me.

Sic 'em Donald! MAGA!!

Thought for the day June 9,2017

Here come Comey!

Comey graduated from the College of William and Mary in 1892, majoring in chemistry and religion. He received his Juris Doctor (J.D.) from the University of Chicago Law School in 1985.

Comey is 6ft inches tall, a very big man, and such looks down on others, literally figuratively.

Most of his working life been taxpayer payroll.

He loves himself.

Consequently, he became enamoured with his 'greatness', his power.

The saying "Power corrupts. Absolute power corrupts absolutely",, is so appropriate in this case.

The FBI spent months investigating Hillary Clinton.

In his speech of July 5, 2016 he laid out the criminal acts of Hilary, and there were many, and everybody knew the axe was fixing to drop.

Suddenly, he concluded there was nothing to charge.

Left the stage, no questions asked.

CASE CLOSED!

Obviously, he had orders from above, and his "impeccable" character wilted.

Thinking Hilary would be elected,(nearly everybody did) he did what he did, to be in the good graces of President 'Clinton" for another 7 years (perhaps more) as FBI Chief.

To his surprise Trump was elected.

Trump inherited Comey. Trump knew Comey was untrustworthy.

You catch more flies with honey than salt.

Trump said nice things to Comey. Comey took the belt.

"I AM GOING TO FILL OUT MY 10 YEARS AS FBI DIRECTOR."

Feeling the power, he resumed 'greatness'

Seeing enough and knowing enough President Trump said "YOU ARE FIRED"!

CASE CLOSED!

Sic 'em Donald! MAGA!!

Thought for the day June 10, 2017

I stole this from Phil Lawyer, whoever he is ?

It is thinking type information!

Those who would erase the past usually have no stake in the future.

Consider these 'non-futurists'.

One noteworthy reality about Europe's current political leadership is summarised here by Phil Lawyer:

- Marcon, the newly elected French president, has no children.
- German chancellor Angela Merkel has no children.
- British prime minister Theresa May has no children.
- Italian prime minister Paolo Gentiloni has no children.
- Holland's Mark Rutte,
- Sweden's Stefan Lofven,
- Luxembourg's Xavier Bettel,
- Scotland's Nicola Sturgeon- all have no children.
- Jean-Claude Junker, president of the European Commission, has no children.

"So a grossly disproportionate number of the people making decisions about Europe's future have no direct persona stake in that future."

Fortunately, Trump has many children, children he loves!

Sic 'em Donald! MAGA!!

Thought for the day June 12, 2017

Looking back at all the supposed crises.

Donald Trump has had to endure, the lies he had to refute, the media Fake News that were proven to be fake, I marvel that he has been able to stay so cool.

Cool Is the word these days.

Too bad Comey lost his cool and turned himself into a great goat.

Sic ’em Donald!

Thought for the day June 13, 2017

Today Attorney General Jeff Sessions has a session with the sessioneers.

Should be an interesting day.

Wonder if clown Schumer will be available to make a fool to himself?

Which one is a Republican?

Sic 'em Donald! MAGA!!

Thought for the day June 14, 2017

HEADLINE

"Boston Globe Has a Problem with Melania Trump Crossing Her Arms in White House Portrait".

It is OK for the Gander, but not the Goose?
Give me a break!
Do they pay people to write this stuff?

Sic 'em Donald! MAGA!!

PS: I noticed in the Jeff Sessions circus session today that Chuck Schumer is not a member of the "Intelligence" Committee.

Figures.

Thought for the day June 15, 2017

I have been hoping expressing this thought would not be necessary, but I have run out of hope.

The second un-Civil war is under way.

Too many entities have been spewing hate for too long and the nuts are coming out of their holes.

Check yesterday's headlines:

"Woman killed, 7 injured in mass shooting in California; shooting: Live updates on the shooting at a congressional baseball practice in Virginia"

(Just days before the Virginia shooting by a Sanders backer, Sanders gave unusually virulent speech, issued a series of stinging and angry attacks against Trump, labelling him "perhaps the worst and most dangerous president in the history of our country" and a habitual liar – his speech revolved around the idea that Democrats have to "take down Trump.")

"Gunman kills 3, then self At San Francisco UPS facility"

The hate being shown and stated by Michelle and Barak, NBC, ABC, CBS, CNN, Bernie Sanders, MSNBC, Soros, Washington post, NY times, Chuck Schumer, may Democrats and others, is all pointed at President Trump and Republicans, and it is swirling out of control.

Social media is filled with hate.

Then we have Kathy Griffin and Trump's bloody head, and Madonna wanting to set fire to the White House.

We have movie ‘stars and late night ‘comics’ using language that is unprintable.

IMPEACH TRUMP! KILL TRUMP! I HATE TRUMP!

The riots we have already had, and last week’s confrontation between the Anti-Sharia law group and Muslims are just samples of what is to come.

Law and order is being burned at the stake and Obama and company are throwing gasoline on it!

Sorry. Sometimes truth hurts. This one of those times. We can only hope Donald gets tough, really tough, in a way only the President can.

Sic ’em Donald!
You are our only chance to MAGA!!!

Thought for the day June 16, 2017

Whoa. Slow down. King sakes. Be calm.

The rhetoric by Democrats, Republicans, Independents, Socialists, Communist, radio, Newspaper, atheists, Muslims, legal immigrants, illegal immigrants, whites, blacks, browns, yellow, Christian, commentators, movie 'stars' and yours truly, has become nauseous, irritating, counterproductive, and divisive.

The seeds being planted are coming up weeds that not even cows, goats, Elephants, or Jackasses can eat.

The American included in those listed above need to vow to work toward making America better. Those who are not Americans need to find a place they like. They are not welcome to sponge off the rest of us.

Sic 'em Donald! MAGA!!

Thought for the day June 17, 2017

This morning I have been sitting here watching short video clips of the election campaign and election day.

And I sit here amazed.

Pryor to Trump's nomination, everyone, and I mean everyone said "No way he will be the nominee!"

After he was nominated, everyone, and I mean every one said "No way he can beat Hillary Clinton.

Hillary will crush him!"

On election day the polls all showed Hillary winning by a landslide.

It was done deal. The glass ceiling was in place for Hillary to break through.

A boat on the river was loaded with fireworks for the spectacular celebration.

The TV network were jubilant.

Then the impossible happened.

TRUMP WON! AMERICA WON!

There was no joy in Mudville, only crying and slashing of teeth.

To the chagrin of Hillary supporters, 7 months later they don't believe Trump won.

Sic 'em Donald! MAGA!!

Thought for the day June 19, 2017

FAKE NEW PART 1 OF 2

A year ago February 13, 2016 Justice Anthony Scalia died in his sleep at a resort ranch in West Texas.

1. The name of the resort is Cibolo creek ranch.it is located 33 miles south of Marfa, Texas. The ranch can accommodate 21 guest at one time, and is basically a DUDE ranch, with swimming, games, a spa for massages, and horseback riding. The restaurant specializes in Mexican food.
2. $900.00 will get you two nights and a horseback ride. Exotic hunting is available for a price.
3. They have an airstrip for private planes.
4. NOW HAVING SAID ALL OF THIS, MY CURIOSITY ABOUT SCALIA'S DEATH IS FARM FROM SATISFIED! There are too many unanswered questions.
5. He came by private plane. Whose plane?
6. He came with a friend. Who paid for him?
7. It was a free ride for Scalia. Who paid for him?
8. Apparently, he was there with 'friends-who were they?
9. It was said he was there with 'friends' to go quail hunting, at place not advertised as a hunting place.
10. It was said he had health problems. According to his Washington, DC doctor, Scalia was examined by his doctor on Wednesday and Thursday and had an MRI, before he left on Friday, Feb. 12.
    Question: Did his doctor tell him it would be OK to fly to this very isolated place, an hour away from the nearest doctor?
11. His doctor said he was too weak to have surgery on his shoulder, but he planned to go quail hunting and fire a shotgun?
12. What happened to his gun (if he had one)?

13. Scalia was known to like red wine so he probably had some with dinner?
14. Coming from Eastern time zone, 9pm was like 10pm to his body, so he went to bed “early”. Who said he felt bad?
15. What was in the wine?
16. He did not wake up.Why?
17. There was no autopsy. Why?
18. His death left a vacancy on the supreme court for Obama to fill.
19. Fortunately, if this were Obama’s plan, it did not work out.

Sic ’em Donald! MAGA!!

Thought for the day June 20, 2017

FAKE NEWS PART 2 OF 2

Who was Anthony Scalia?

1. Son of Italian immigrant, Married, had nine children
2. Associate supreme court Justice for 30 years.
3. Conservative constitutional origin list voted against same-sex marriageVoted against Obama care. Called it SCOTUSCARE.
4. Quote "Subsides to help Americans buy health insurance is 'interpretive jigger-pokery
5. Opposed Obama progressive agenda. Pro 2nd amendment
6. One of 36 guests of John Poindexter's Cibolo creek ranch. Only known guest. 36 unidentified. Why?One unnamed guest came with him from Washington?
7. Why was he there?
8. He was a member of the exclusive Order of St. Hubertus hunting societyExotic hunt were available at Cibolo. With bad health and bad shoulder,Why was he in middle of nowhere?
9. He was scheduled for a hunt Saturday morning. He woke up dead.

What happened?

A number of strange and, until now, unexplained things. Friday he flew from Washington to Houston, took private plane to Cibolo. Had enjoyable dinner with friends. Probably drank some red wine. Since he had a hunt scheduled early Saturday he chose to go bed around 9PM(10pm WASHINGTON). So far, nothing strange.

Saturday morning Poindexter tells the story that at 8:30 he knocked on Scalia's door. No response. He then takes some guests on a hunt. 3 hours later he returns and again knocks on door. After no response now, he forces way into the room. Scalia is dead 'with pillow on his head' (later changed to above' head which is also a strange place for a pillow.)

No doctor present. He calls judge Cinderella Guevara, a Democrat, 50 miles away, to report his death. Cinderella orders autopsy. Cinderella talks to Scalia's doctor 2000 miles away in Washington. He said Scalia had bad heart. Probably had heart attack. Cinderella becomes Santa Claus. Gives Poindexter a present. Voids autopsy order. So.... A doctor 2000 mile away diagnoses cause of death, and a judge, 50 miles away with no medical expertise, agrees with doctor.

Case closed.

Jan. 20th, continued

Scalia's body rushed to El Paso, flown to Washington, DC, funeral arrangements hastily made and he had an honourable funeral.

About Poindexter.

He is a multi-millionaire.

Did he gain financially having 35 still unknown (to us) guests at Cibolo?

He donates to Democrats.

Obama presented Poindexter with a distinguished award for service of his Vietnam unit. Did Poindexter do Obama a favour?

Just wondering, Obama did not attend Scalia's funeral.

Poindexter did not attend Scalia's funeral.

People die in different ways. How did Scalia die?

Thought for the day June 21, 2017

I thought to myself this morning...

I said, "Self, What is an American?"

Well, when I started to tell self what an American is, I started getting ambiguous answer.

So, I checked the dictionary for a definition.

No luck really. What I found was paragraph after paragraph trying to define AMERICAN.

An American is many things.

1. He loves and appreciates life.
2. He wants what is best for himself, his family, friends, & country.
3. He will pay the price, with action and work, to achieve the best.
4. He will use his mind to acquire the knowledge for good, not evil.
5. He believes. "man has a right to live his life in freedom"
6. He believes he has the right to live as he sees fit.
7. He believes In the right to worship as he pleases.
8. He embodies freedom for the human spirit!

Now think about this. There must be millions of people all over the world that holds to these beliefs. They may not be able to enjoy these things. But believe and, By definition, they are "American".

Ooops. You don't agree? Being a 'United States eon' gives you that right. But there is a North America and a South America. I learned that many people in South America think of themselves as American.

Check "American" above again. Think on it. Dwell on it. Then you will realize a new breed of people is being created in the United States and they ARE NOT AMERICANS!

They really are not "United State eons".

Sic 'em Donald! MAGA!!

Thought for the day June 22, 2017

Otto Warm bier died in a North Korean prison in March,2016.

Medical science preserved his body.

On June 12, 2017 his preserved body was released from Prison, and flown to his hometown in Ohio.

Otto died again Monday June 19, 2017.

The world in some places has a semblance of civilization.

North Korea is not one of those places.

Kim Jong-un is the “leader” of North Korea.

Calling him a barbarian would be a high compliment.

Since coming to power in 2011 as a 26 years old idiot he has had his uncle and brother assassinated.

There have probably been more, including Otto.

He really is a unstable person, capable of stupid acts.

Be prepared. If he should make the wrong act, he will be obliterated. Write it down.

Sic ’em Donald! MAGA!!

Thought for the day June 23, 2017

There is an old saying.....

“He that tooted not his own horn, his horn shall remain untooted.”

Defiant Pelosi isn’t going anywhere.

‘I am a master legislator,’ Pelosi told reporters as she hit back at Democratic colleagues pushing for here to step aside.

TOOT TOOT, NANCY!

“I am a master legislator” Pelosi declared.

“I am a strategic, politically astute leader.

My leadership is recognized by many around the country.

That is why I am able to attract the [financial] support that I do, which is essential to our election, I am sad to say,”

Personally, I don’t give a hoot for your toot!

Sic ’em Donald! MAGA!!

Thought for the day June 25, 2017

I woke up this morning thinking "what can I think about today".

I was blank.

So, I got up, looked in the mirror.

That is usually a mistake.

My mirror lies to me. Many times, especially early in the morning, I don't even know the person in the mirror.

Suddenly I thought "That's you! You're still here!"

Wow. The Lord has given me one more day.

Plus, today is Sunday, the Lord's day, a day to be grateful and thankful.

As I have said before "my bucket runneth over".

While today is extra special day is special for me.

So, that's what I am thinking about today.

I hope today is extra special for you, too!

Sic 'em Donald! MAGA!!

Thought for the day June 27, 2017

Yesterday, June 26, 2017, The Supreme Court of the United States, SCOTUS, Upheld President of the United States, POTUS,

Ban on immigrants from certain terrorist countries by a very unusual vote of nine to zero.

That is 9-0.

In effect, the ruling agrees with constitution that the President has the right and responsibility to take whatever actions necessary to protect us, the citizens of the United States.

And the ruling was a kick in the butt to the lower Federal Socialist Courts that said Trump DID NOT have the right!!!!

Sic ’em Donald! MAGA!!

Thought for the day June 28, 2017

Health care!

Sanders "Pass this GOP health bill and thousands will die!"

Pelosi "Pass this GOP health bill and thousands will die!"

Franken "Pass this GOP health bill and thousands will die!"

Schumer "Pass this GOP health bill and thousands will die!"

A few facts for the scare-mongers:

YOU MAY NOT BELIEVE IT, BUT EVERY BODY WILL DIE-EVEN YOU.

2,500,000 DIE EVERY YEAR IN THE USA.

6849 AND ½ PEOPLE WILL DIE TODAY.

DO YOU KNOW WHERE THEY ARE AND WHO THEY ARE?

MOST HAD INSURANCE AND STILL DIED. A FEW HAD OBAMACARE.

SCUM BAGS. WHEN IT IS YOUR TIME, YOU TOO, WILL DIE.

It seems your ONLY talent is scare tactics. Create panic.

The sky is falling!

Stop this "throwing Grandma off the cliff stuff".

You had your glory with "Pass it so we can know what's in Obamacare'. Your 'glory' has faded away. As usual, every idea you have is counterproductive trash, and ends up in the cesspool of Socialistic junk!

Sic 'em Donald! MAGA!!

Thought for the day June 30, 2017

When I was boy in East Texas, there were few paved roads.

When It rained, muddy placed developed. Often time cars would get stuck and would have borrow a neighbour's mule to pull them out.

However, experience drivers, knowing where the mud holes were, as they approached one, would go really fast, maybe 30 or 40 MPH, and try to fly through the mud hole. So, if they didn't stop, they did not get stuck.

It dawned me, Life is like that. if you don't stop. You won't get stuck.

So, I adopted that my philosophy of life. It has worked for me a very long time. I play golf when I hurt. I bowl when I hurt.

As long as I can, I refuse to stop. I will not sit in my easy chair and die!

I will enjoy life as long as there is life!

But eventually, we all get stuck.

That's life. Think about it.

We were born to die.

AMEN

Sic 'em Donald! MAGA!!

Thought for the day July 1, 2017

The year is half over. The last week of June was an uneventful week, full of pomp and circumstance which added nothing to the betterment of America.

We are going backwards actually.

The house passed the bill for Kate's law and defunding Sanctuary cities and sent it to the Senate.

A waste of time.

It will die in the Senate. Why?

Because the Democrats don't care if people like Kate get killed by ILLEGAL IMMIGRANT CRIMINALS.

Democrats don't care, in fact they endorse Sanctuary cities harbouring and protecting criminals, both illegal immigrant criminals and American born criminals.

This week, also, despite all the good President Trump has done so far,

24 Democrats have formed a pact to remove Donald from office by any crooked means they can contrive.

It became more obvious each day

THE DEMOCRATS DO NOT CARE WHAT HAPPENS TO AMERICA, THEY WANT THEIR POWER BACK—AT ANY COST.

Sic 'em Donald! MAGA!!

Thought for the day July 3, 2017

A friend of mine expressed concern and dismay over the "UnPresidential" behaviour, of OUR President, and I have this to say.

The Networks, especially MSNBC and CNN have become downright vicious with their lies, distortions and innuendoes.

They have partnered with their socialist "friends" in an outright assult, determined to destroy OUR President.

Sometimes ago I warned you not to fall for the propaganda.

It warps your mind.

The Socialist, Communist, Obamaites, are purposely distorting news, distorting stuff that isn't news, making up what if stories, repeating lies, innuendoes.

A friend of mine told a little story one time that illustrates what they do. He said what if a newspaper put out a front page headline

"—— ——— SAYS HE DOES NOT BEAT HIS WIFE"

He could deny, deny, deny, but some people would always believe he beat his wife.

So that's their game. Don't fall for it!!

From the beginning, way back in 2015, that have attacked, maligned, call him every uncomplimentary name there is, even "another Hitler".

And they have shown no mercy toward Melania, his family, and even his little son.

They have been, and will continue to be,

Unmerciful in their assault to destroy him, destroying America in the process.

Scarborough and Mira called Donald nearly every name in the book, but wanted to crash his New Years eve party.

AND THEY ADMITTED SHE WAS BLEEDING A LITTLE BIT FROM THE CHIN.

SO WHAT HE SAID WAS TRUE. MAYBE NOT CUSHY NICE, BUT TRUE.

WE ELECTED A FIGHTER. HE CAN'T WIN IF WE TIE BOTH HANDS BEHIND HIS BACK. HE IS NOT A PUSSY FOOT DIPLOMATIC LIKE BUSH, HE DOES NOT FIT OUR PRECONCEIVED MOLD FOR PRESIDENT, BUT HE IS WINNING.

LOOK AT THE LONG LIST OF THINGS HE HAS GOTTEN DONE ALREADY.

We have a fighter!!

BE PROUD OF DOING SOMETHING RIGHT! 

Sic 'em Donald! MAGA!!

Thought for the day July 5, 2017

Pay attention: GLOBAL WARMING HOAX!

This was published in the Washington post November 2, 1992.

It was republished and circulated worldwide by Al Gore in 2001 AFTER HE LOST THE ELECTION TO GEORGE BUSH.

And the suckers bought it. It is his revenge!

"The Arctic Ocean is warming up, icebergs are growing scarcer and in some places the seals are finding the water too got according to a report to the Commerce Department yesterday from Consulate at Bergen Norway.

Reports from fishermen, seal hunters and explorers all point to a radical change in climate conditions and hitherto unheard-of temperatures in the Arctic zone.

Exploration expeditions report that scarcely any ice has been melted as for north as 81 degrees 29 minutes.

Soundings to a depth of 3, 100 meters showed the gulf stream still very warm.

Great masses of ice have been replaced by moraines of earth and stones, the report continued, while at many points well known glaciers have entirely disappeared.

Very few seals of herring and smelts which have never before ventured so far north, are being encountered in the old seal fishing grounds.

Within a few years it is predicted that due to the ice melt the sea will rise and make most coast cities uninhabitable."

(MAYBE WE NEED TO START BUILDING SOME NOAH'S ARKS????)

It's a bad joke.

Sic 'em Donald! MAGA!!

Thought for the day July 6, 2017

Man is barbaric by nature. Since Cain killed Abel, man has been killing man. And he is ingenious in finding ways to kill.

Excuses for war is the big one. Then there is starvation, annihilation by the sword, hanging, shooting, drowning, fire, freezing.

The roman Gladiators fights were a 'civilized' way of killing.

Two (are more) Gladiators were put in the arena of the Coliseum.

One was usually protected with heavy armor, (like a football player,) while the other might choose no armour to maintain speed and agility.

They fought until one was dead and the crowd, in unison, stood and praised the victor.

During the early Christian era, to please the crowd, the Romans executed included dog, bear, boars, and lions.

NOW..............

Visualize a NASCAR race. 200,000 people paid big money to see bunch of cars run around the oval track.

Such fun, round and round and round they go.

Boring, boring. Is this really what they came to see?

Not hardly.

Suddenly, there is a 5-6 car pileup. Cars burst into flames.

Drivers are hurt, maybe killed. The crowd roars.

This is what they paid their money for, and they go home happy.

Without a ‘killing’, they wasted their money.

The same concept applies to football, hockey, soccer, boxing,

Man is barbaric, some JUST more barbaric than others.

Just look around the world. People killing people IS GOING ON EVERYWHERE.

Thought for the day July 7, 2017

My birthday is not until October.

I get all sorts of stuff in the mail, notepads, calendars, chances to join something, win something, cards, etc.

It is all free, really free. I can keep it.

It is mine. They "Why didn't you donate Police" won't come knocking at my door to get my 'free' stuff back.

Occasionally, I get something that amusing.

As I said my birthday is in October.

Yesterday I received some really nice BD cards.

Of course, there was a bleeding-heart message saying "Please contribute $30.00 or more to Such and Such Organization."

"You can save the world by making this a monthly contribution!"

On one card the message was

"May you live all the days of your life."

I thought about that for a minute, then I said to myself "Self that is a good idea."

So that is what I plan to do—

Live every day of my life (and not one day more.)

What about you?

Sic 'em Donald! MAGA!!

Thought for the day July 8, 2017

Round one!

You have every right to be proud of OUR President!!

The MASTER BUILDER, NEGIOTATOR meets the KGB.

Round 2 today!

Sic ’em Donald! MAGA!!

Thought for the day July 9, 2017

It is Sunday again and I sit here worrying about World affairs.

Why do I do this?

Why do we do this?

There is not a good answer.

I know there are thousands who are bent on making my life worse, many of them are at the G 20 Summit, in Germany, protesting.

Protesting what? They do not know, but are happy to fight with police, destroy property, steal stuff, all the while wearing hoodies to hide their identities.

It is a weird thing.

And there in the middle of the protestors in none other than nut job, (there are other word probably more descriptive than nut, but nut works for me)

Bill de Blasio, Mayor of our New York City,

ON AN ALL EXPENSE PAID TRIP TO MEDDLE IN THE AFFAIRS OF OTHERS!

Paid for by whom? George Soros? Obama? The taxpayers of New York City?

By whom?

Some nuts are easy to spot.

De Blasio in one.

Sic 'em Donald! MAGA!!

Thought for the day July 10, 2017

I want to throw out something for you to think about.
And I hope you are obliged to comment.
I am not a billionaire, or even millionaire.
I am not a billionaire, or even millionaire.
I am, fortunately, a thousandaire.
As such I live comfortably with very few unsatisfied wants.
I have no way of knowing about the life of a billionaire, or millionaire.
If one is happy, it is probably a very good life.
Now hear this.
Donald Trump is a multi-billionaire and a happy one,
So he can buy anything else he wants.
So why did he want to be President?
Not for the money. It is nothing.
Not to make friends. His enemies have multiplied 100-fold.
Today he doesn't really know who his friends are.
His enemies criticize, condemn, and profane him.
He is flying here and there, giving America first speeches, sleeping very little, meeting with foreign heads of state, who speak very little, if any, English, all of which have a different agenda than his.
Wrestling with members of his own party for nothing,
So, WHY?
To satisfy his ego?
Because he is Patriotic? And remembers a different America?
Personally, I have to eliminate EGO. What he is going through is a pretty high price for billionaire to pay for a satisfied EGO.
So that leaves Patriotism and a strong desire to
MAKE AMERICA GREAT AGAIN!!
To me, that's WHY!
What do you think?

Sic 'em Donald!

Thought for the day July 12, 2017

I don't care.
When I was much younger and trying to make a living for my family.
I tried to be prim and proper, and courteous.
I laughed at a customer's corny jokes.
I said "Yes sir" to my boss and my elders.
In short, I did what I did, hoping people would like me.
I really cared what people thought about me.

I was kinda like that nursery rhyme:

Little Jack Horner
Sat in the corner,
Eating a Christmas pie;
He put in his thumb,
And pulled out a plum,
And said "What a good boy am I"

But as the years have come and gone,
MANY things I once thought important,
ARE NOT IMPORTANT AT ALL!
I don't have to say Yes sir! To my elders because I don't know any.
I am not grouch, but if a clerk in a store or restaurant makes a mistake in their favour.
I am not ugly, I am not nice. I want it corrected.
If it is in my favour, thoughtful consideration is required.
I still want people to like me and say nice things, BUT,
I am fully aware that worrying about what people think, won't change anything, and if truth be known, most people I know DON'T THINK ABOUT ME ANYWAY!!
And I don't care.
In the December of my life, where the resting place for my soul will be, is my biggest concern.
I have in my request for a one-way ticket to Paradise.
In this matter, I DO CARE!

Sic 'em Donald! MAGA!!

Thought for the day July 15, 2017

The biggest problem we have in Washington, DC is we have too many

Spare horse parts. 

Sic 'em Donald! MAGA!!

Thought for the day 16, 2017

Amazon- something you may want to know.

Last month I ordered some golf shoes thru amazon and paid on my Discover card. On July 4th, a charge for Amazon Prime Membership showed up on my Discover acct. It was an inauspicious amount of $11.90.

I did not consciously, or unconsciously, authorize this charge

I called yesterday and they were "happy? To credit my Discover bill, after she had ordered some shoes. Actually, she was charged a second month before she noticed it. SO IT WAS GOING TO BE MONTHLY CHARGE, NOT JUST ONE TIME CHARGE!!!!

Make me wonder "How many $11.90's Amazon has collected this way?

Do they have any of your money?

Just asking.

Sic 'em Donald! MAGA!!

Thought for the day July 17, 2017

20 YEARS FROM NOW...........

As I have said many times I am 91, 3 months shy of 92.

I am pretty sure, although not positive, that I will not be here 20 years from now.

I look around at people, at my neighbours, and my friends at church, and others what I know, and I know many of them will not be here either.

I am not being morbid, just realistic.

I sit here griping about the people I do not like running our government. Then I realize, they won't be here either.

So, who will take their place?

Who will be running things 20 years?

1. Will the protestors of today somehow how become statemen and lead America to greater heights?
   Probably not.
2. Will the nerds and snowflakes, that Universities and Colleges are turning out by the thousands, even be able to find their own bathroom, much less run our country?
   Probably not.
3. There is another group that gives me hope. I know a few them and I am sure you know some, also.

They are relatively young, well educated, proud to be an American, with a brain filled with garbage, some are married with children, looking for a welfare check, but willing to work, at whatever, to provide food, clothing, shelter, AND ISURANCE, for the family they love.

Maybe, just maybe, they will take the reins of government, and continue to MAKE AMERICA GREAT AGAIN!"

That is my hope.

Sic 'em Donald! MAGA!!

Thought for the day July 18, 2017

SEE HOW MANY RUSSIA'S YOU CAN READ ALOUD IN 5 SECONDS WITHOUT STUMBLING!
(I got 27, then blathered)

Russia Russia Russia Russia
Russia Russia Russia Russia Russia Russia
Russia Russia Russia Russia
Russia Russia Russia Russia Russia Russia
Russia Russia Russia Russia
Russia Russia Russia Russia Russia Russia

I am sick of hearing about this, So far,
it has filled my head with nothing-nothing-nothing!!!
So, I am scratching if off my list.
If the sick subject shows up on my TV,
CLICK ***** channel change or OFF!!!

Sic 'em Donald! MAGA!!

Thought for the day July 19, 2017

A woman you know as lying, crooked, Hillary made a speech in Reno, NV yesterday. She spent the whole of her speech casting supporters of Donald Trump, such as me and you and America First, as racist. Personally, I felt insulted until I considered the source. The Alt-Right are America First patriots who, like me, believe in placing the needs of Americans above the needs of foreign countries, illegals, or refugees. That's not RACIST, that's COMMON SENSE. The term "Racist" is what Liberals and progressive start yelling when they are losing an argument, and believe me, she is losing, (perhaps in more ways than one), and the scandals on her back is losing it, (perhaps in more ways than reason she only comes out her hole every three-four days is---she has to rest. Meanwhile, she is married to a man constantly accused of rape and sexual assault, she took MILLIONS from Middle East countries who abuse women and execute gays, and she also "made out" with a KLU-KLUX-KLAN Gran Dragon, who she and her husband proudly called a "FRIEND."

I am NOT a racist but she is a BIGOT!

Sic 'em Donald!

Thought for the day July 20, 2017

John McCain has brain cancer.

In each life some rain must fall this is a sad song that applies to all of us, But in John's case "some" is not the word.

'Torrential' rain has fallen on him.

During the Vietnam war, his plane was shot down on his 23 third missions. He survived the crash, with a broken arm and leg, was captured and spend 5 ½ years as a prisoner in North Vietnam.

Somehow he stayed a live while enduring unimaginable pain and torture. IT WAS A MIRACLE.

Now brain cancer treatment will be painful, and, he survives, it will be another miracle. So if you like John or not, we have to be grateful for his patriotism and his service to our country.

God bless John and God bless the USA!

And God bless our President Trump!

Thought for the day July 22, 2017

Bathroom bill! Bathroom bill!!

Why is this a subject of conversation?

Why are legislators spending time and money try to write a bill to solve a problem that for thousands of years was not problem. I know you say, by freak of nature, some boys think they are girls. But close examination of their anatomy would reveal a male's tools.

It must be frustrating to such people who honestly feel like a woman, while being deprived of the main function of a woman-having a baby.

It aint gonna happen.

The world is full of actors. A man can say

"I am a woman" and act like a woman, but does that make him a woman?

I saw Hillary bark like a dog on TV. Did that make her a dog. Well, maybe. Probably not.

They say Bill Clinton was horsing around. Did that make Bill a horse?

What I am trying to say is-How many men, who are men, acting like a woman, be using the bathroom along with your wife or daughter, who are not men.

The world is full of actors. Some of them are B-A-DDD actors.

Sic 'em Donald! MAGA!!

Thought for the day July 23, 2017

People play games.

There are many games played with dice,

Monopoly, canasta, Yahtzee, poker, etc.

Some games use cards, bridge, solitaire, etc.

Many games use a ball.

Balls come in different sizes and shapes.

There is football, soccer, tennis, basketball, baseball, and golf.

Take baseball, for instance. A man stands at 'home' plate, in a fixed position, with a stick in his hands. Another man stands 60 feet away with a ball in his hand. He winds up and throws the ball toward the man with the sick at speeds up to 100 mph, daring him to it.

The ball has no sense. It only does what it is told.

Sometimes it hits the man with a stick, at 100 mph, that hurts.

Stupid game, but today a million or more people will pay good money to watch.

Many will want the man with the stick to hit the ball.

Many will want him to miss it.

Many will have popcorn and hotdogs, drink sodas or beer.

All will yell at the players or umpires.

Some will go home happy.

Some will go home feeling like they wasted their money.

Games are all alike. There are winners and losers.

Life is a game. Play it to win.

Sic 'em Donald! MAGA!!

Thought for the day July 24, 2017

I started playing golf when I was 12 years old, and at 91, I am still playing 1-2 times a week. Golf is a 'gentleman's game. Plus, it teaches patience and self-control. And it humiliates you. It also, is the only game that you can begin your game on the first hole with 3 brand new "friends" and finish all 18 holes with 3 new enemies.

Jordan Spieth won the British Open yesterday.

3 years ago, I 'adopted' Jordan as my favourite golfer.

Thursday, Friday, and Saturday, Jordan was leading the tournament and I was so proud of him. He is such a fine young man and I really wanted him to win.

Sunday, he started the day "floating on air" thinking he could win.

But golf is a fickle game. About the time you think you have it mastered, it humbles you, AND BREAKS!

Jordan was humbled yesterday. The first hole, a sense, brought him back to earth.

Everything started downhill on the first hole and continued through the 13th, where he finally lost his lead.

Things looked really dark. The ultimate crash, and a sad lesson in humility seem imminent.

But, on the 14th hole, with grit and determination,

Jordan shook the gods off and went 5 under par on the next 5 holes.

He won!

He also was reminded of something he already knew,

Golf is a fickle and humbling game.

Yesterday, July 24, 2017,

My beautiful wife celebrated her 92nd birthday.

I am proud and grateful husband!

Thought for the day July 26, 2017

What is your measuring stick for Trump behaviour?
Obama?
Bush?
Clinton, either one?
McConnel? Paul Ryan?
Cruz? Rand Paul? Rubio?
Schumer? Al Franken?
Maxine Waters?
Come on. He is what he is. One of a kind. He has not changed.
You elected him President because he promised to make changes you wanted...
Now that he is elected, and doing what he said he would do, YOU WANT HIM TO CHANGE AND BE A SWEET-TALKING POLITICIAN?
Come on. He is what he is. One of kind not changed!!! Politics as usual will not drain the swamp
You have to understand, the Progressive Movement took a giant step forward with Obama, and they planned for Hillary to complete the destruction of our republic.
They are fighting and clawing, using every tactic possible to destroy Trump,
Because if he succeeds, their dream becomes a nightmare.
They feel they have come so far, so close to their goal, that they will pay any price to destroy Trump.
Just stop and look at what they are doing. It ain't pretty, but they want blood!
Trump is fighting the only way he can. Diplomacy, the way you think, will only get his throat cut!!!
Donald is for us. Donald is for America the Beautiful.
Faint heart will never win a beautiful America!
Donald has guts! He is a fighter! Be thankful!

Sic 'em Donald! MAGA!!

Thought for the day July 30, 2017

Today is Sunday, one of my favourite days.

Of course, Monday-Saturday are favourites, too.

But Sunday is really special.

First, it is church day and I get to go commune with the LORD.

Second, Clarene and I were married on a Sunday.

Third, I am reminded of a momentous occasion.

When I graduated high school, at age 16,

I was offered a football scholarship at Texas Tech in Lubbock, Texas. At the time, with the war going on, they were building Lubbock Army Air Force base, so I went to Lubbock and got a job. It paid minimum wage of fifty cents/hour. I worked 6 days and on Sunday,

I went to church. Understand, in 1942, the businesses open on Sunday were grocery stores, filling stations, churches, and the funeral home.

Being naïve of the world, it did not occur to me then I was supposed to work on Sunday.

Monday morning when I reported for work, the foreman said "What are you doing here?"

"I have come to work."

"You don't work here! Where were you yesterday?"

What a shock! I WAS FIRED FROM MY FIRST REAL JOB!

For going to church!

Sic 'em Donald! MAGA!!

Thought for the day July 31, 2017

Today is 6 months, eleven days into the Presidency of Donald Trump.

A lot has been accomplished, but there is much to be done.

The swamp is still full of critters, but the draining has begun.

Donald is a fighter and, fortunately, does NOT have a faint heart.

I don't either. Hope you don't!

Sic 'em Donald! MAGA!!

This is the end.

I hope you have enjoyed my thoughts!

When I started my thoughts for the Day 2 years ago,

It never occurred to me they would be in a book

And read my millions!

It has been a delightful and exhilarating experience.

Thanks for reading.

CPSIA information can be obtained
at www.ICGtesting.com
Printed in the USA
LVOW12s0325270118
564207LV00001B/3/P

9 781641 663632